TURNING
OUT

Cover Artist: Simply Defined Art

Editing: 3P Editing

Proofreading: Judy's Proofreading and Lori Parks

Formatting: Rainbow Danger Designs

Paperback: 978-1-9994727-3-3

Ebook: 978-1-9994727-2-6

It's not supposed to be easy
    That's why it feels so fucking good —

AWOLNATION, "JUMP ON MY
SHOULDERS"

ONE

OCTOBER

BORED. THAT WAS THE only way I could describe how I'd felt this year; completely and utterly bored. It was my fourth year of med school, and I was low on free time while I finished up my last rotations. I should have been doing something productive—like sleeping—or brown-nosing to further my future career, but I wasn't. What was I doing? I was sitting up in Christy Ashton's apartment in Downers Grove smoking a blunt and wondering why I'd been avoiding making eye contact with her. We'd been doing this—whatever *this* was—for nearly a year. We'd hang out, we'd smoke up, and we'd fuck. It was simple and easy, and she's hot as all fucking get-out. Even so, I couldn't shake this feeling I'd been having for the past few months. It was almost as if I'd been at the same routine too long and the residual sediment was weighing me down. Or maybe it was the late October chill creeping in through the open window. What-ever the case, I didn't fucking like it, and it was indeed time for a change. Christy and I weren't dating so it wouldn't really be breaking up, but merely a change in scenery. Downers Grove was too damn far away from my place down-

town, anyway, and I didn't have a car. Money for an Uber—
and the occasional lift from my favorite big bro—wasn't an
issue, but that wasn't the point. I was fucking tired and busy
and over that situation. It was like a resolution; New Year,
new me. Except it was only October, so not really—the gist
was the same.

My attention caught on Christy when I heard the unmis-
takable click of a butane torch, and I saw her heating up her
favorite titanium nail. I glanced down at the table and
noticed that she'd dipped into my shatter at some point. I
raised a brow, though I couldn't really be fucked about it.

The sound of the metal scraping the glass beckoned my
attention again, and Christy was leaning into my blue glass
rig and inhaling the smoke. She raised glazed-over blue eyes
at me, and her full, cock-sucking lips curled up at the
corners. I knew this look, and what it meant and I knew it
well. She wanted my dick and, hell, I'd never been the type of
guy who was unwilling to share. I cocked my eyebrows at her
and squeezed the half-chub I'd gotten from seeing her lips on
my rig a few moments ago. She bit her lip and crawled over
to my chair, sliding her soft hands up my thighs once she'd
reached me.

When Christy's fingers touched the edges of my boxers,
she yanked them down. They caught on my now rock-hard
dick, and she tugged again. I lifted my hips to help out,
suddenly craving the wet heat of her mouth. She gave me
another hazy smile and sank those lips down on my cock.
My eyes rolled back, and I instinctively inhaled a sharp
breath. One last blowjob then it was time for a fucking
change.

I'D JUST GOTTEN off a ten-hour shift at the hospital and

stopped home to change into some fresh clothes. As fucking dead as I felt, I knew going out with my squad would resurrect me like it always did. I threw on a pair of questionably clean jeans and a red zip-up sweater and made my way out the door. The bar was a couple blocks away, and it was only late October, so I walked.

Walking always helped clear my mind, anyway. And it was the only exercise I'd been getting lately, which wasn't enough—so said Dani, but whatever. I loved her to death and didn't know what I'd do without her. No, that was a lie. I knew exactly what would happen—I'd wither up and die. Okay, maybe I was a bit dramatic. I might not *literally* die, though I'd be a fucking mess. More so than I'd been for the last year.

After coming to my senses a few nights ago, I broke things off with Christy, and it went just as I'd expected. We briefly talked, we smoked, and we fucked. Twice. Nice and easy, the way I like things to be. Dani never liked Christy so I was sure she'd be hella pleased when I told her the news. I should have listened to her and ended things months ago, but what could I say? It took me a little longer to realize it wasn't working for me, but I got there. The biggest red flag should have been when I realized that I didn't want her to meet my brother, Theo. After seeing what he and his boyfriend have and how happy they are, I realized that I wouldn't mind having that too. Someday. My schedule was a little crazy, though things would calm down for a hot minute after Match Day—until residency started in June.

It's not that I craved the companionship, but maybe how *I* could change. Before my brother met Masa he was a mess. After his best friend died, he closed himself off from everyone, including me, to an extent. The life in his eyes was gone. He still smiled at me and went through the motions, but I felt like I was losing him—or worse, that I'd already lost him and I was just in denial. All of that changed after he found Masa. I'd never seen Theo so damn happy, and that's the best damn thing. He made me realize that maybe I could change too. I'd never been depressed or shit like that, but maybe there was something more that I hadn't found. I didn't know what the fuck that something more might look like, but finding out fired me up. I lost sight of that while I grew too comfortable with how things were with Christy, so losing her was the first step.

It had always been in the back of my mind. Theo coming out to me also stirred up some questioning about myself. I'd always loved women—maybe more than I should have. At the same time, I'd also always known that I wasn't exactly *not* attracted to guys either. Girls were always just so accessible so I never gave my attraction to guys any thought. In the back of my mind, I knew things would be easier if I ignored those feelings and just went with what was easy and expected. Theo changed that for me, so maybe it was time I manned the fuck up and explored.

Someone bumped into my shoulder hard and didn't apologize, momentarily jogging me from my thoughts. Not feeling particularly confrontational, I shrugged it off and kept walking. It was a bit colder than I was expecting, but nothing I couldn't handle. A few more minutes later, the familiar sign to the bar came into view. I opened the door and was greeted by a blast of hot air and practically vibrated at the familiar smell of beer and tasty fried food. It was nearly midnight on a Tuesday, but the place was still packed. I scanned the patrons until my eyes settled on close-cropped, bleached blonde hair, then made my way through the crowded tables.

When I was about fifteen feet from the table, Scotty turned around and greeted me with a wide smile before turning back to the others and yelling, "Ay, my favorite *oyinbo* is here! No offense, ladies." He animatedly clapped his hands together over his head in mock prayer and bowed his head low to our fairer-sexed companions, Dani and Roz. As usual, Roz was perched on a high stool between Scotty and the ever stoic Patrick. Dani sat across from Roz and raised her chin in greeting when she saw me.

I greeted my friends with a series of fist bumps and mildly inappropriate comments before taking the empty seat between Dani and Scotty. Dani gently squeezed the back of my neck in that place that makes me fucking melt and slid two full shot glasses in front of me. God, this girl was my savior.

"Drink up. We're three rounds—"

"Four rounds," Scotty quickly interjected with a noticeable slur to his speech.

"Okay, three *or* four rounds ahead of you. I wasn't sure when you'd arrive so I held off on getting you a beer."

I leaned in close and rested my forehead on her bare arm. She often wore fitted T-shirts and tonight was no different. "Thanks a million, love." I sat up and hammered the shots back in quick succession before slumping back in my chair and eyeing my friends. "Aiight, fill me in on what I've missed."

Scotty rolled up the sleeves on his light denim button-up and flashed his signature mischievous smile at me. "Well, you remember that hot Ukrainian nurse on the fourth floor at Mercy?"

"You sly dog, you didn't!" Though I already knew he did. Scotty was a smooth bastard. He normally spoke with a mild Nigerian accent, but really played it up and laid on the charm when chatting up girls and it *always* worked. It also helped that he was six foot two, had full, sculpted lips that always seemed to be curved into a smile, broad shoulders, and always had a fresh fade. I could admit that the dude was damn attractive and it didn't surprise me that his charm always worked. Except with Roz. That little firecracker was immune to all of our best come-ons. At a modest five foot three, she sat up on a high stool while the rest of us sat in chairs. It was her bleached hair that caught my eye through the crowd. Our lovely Roz might be a small package, but her personality was anything but. Her smokey eye makeup made her crystal-blue eyes really pop, as did her naturally thick, dark brows. Her look was finished off with dark purple—it's actually called plum or black cherry or some shit that I refuse to remember the name of—lipstick and a white lace bralette as a shirt.

"Boy, you know I did! Almost four weeks of effort that finally paid off a few nights ago. Several times, if I'm being honest. That was the hardest I've ever had to work, but it was so worth it."

"I'm glad you spent nearly the entirety of your rotation at Mercy focusing on what was really important instead of worrying about those pesky patients and medical procedures," Pat said in that dry sarcastic way he was famous for. God love 'em.

Roz and I laughed while Scotty smiled triumphantly. Dani shook her head. "Don't worry about him, Patrick," Dani started, "he's not going to be an OB/GYN, so no one will suffer from his misguided attention."

"Hey now. I haven't decided what my focus is going to be. I love women; maybe I will be a gynecologist."

Roz choked on her beer and turned toward Scotty. Pat sighed dramatically. "Oh, please. If you truly love women, believe me when I say that you do *not* want to be a gynecologist," she said knowingly.

"I imagine it's kind of like when I saw that video on how hot dogs were made a few years ago." I paused for dramatic effect and looked Scotty in the eyes. "I haven't been able to eat one since." He wrinkled his face at me while his eyes rolled up—the tell-tale sign that his gears were turning while he processed this information.

Dani huffed next to me, garnering everyone's attention. "You're a lying sack of shit, Jamie."

I turned to her, and her hazel eyes blazed so hot it was all I could do not to flinch away. "Am not."

"I saw you eating hot dogs last summer at my cousin's birthday party."

"I'm inclined to believe her over you, Jamie," Roz said with a smirk.

"Cannot trust *oyinbo*—always lie!" Scotty pointed at me and shouted in an exaggerated accent. Ever-reserved, Pat shook his head at our antics and took a slug from his bottle of craft beer. He was easily the classiest among our rag-tag group. No matter the occasion, he wore dress shirts fully buttoned up. In recent years, he came around to wearing dark-wash jeans instead of slacks occasionally, though the dress shirts remained. If he had enough to drink, Roz had varied success in getting the top few buttons undone. He said his formality was to appease his mother and that until we knew what it was like to grow up with an overbearing Chinese mother, we should shut up about it.

Except I did know. I knew Pat growing up and met his parents several times at parent-teacher meetings and various sporting events and graduations. His mother was a very sneaky woman; serene and soft-spoken at first glance, but forceful and unyielding upon closer inspection. His dad was the complete opposite—a middle-aged Irish guy who swore like a sailor and didn't care if his son was top of his class or not. My dear Pattycakes was a good boy, so he tried for his mom, even after he moved out of their house. Scotty, on the other hand, was trouble through and through.

"You can totally trust me, Scotty. If I ate hot dogs—and I'm not saying I did—"

"You totally did," Dani deadpanned.

"—I was so shitfaced that I don't remember it, so I don't think that really counts."

"Wait, D, how old is your cousin again?" Roz asked.

"She's eight."

Roz turned back to me with a pointed finger. "You got smashed around a bunch of kids?"

"That's low, even for you," said Pat.

"Oh, cut the shit, guys. Kids are insufferable without alcohol. Besides, they fucking loved me. I was sore for three days from all the pony rides I gave. You try going through *that* without at least seven shots and see how you fare." At that, they all laughed at me, so I took a gracious bow and stole a swig from Dani's beer. After I set the glass down, she punched me in my side. "What the hell, D?"

"You can keep the beer. I don't know where those lips have been." She shuddered.

Ah, the perfect segue. "Funny you should say that—"

"It's not funny, you're just a whore," Scotty said with a hand grasping my shoulder.

"Do not dare slut-shame me. Besides, these lips haven't touched anyone in like, a week. I ended my… arrangement with Christy," I said proudly. "It was time for a fuckin' change." My declaration was met with excited hoots and hollers, and they all told me how much they hated Christy. Pat, Roz, and Scotty had even placed bets on how long it would last. Roz came out the winner, much to the guys' displeasure. While the three of them bickered, Dani knocked her knee into mine and nodded her approval of my super-adult life choice. Or maybe it was because she hated Christy. Who really knew what women were thinking?

The server's arrival broke up the argument over the bet.

More shots and beers were brought to the table and we all relaxed into our familiar rhythm. Med school wasn't easy, but having friends and future colleagues like these guys made the effort worthwhile. That and the money. And you know, helping people and saving lives and shit. Fuck, maybe I had a God complex.

After several rounds, Roz shifted onto Pat's lap, and had managed to unfasten the top four buttons on his shirt. She was telling him about a patient of hers while he actively listened as much as a drunk guy could. Scotty was leaned over the table on his elbows getting advice from Dani about how to talk to women who were immune to his charms. At one point, he twirled Dani's long, silky brown hair in his fingers then cried out when she twisted his wrist and applied pressure. I bit back a smile and sipped my beer while I continued to watch my friends. I must have zoned out because the next thing I knew, Dani was snapping her fingers in front of my face, and Scotty was engaged with Roz and Pat.

"Where are you?" Dani asked me.

"Sorry. Miles away for a sec. What's up?"

She groaned and nodded toward the other three. "They're talking about sex again."

Dani always disengaged when the conversation shifted in that direction. She'd said over and over again that it was none of our business and that she frankly wasn't interested in who we were sleeping with. Even in private she never wanted to talk to me about it, and compared it to her discussing sex with her brother. She'd wrinkled her nose at the thought while I'd just beamed that she regarded me like a brother. There once was a time where I'd asked her out—because she's cool and fucking gorgeous—but she shot me down, and it was the best thing that could have happened. We were best friends, and our bond was pretty unshakable. I was convinced that it could survive anything after what happened when I set her up with my brother and it epically backfired for all parties involved. Whoops.

"Damn straight we're talkin' 'bout sex again!" Scotty announced with a wide smile.

"Don't be crass. We were discussing the prevalence and social acceptance of anilingus recently," Pat simply said.

I stared at him blankly and slow-blinked a couple times. I heard his words, but my mind was screaming "does not compute." I replied, rather eloquently, with, "Um, wut?"

"Eating ass, *oyinbo*," Roz clarified. She cocked an eyebrow at me, challenging me to say something about the nickname reserved for use by Scotty.

I pointed at her and twisted my face in mock offense. "*You* don't get to call me that. You're fucking whiter than I am." Roz shrugged her smooth shoulders and winked at me.

"'Eating ass, *oyinbo*!'" Scotty echoed.

Dani leaned back and hung her head while her shoulders shook with silent laughter. Pat huffed at Scotty and Roz then looked up at the ceiling when he spoke. "Thanks for the clarity, guys." He shifted his gaze down to me and shook his head. "I'm too tired for this shit."

"Quit actin' like you don't love us," Scotty whined.

Pat sighed, but I could see his lips twitch, trying to hide a smile. "Is it an act?"

"Rude," Scotty pouted. Roz grabbed Pat by the collar of his shirt and whispered something to him I couldn't hear. It made him blush. Scotty paid them no mind, focusing his attention on me. "I was jus' tellin' dem 'bout Natalia."

Oh, yes, he was donezo. "Who?" I honestly asked before draining the glass in front of me.

Scotty's eyes went wide, and he grinned like an idiot.

"Natalia! Nurse at Mercy! She was kinky as fuck. So she was blowin' me, and you know—"

"And this is when I zoned out before," Dani mumbled beside me.

"—it was great 'n all but she started goin' lower 'n started rimmin' me!" He waved his hands around like he was telling an epic tale and, really, it was kind of adorable. I always loved drunk Scotty.

"Tell him the best part!" Roz said excitedly.

Scotty opened his mouth to speak again, but Pat cut him off with a quick hand to cover his mouth. "Nope. I refuse to listen to that again."

Scotty pouting like a scolded child made me laugh, and I spoke before I could think any better of it. "I've never had it done to me. I've done it to a few girls, though." Shit, maybe I was drunk too.

"Wait, seriously?" Roz stopped laughing.

Scotty cocked his head like a puppy trying to understand an unfamiliar command and eyed me disbelievingly. "You dated that music chick for a year 'n she never tossed ya salad?"

"Dude. One, we weren't dating. Two, she was a ballerina —and mind-blowingly flexible, if I dare say—and three… I dunno, I guess it's just something that never crossed my mind." That was a lie. I thought about it all the fucking time but didn't want to be weird and ask. No, weird wasn't right. Whatever. I was trying to sort my shit out and figure out what I wanted.

Pat sighed and nodded his head. "I guess that's fair. Not much crosses your mind."

The table laughed at my expense, though it was all in good fun. "I would be mildly offended right now if not for the fact that that's not entirely untrue."

Scotty clapped his hand over my shoulder again and

squeezed. "It's all good, man." He shifted his hand and cupped my chin gently. "You're pretty enough that I'd take one for da team and do ya a solid," he said, then winked at me. My crazy buddy, Scotty. Fuck, he probably would too.

"That, or Handsome Tom might be around here some-where. I'm sure he'd treat you right." Handsome Tom was a regular at this bar. A bit of an enigma, he always seemed to be there when we showed up. He was handsome as fuck, hence the nickname, and a grade-A charmer.

I shook my head and took a drink to hide the smile that pulled at my lips. "Fuck you. Both of you," I said without a trace of malice. That cocky bastard Scotty waggled his eyebrows at me and damned if I didn't want to stir in my seat. Dani saved me by announcing that it was time for more shots. No one argued.

The rest of the night was more of the same. A few hours later I found myself stumbling home, dreading how I was going to feel in the morning. Normally I'd be able to sleep it off and show up to the hospital like a brand new fucking man, but I had to go home and visit my mom. We had a breakfast date planned, and I had to cancel the last one because of work. I wouldn't miss it twice in a row. Dani asked me to go costume shopping the morning after next, but I couldn't do two early mornings in a row. I'd beaten her down to noon, though I still felt like I'd lost somehow. Damn her.

There were significantly fewer people out now that it was so late. Or early. However you wanted to look at it. There was a breeze coming off the lake, sweeping through the streets, though the burn of alcohol in my system had me wanting to peel off my clothes on the sidewalk. Luckily, my place was just a few more blocks away. After another block I promised myself I'd call a fucking Uber next time.

I was late meeting up with Dani—surprise! She was waiting on a bench a few feet away from the store wearing large sunglasses and holding a paper bag and two coffee cups. I apologized for my tardiness, but she knew I would be late and stopped to get me a café mocha and a bagel. I thanked her and lavished her in praises before tearing that bagel apart in a display of hunger reserved for apex predators in the wild. Dani laughed at me and guided me inside the store then removed her glasses. Despite how chipper she seemed, I saw the bags under her eyes and knew she'd probably had a rough night as well. Perhaps she was handling her exhaustion with more grace than me, but grace was never my forte. Inside, I unzipped my sweater and took a sip from the paper cup. Dani looked at me with her eyes squinted. The freckles across her nose and cheeks distorted as she wrinkled her nose at me.

"What are you giving me the stink eye for now?"

"Looks like you found yourself a succubus last night," she said, motioning to my neck.

Oh. Right, last night. "Katrina texted me last night while I was at the hospital. She wanted to hang out after my shift."

She rolled her eyes, grinning at me. "Mhm. I see that went well for you."

"I've had worse nights. Is my neck really noticeable? I asked her to go easy on me, but I think that just made it worse."

"Judging by the hematomas on your neck"—she reached out and pulled the collar of the T-shirt to the side—"and clav, I'd say you'll be marked for a week if you treat it. Longer if you don't." She released my collar and gently pulled on a small clump of my overgrown wavy hair.

I cried out, which just made her laugh as she walked away, sipping her coffee. "Thanks, Dr. Gallo," I mumbled.

It was far warmer inside the store than outside, and I

needed to cool down. I eyed a display cabinet over to my left by a wall and made my way over. I set my cup down and pushed the sleeves of my hoodie up to my elbows. I tugged on my white tee and fanned my chest with it a few times to cool down before picking up my café mocha and scanning the floor for Dani. She was nowhere in sight. I could smell her Brazilian dark roast coffee, so I followed the robust scent. She took it black, and the smell was always so strong. I'd been enticed into trying it a few times, despite hating coffee. It was a fucking mistake every time because it tasted disgusting, but it smelled damn good.

I followed the rich scent through aisles of witches and ghosts and found Dani feeling the fabric of… I didn't know what the fuck it was. "Umm, what's that?"

"*Sharknado.*" She held up an attached bag with attachable shark heads in it.

"Oh God, why?"

Dani just shook her head and moved on. We commented on a few more tragic costumes, and the longer I observed her, the more I noticed that she looked beat. I waited until the other shoppers in the aisle moved on, and when we were alone, I donned a dark brown pirate hat and dropped my voice to a semi-serious tone. "How's things, D?"

She sighed deeply. "I'm tired. Between rotations, studying, the restaurant, and family drama, I'm feeling run-down. We've just got a few more hellish months left."

"Yeah, and then the real fun begins with res," I added dryly.

"No, then we get a few months off before residency. I thought I might take a trip with Andrew. We haven't seen each other enough."

"Ah, how is ol' Indy doing these days?"

"He still hates it when you call him Indy," she said in a flat tone.

I shrugged. "Not gonna stop. He should embrace it and be flattered. Who doesn't want to be Indiana Jones? Other than Andrew Jones, distinguished forensic accountant," I said teasingly. Dani snickered and shoved me with her shoulder. I did like Andrew. He was a bit of a stiff when I first met him, and he might very well hate my guts, but he'd been keeping Dani happy, and hadn't been making a huge fuss over how busy she was. If my brother was anything to go by, Andrew was definitely Dani's type. He fit what I liked to refer to as the four S's; suit and tie, shit together, self-sufficient, and straight. My brother kind of made the last entry super important. They were back on good terms now, and could joke about it. All right, they didn't joke about it, but I sure did.

"Nah, Andrew's not so bad. What was the family drama you mentioned? Is your dad drinking again?"

She sucked her teeth in an unusual show of frustration. "No, it's not that. Dino came back again earlier this month, and things have been *strained*."

The prodigal son has returned. I'd never met Dino. He'd already moved out of the city by the time Dani and I became friends. He visited a couple times a year but never stayed more than a few days. "Why didn't you tell me sooner? How long is he staying this time?"

"I meant to, but you've seemed bummed enough lately. New York hasn't been working out for him, so he's home for good. For now, at least. I love him to hell and back, but he and Pop can't agree on anything. He already moved out and is looking for work now."

"Your parents didn't want him back at *Ciao Bella*? You said he worked there years ago before he left town."

"Nah, they offered, but he said no, which sparked the fight that ended in Dino moving out." I nodded my head, unsure of what to say, but Dani spoke again before I had to.

"Enough of my shit. What's going on with you? I can tell you've been keeping something from me, *James*."

James. Damn, no use mincing my words. She only called me James when she was serious about something. I looked around the aisle once more to make sure we were alone and took a deep breath. "I ended things with Christy because I felt like I was stuck in a rut and unable to move forward and it was kind of exhausting. I didn't love her, but she gave really, really great head and, I'll be honest, that made me put the decision off a lot longer than I should have, but can you really—"

"Jamie, stay focused."

"Right, sorry. Anyway, Christy isn't what I wanted, and she was keeping me from figuring out what I do want."

"Which is?"

"I don't know, exactly," I answered honestly. "Something more. I want to be happier."

Dani nodded slowly and smiled at me. "I get that. I'm proud of you, *fratellino*. You're finally starting to grow up," she teased.

At that point, I figured I might as well tell her everything. "I'm also questioning my sexuality and think I might like guys," I blurted out.

Her eyes went wide, and she stopped herself from gasping. "What the fuck, Jamie?"

"Well, guys and girls. I still love women, I do. But I think maybe, I'm attracted to guys too."

"So, you're not questioning?"

"Ah, I guess not. I've never been with a guy before, but I've definitely been sexually attracted to them since puberty." Dani was silent then and stood stock still. I couldn't take the tension, and looked down at my feet for a few seconds. Forever.

I didn't see it coming when she pulled back and punched

me in the jaw. I stumbled back, shocked more than anything and shot my gaze to hers. Shiiiit, she was pissed.

"What the fuck is wrong with you damn Rey boys? *Che cavolo*!" Unsure of what to say to defuse the situation, I stood there with my mouth shut—and sore, goddamn—and chanced a tentative grin at Dani. "I'm not angry at you because of this, Jamie. Understand that I'm angry with you for keeping it from me." The calm had started to return to her voice. She huffed and crossed her arms. "Speak."

"I'm sorry I didn't tell you. I didn't tell anyone. I haven't even told Theo yet!"

"Why not?"

"It wasn't ever something I thought about. When I was younger, I figured that I could ignore it since girls satisfied me. When Theo came out last year it made me think about it more and really look at why I hadn't, um, explored that side of myself. He and Masa were super happy, and I got to thinking."

"You had the hots for Masa, didn't you?" she asked, deadass serious.

"Um, maybe a little? And only at first!" Dani burst into a fit of laughter that made me realize I should have lied. Ugh, fuck my life. "Please don't tell Theo, he'll kill me. Like, he'll legit probably try to strangle the life from my body."

Still laughing, Dani pulled me into a tight hug and took the pirate hat off my head. She tossed it aside and combed her fingers through my loose curls. "You're an idiot, but I love you, Jamie." She kissed my cheek before pulling back. "Now help me pick out a costume that doesn't scream 'I'm a slut.'"

"But it's not a good Halloween costume if it isn't slutty," I said matter-of-factly.

"Oh, so you're going to wear something slutty?"

"Abso-fucking-lutely."

TWO

OCTOBER

THE HALLOWEEN PARTY IN Lincoln Park was already bumpin' by the time I arrived. Loud bassy music boomed from down the street as I made my approach. I didn't see anything too debauched until I walked through the front door. So that was an improvement over last year's Halloween shit-show. I'd walked over from visiting with my mom in my family's home in the neighborhood. Stopping by home before the party also meant a chance to dip into my dad's prized scotch collection. So, I was already good and buzzy when I arrived at the party.

The music was so loud that I couldn't even make out what it was, but it felt good pulsing through my body. *I* felt good. Warm, light, blitzed. Yeah, maybe I smoked a few J's on my way over, so I was feeling pretty fucking good. I scanned the swaying bodies in the living room for familiar faces and found several, but not the ones I was looking for. Dani, Scotty, Roz, and Pat were here somewhere, but I wasn't in a huge rush to get to them, so I didn't bother texting.

I made my way into the kitchen and filled a red party cup full of beer from the keg on the table. The liquid was ice cold sliding down my throat, and it was everything. I decided to wander around and take a peek at all the costumes for a bit and much to my surprise—noooooooot—there were a few buff guys dressed as Goku or Superman, some Marvel costumes, doctors, vampires, and tons of last-minute slutty cat and deer costumes with whiskers drawn on with eyeliner. How did I know it was eyeliner? Because I was fucking wearing it too. That's right, folks. When I told Dani that costumes should be slutty, I fucking meant it. I was rocking a hot-as-fuck smokey eye and super pale foundation to make my eyes pop. I'm dressed as slutty Beetlejuice with the black and white striped suit, sans the white shirt, with a black tie lying against my bare chest. The band of my CKs was on display for added flair. It was brilliant and much more inventive than when I went as Post Malone last year.

An insanely attractive girl in a not-so-practical latex nurse uniform bumped into me, sloshing some of my beer on the floor. Her cheeks were flushed, and her pupils dilated—she was donezo.

"Oh my God! I am so sorry!"

I flashed her my sweetest smile and shrugged my shoulders loosely. "It's all good, love. Just slow down a little, yeah?"

She returned the smile and enthusiastically nodded her head. "For sure. Hey, are you supposed to be Robin Thicke? You are, aren't you! I totally forgot about him."

"Wait, wut?"

"Blurred lines? Robin Thicke?"

I waved my hand off dismissively. "No, yeah, I remember that. But that's not who I am." She tilted her head in confusion. Oh boy. "'Say my name three times!' No? Nothing?" She just blinked at me and smiled harder. "God, how *young* are you?"

"I'm eighteen, what about you, cutie?" She slowly slid a painted red fingernail down my chest.

"Oh God, you're a child." I stepped back, saluted her, and walked in the opposite direction with my half-empty drink.

Back in the kitchen, I found Roz filling up two beers and sidled up next to her, leaning against the edge of the table. She looked dazzling in a tailored black suit and bright red lipstick. "Damn, sweet dreams really are made of this." Not my best line, but remember, blitzed.

Roz leaned into me without looking, and I wrapped my arms around her and kissed the top of her head. "Hey, baby boy." A nickname courtesy of being the youngest in our group. "We're all out by the pool."

"Isn't it a bit cold?"

"Drink enough, and you'll be warm. The water is heated too. Scotty jumped in already."

"Of course he did. All right, leggo."

We passed by several people who thought Roz was Miley Cyrus or Lady Gaga and that I was Robin Thicke or a damn criminal before we reached the rest of our friends. Scotty was indeed still in the pool, taking his Aquaman costume far too seriously. After greeting everyone and having a few laughs, we determined that we were probably some of the oldest people there and the thought was beyond depressing. Dani ended up going with the costume I picked, and she fucking killed it as Lara Croft. People knew who she was, and she got hit on more than she'd have preferred. I just took that as a win on behalf of my costume selecting skills. The best part was that Lara Croft was basically femme Indiana Jones, and I'd hoped Andrew would pick up on the dig when Dani told him. Pat wasn't big on costumes and went as a doctor, as usual, and wore one of his actual lab coats. No matter how uninventive it was, he had the attention of a super cute doe, so I couldn't knock him.

The sound of disturbed water caught our attention, and I

looked over to see Scotty hauling himself out of the pool along the edge instead of just using the stairs. I had to quickly look away, so I didn't see how his biceps flexed with the action, or how his costume clung to his toned body. Nope. I didn't notice those things at all. Noticing guys more was going to take some getting used to, but I sure as hell wasn't going to start with my friends.

Scotty came up beside me and greeted me with a fist bump. He rubbed his hand down his face, clearing off the dripping water and shook his head, getting water drops on my bare skin. "S'up, man? Are you supposed to be a stripper or something? And are you wearing makeup?"

"Fuck you, fish boy. I'm slutty Beetlejuice! What's wrong with you people?" Scotty snorted, and his perma-smile widened. "Oh, shut it. I didn't mean it like *that.*"

"Ah, *oyinbo*, you never learn."

"Yeah, yeah, whatever."

"You two," Dani said to Scotty and me, "get over here for a pic before we go inside."

Roz stood between Pat and Dani, while I was sandwiched between Dani and Scotty. I put my arms around Scotty's shoulders and Dani's waist while she held her phone up for a super cramped selfie. Looking at ourselves on her phone display, I saw Scotty smirking and squeezed his shoulder. "Dude, better make sure you smile with some teeth so we can find you in the pic, it's a little dark out here, bruh." Muhahaha!

Dani and Roz snickered while Pat turned away, but I could still see his smile on the screen. Scotty pulled me closer, and I felt his laughter against my body before I heard it. He kissed my temple and ruffled my hair. "Damn, I'll give you that one."

We didn't make it past the kitchen because Scotty was

fucking soaking wet. A house like this would no doubt have a regular cleaner, but Dani and Roz insisted that he wait on the tiled floor of the kitchen while they went to get him some towels. Scotty complained, so Pat and I got roped into keeping him company.

"You really didn't have to jump in the pool," Pat said.

"He was probably just proving that black dudes can swim, amirite?" I added with a shit-eating grin. My favorite kind, truly.

"You're on fire tonight," Scotty replied.

"Dude, you're making it way too easy. Although I should probably stop before people overhear and think I'm a racist." Yeah, that would be bad.

"Don't worry, *oyinbo,* I'd save you. Anyway, I was in the pool because a cute little kitty asked who I was. When I told her it still didn't really click."

"Sooooo, you jumped in the pool to prove that you were the King of the Seven Seas?" I asked facetiously.

"More or less," Scotty replied with a shrug of his broad shoulders.

"Did it work?"

Scotty licked his lips and grinned. "Her name is Lauren, not Laura, she likes the nineties, and I've got her digits in my phone."

I held up my fist, and he bumped it. "My man."

Pat audibly sighed and crossed his arms. "Are you two done?"

As if on cue, the girls returned with several dry, fluffy, white towels and began patting Scotty down, wicking the water out of his costume. He reveled in the attention, getting even more excited when Roz shoved a towel in Pat's hands and forced him to help. When Dani tried to do the same to me, I took a step back and held my hands up.

"Sorry, no can do." Dani cocked an eyebrow at me,

which I knew meant I had to elaborate if I had any hope of getting out of feeling up Scotty.

"I need to use the little boys' room," I answered as innocently as possible.

"Fine. Go."

"Roger that," I started off toward the living room, though I didn't make it more than a few steps before I backtracked and bent down to ask Dani a question. "Um, where is it?"

"Up the main staircase, fourth door on the left. Fifth on the right. There're a few on this level, but the ones upstairs don't have lines."

I blew Dani a kiss and headed off toward the front entrance and up the main steps. By the time I got up there I was ready to burst from how long it took to weave through the throng. I relieved my screaming bladder and instantly felt, like, a bazillion times better.

Back downstairs, I took a few moments to take in partygoers. The male partygoers in particular. It still felt a bit strange to be openly looking at guys, but I was trying. There were plenty of hot guys seeming to be occupied, be it with talking to girls or their friends. How the hell was I supposed to know who else was into dudes? It would appear that none of them were. Statistically speaking, I knew that wasn't true, though the scene at the party was confusing as fuck. I made a mental note to talk to Theo and Masa about any tips or cues I could try looking for. Er, maybe just Masa. My brother had only ever had one boyfriend—but that was more than I'd ever had. I looked back out at the crowd and noticed that the guys also kind of all looked the same. Generic, rich, university bros separated into two categories: sporty guys and hipsters. There were a few exceptions to the rule, but no one really caught my eye enough for me to go risk hitting on a straight guy. God, I didn't need that type of drama. How did I even go about picking up a guy, anyway? Ugh, this bi thing was too confusing for me to process with my fading high. I didn't know much, but I did know that I didn't want a guy who looked like me, which greatly diminished the possible options before me.

"You look lost," a smooth, feminine voice said from behind me. I turned around to see a brunette knockout dressed in a tied-off red and black plaid flannel, itsy bitsy jean shorts, and spike heels. If the twitch in my boxers was any indication, it was safe to say I *definitely* still liked girls. Dayum.

"Maybe I was just waiting for you to find me," I replied with ease. "You make a pretty good Daisy, by the way."

She cocked a manicured eyebrow at me. "Just pretty good?"

"Well, Catherine Bach was one of my childhood crushes, so that pretty much makes her an untouchable goddess"—I turned up my smile—"but if I had to reevaluate without bias, Ms. Bach might be shit out of luck next to you." That did it. She bit her lush bottom lip and smiled at me with budding desire in her eyes.

She raked her eyes up and down my naked torso. I was by no means a muscly guy, but I wasn't exactly stick-thin either. I used to run track and have always been on the lean side. "You're not so bad yourself."

"Care for a dance, Ms. Duke?"

"Erin. And yeah, I'd love that."

We danced for a couple of songs then I went to go get us drinks. We found the arm of a couch to sit on and talked while we nursed our beers. Erin was twenty and wanted to be a geologist. Huh, fancy that. I told her I was a student, though I didn't specify. I made a habit of not telling people I was in med school, to avoid any assumptions about me someone may be inclined to make. A song she really liked came on which meant it was time to chug and dance more.

Her body was glued to mine, and she felt fucking amazing against me. She was soft in all the right places and fit against me perfectly. With her back against my chest, she tilted her head to the side and reached up and cupped the back of my head. I took the cue and leaned down to kiss her exposed neck, and nibbled on her lobe a bit—something I always liked done to me.

A gust of cold air made me turn toward the front door, and that's when I saw him. Quite possibly the sexiest guy I'd ever seen walked through the door and stopped at the edge of the living room, scanning the crowd. I couldn't help but stare as everyone else in the room instantly became irrelevant. This guy was unlike everyone else at the party. He was tall and broad in a way that made me wonder what it would feel like to be pressed up against him. He wore a red leather-looking... was that a damn harness? I guess it was a harness, under blue denim overalls. One strap was unhooked, displaying a strong, hairy chest so masculine that I felt like a prepubescent boy with my mostly smooth chest exposed. One of his arms was heavily tattooed, though I couldn't make out the details from how far away I was. Upon further inspection, I noticed he was wearing white gloves and a red snapback. Fuck me sideways—he was motherfucking Mario. A man of class, I could tell. I felt my lips pull into a smile as I continued my blatant exploration and took in his well-groomed, thick, short beard and shapely lips. My smile faded when I got to his eyes and realized he was watching me gawk at him, probably with a dumb grin on my face. Shit, shit, shit! I looked away and closed my eyes, focusing solely on moving with... shit, I forgot her name.

The song ended and morphed into another that sounded alarmingly similar. Um, Daisy, I guess, still had her back to me, so I chanced another look at the door, dismayed to find that hunky Mario was no longer there. I turned back toward Daisy—God, I was terrible—and nearly jumped when hunky Mario was watching me from his vantage point against the wall, directly in my eyesight. That time I fucking froze. His dark brown eyes had me pinned, and I barely remembered to even breathe. I was vaguely aware of Daisy turning in my arms and giving me a questioning look, but I couldn't tear my attention away from *him*. She tapped my shoulder and followed my line of sight when I didn't respond. When she turned back to me she finally spoke.

"Ah, I get it." She withdrew her arms from my shoulder and hip. "All the good ones are gay these days," she said before walking away and getting swallowed up by the dancing bodies.

I remained standing in place, eyes locked with hunky Mario. He licked his lips, and my heart rate skyrocketed. I didn't know what was happening, but it was intense, and my dick certainly liked it if my semi was any indication. He cocked his head back, and I nearly groaned at the sight of his neck stretched tight. I *did* groan when he swallowed, and his Adam's apple bobbed up and down. Fuck. Was a guy's throat always so sexy? Why hadn't I ever noticed like that before?

All thoughts died when he started walking toward me. Seeing him up close, I noticed he was quite a bit taller than my five foot ten, maybe four inches so. Damn, that was hot too. He leaned in close enough that I could feel his hot, minty breath on my neck and I shivered.

"*Beetlejuice, Beetlejuice, Beetlejuice,*" was all he whispered before he pulled back, motioned toward the stairs behind us, and walked away. He managed to make it sound filthy as fuck with his deep voice, leaving me rooted to the floor. I managed a glance over my shoulder and saw him watching me as he ascended the steps. Oh, I guess this was how it happened between guys.

Move, Jamie! I felt like screaming at myself. I wanted to follow him, but then something else held me in place, something I wasn't used to feeling; fear was a wicked bitch. What would happen if I went upstairs? Who would I be? What would people say? What would they think? No, that type of thinking was why I said I needed a change in the first place. The old Jamie wouldn't give two fucks about the answer to any of those questions, and he wouldn't be scared. It was simple. I asked myself what I wanted at that moment, and before I could think of the answer, my legs were already moving toward the stairs.

He was leaned against the wall with his arms crossed, facing the steps when I reached the top of the stairs. The music was subdued upstairs, and when he spoke, I caught the full timbre of his deep, slightly gravelly voice.

"I wasn't sure you'd follow, but I'd hoped you would." He took a step toward me, and I felt the air leave my lungs almost violently. He reached out and grabbed my tie, wrapping it around his fist, before walking backward down the hall, hauling me along. The white gloves were gone, though their whereabouts were the last thing on my mind. He pulled me into the bathroom and instructed me to close and lock the door behind me. As soon as the lock clicked, his hands were flat against the door on either side of my head, blocking the escape I didn't want access to. My head didn't know what to do, but my fucking dick sure did; I was hard and straining against my ridiculous striped pants. Neither the thin material nor the busy pattern did a damn thing to hide my raging erection. Hunky Mario smiled when he saw it. Jeez, that nickname needed to go.

"What's your name?" I asked.

His only reply came as a rough kiss, unlike any other I'd ever had. The scrape of his beard against my clean-shaven face almost hurt—in a good way? Yeah, it was definitely a good hurt. He was hella skilled with his tongue and expertly attacked my mouth with a kind of fervent energy no other partner ever has. I'd like to say I led the kiss—because I was a damn good kisser—but I'd be lying. He seized control, and I couldn't have fought him for it, even if I wanted to. He broke the kiss, spun his hat around, and nipped along my jaw while his hands settled on my hips. Without his taste in my mouth, I was able to think for a moment, and I asked him again what his name was.

He ceased his exploration of my jaw and pulled back just enough to look me in the eye. "Don't worry about it." His eyes raked up and down my body and I thought I was about to burst into flames. "You're a bit skinny, but you're fucking cute." He rushed my mouth again, his lips crashing against mine in a bruising kiss. One of his hands fisted my hair while the other skimmed my treasure trail and the band of my boxers. I took that as all the permission I needed to get handsy in return, and I tentatively put my hands on his waist. He was firm and not at all curvy like most of the women I'd been with. I wanted to touch him more, to map out every inch of his body, but I fucking froze again when he firmly grasped my cock over my pants.

"Oh, fuuuuck," slipped past my lips. He chuckled triumphantly and kissed me again while he undid my pants and slid a hand inside my boxer briefs. I moaned into his mouth, and he swallowed every single one of my curses. After a few strokes, he pulled back from the kiss and glanced down at my cock in his hand.

"Circumcised, huh? I like it." He released me and looked around the bathroom, eyes settling on a pump bottle of hand lotion near the sink. He got two pumps from the bottle and grabbed my cock with a now very slick hand. I wanted to reciprocate, but it wasn't going to happen so long as he was touching my cock. He knew exactly how to touch me, and when to apply more pressure—it drove me fucking wild. Too damn much. I was about to come and was powerless to hold it back. He kissed me again like he knew I was close and when his tongue swiped across the roof of my mouth, I was fucking done. Done. Donezo. I came all over the inside of my boxers, and he stroked me and kissed me all the way through it.

"Oh my fucking God," I ground out between gasps. He smiled at me and gave my softening cock one last firm squeeze—causing me to wince and shudder—before withdrawing his hand from my softening cock.

"Damn, you're fun," he said with an evil grin. He held up his hand, and my cum was strung between his fingers like the lewdest spider web. I was about to apologize for not giving him fair warning, but the words died in my throat when he licked his palm. His tongue moved on to each of his soiled fingers, saving his thumb for last. When his thumb slid free from his lips, I was transfixed and staring at his mouth with bated breaths. He smiled and pulled me by my tie once again into another kiss. I could taste myself on his tongue, and I wanted more. I wanted everything.

Then he broke the kiss and stepped back. He washed his hands in the sink, and I took that opportunity to step around him and clean myself up as best I could with toilet paper. Luckily, the mess was pretty contained, but I was in for a fucking uncomfortable night. Was it worth it? Hells yeah, it was.

He finished drying his hands on a hung up hand towel when I had my pants fastened again. There was so much I wanted to say to him, though I didn't know where to start.

My stupid mouth didn't get that memo. "That was awesome."

He snorted a laugh and turned his snapback around properly. "You're welcome. Look"—he pointed to the door behind him—"this was fun, but I'm gonna head out." He spun around and opened the door and was halfway into the hall before my stupid mouth caught up with my brain.

"Wait! Can I at least get your name and number or something?"

He halted his exit, stood still for several long moments before ultimately shaking his head. He shot me one last smile and closed the door behind him.

"Fuck!" I whisper-shouted to myself. I washed my hands and bolted out of the room and down the stairs hoping to catch him and demand something—*anything*—but he was gone. I inwardly cursed and pulled out my phone out of habit. I had dozens of texts from my friends, demanding to know where the fuck I was and who I was fucking. I thumbed out a reply to Dani saying I'd be right back and to have some fucking shots ready when I got there.

I was late meeting Theo for lunch the next day. We had lunch at least once a week to stay in touch. Thursdays worked best for me with my current rotation and, as usual, Theo was very accommodating for me. Theo had his eyes glued to his phone as I approached the table. He was smiling, so I could only assume he was texting Masa. Theo was a handsome dude. When he smiled it definitely kicked it up a few notches. He had short wavy chestnut-brown hair that was usually styled back for work, and blue eyes a shade darker than mine. More often than not, he kept well-groomed scruff on his jaw, and as much as I liked to tease him for it, it really did look nice. I couldn't grow a beard like that, so maybe I was a wee bit jealous. Just a smidgen. He was six years older than me, so I still had time to catch up. Theo was super fit and took care of himself in ways I doubted I ever could. Sometimes I'd think about what it would be like to be a bit more traditionally masculine. The attitude, the beard, the body hair, the muscles. It just seemed like such a departure from who I was and, frankly, something wholly unattainable.

As I closed in on the booth where my brother was seated, he looked up and smiled at me. He slid out of the booth and stood up straight to embrace me in a hug—something relatively new to us. Theo was a couple inches taller than me, and our bodies were very different. We shared similar facial features, being brothers and all, but he was sharper where I was softer. Basically, he was a more handsome version of me. He also dressed pretty fancy-schmancy, though I didn't envy that. The idealized version of myself I'd never be. And I used to be okay with that. Then last night I wanted to be more. When I had my hands on that guy and he said I was skinny, I'd wanted to be more like him. And that was fucking wild. I'd always been confident in my appearance and had never received any complaints from partners. I mean, hunky Mario didn't complain, but still.

Theo released me from the hug and cupped the back of my head, gently squeezing my neck, before releasing me completely and sitting back down. I sat in the booth across from him and drank half of the glass of orange juice he'd ordered for me.

"It's good to see you, Jay, but I've got to be honest. You look like death warmed over."

"Ugh, I feel worse." After I met back with my friends, things got a little crazy. I didn't remember much after the tequila came out.

Theo's brow furrowed, and he looked at me closely. "Are you wearing eyeliner?"

"Turns out expensive makeup is hard to get off without makeup remover. What the fuck, right? This is the best I could do."

"You should pop over to Dani's and get that cleaned up. You look like a fourteen-year-old girl with a broken heart." He smirked at his dig, something else he never used to do. The new Theo really was my favorite.

"If we're going to start out with honesty, then I'll admit that I kinda do feel like one. Well, maybe fifteen. Fourteen-year-olds don't really have the scope to understand their feelings, but I feel like I've got more—"

"Jamie. Focus."

"Right, sorry. What I'm trying to say is that I met someone last night."

Theo snorted a laugh. "What else is new?"

"Fair. Okay, I guess I shouldn't have started there. So, new development that isn't really all that new, but that's not the point. God, I'm rambling. This was a lot easier when I told Dani." I rubbed my sweaty palms on the thighs of my jeans.

"Jay, are you okay? *Truly* okay? You're acting strange, even for you." Theo looked genuinely concerned for me, and I inwardly cursed myself for my lack of communication skills.

"I like guys and girls. Sexually. Possibly emotionally, but I really don't know that yet." Saying sexually probably wasn't fucking necessary, but oh well, it was out. *I* was out. If I didn't feel like garbage from mild-to-severe alcohol poisoning, I might have been feeling something a bit more gratifying.

"Are you serious?" Theo asked neutrally.

I nodded my head and hummed. "I've known for a really long time. Dating girls exclusively had always seemed way easier—you know, with Dad and all. I'd been thinking more about what to do about it when you came out to me. You were really the catalyst in getting me to sort my shit out and stop ignoring this... aspect of myself." I nodded again, maybe a bit frantically.

Theo nodded in a much more controlled way and rapped his knuckles on the table before he spoke. "Thank you for telling me."

"Of course I'd tell you. I wanted to tell you first, but I kind of blurted it out to Dani the other day."

Theo laughed quietly. "That sounds like you. It's okay, Jay. I'm not upset that I wasn't the first to know. Tell me something. You said you've known this for a long time. How long?"

I shrugged. "Since I was about thirteen or fourteen." Theo's jaw tightened. He looked grim. I could tell he was thinking about something and doing that thing he used to do where he blamed himself for all of the world's problems. "Hey." He looked up from the table and met my eyes. "I don't want you to sit there and think I didn't speak up because you didn't. Don't put that on yourself, okay? I didn't bother with it because it was easier not to, and I liked girls just fine, so I left well enough alone. It's not your fault." I leaned forward and pointed my index and middle finger at him—the two-finger point was so much more dramatic. "So don't you dare twist yourself into thinking that." I dropped my hand and settled back against the booth, satisfied with myself and momentarily forgetting that I might hurl on the table.

A joyless smile pulled at Theo's lips. "Am I still so transparent?"

"You know what they say. Old habits and shit like that."

Theo huffed and smiled more genuinely that time, which in turn made me grin. "So, have you met any guys you like?"

"Kinda. That's what I was trying to say when you likened me to an emo adolescent girl."

Theo winced. "Sorry about that."

"Nah, don't be. It's true. I met a guy last night. Well, it's more appropriate to say I had an encounter with a guy last night. I didn't catch his name."

"Too preoccupied with something else?"

"Yes and no. I asked him for his name three damn times, and he wouldn't tell me! He totally rocked my world, and I came in like two minutes like some inexperienced virgin." Ugh, the worst.

Theo took a drink from his water, but I still saw him smiling. "Tell me about him."

"God, Theo. He was so fucking hot. He was older than me—he had to be. Tall, beard, tattoos, muscles. Like, *hot dayum*."

"Interesting," Theo drew out. "That's not the type of man I'd have pictured you with."

"Yeah, well, he's not with me, remember? The sexy bastard wouldn't give me his name or number."

My brother eyed me carefully like he was looking into me, and I shuffled nervously. "What else is going on? There's something else bothering you."

Blah, I had to say it out loud. "He called me skinny in an offhanded comment, and I'm a little messed up about it." Theo's brow wrinkled, but he didn't say anything. I took it as my cue to keep going. "I've been feeling a bit weird lately. I've wanted to make some changes to better myself and make me happier. You've been a big inspiration for me, actually. How you've changed and how hard you work at keeping things that way. You've shown me that there's always more if you try for it. I guess we never stop idolizing our big brothers," I said with a smirk.

"Jesus, you really think that about me?"

"God, it's Jamie, not Jesus. Get it right. And yeah, you're a superstar in my eyes, bro."

"I don't know if I deserve that, but thank you. What was it about his comment that bothered you so much?"

"That's where it gets tricky. Part of me thinking about this whole bisexual identity was a re-evaluation of what being a man meant to me. Meant for me. I never cared much about it before, and now it's popping up more and more. I'm not sure what to do. It's driving me a bit batshit."

Theo nodded knowingly. "You've got a brand new set of standards to hold yourself to on top of dealing with an identity crisis. Oh, Jay, you're more like me than you think."

"That guy was kind of like how I see you; he was every bit the man I'm not. A man I don't know that I could be, but maybe I can find my own version of it. Does that sound dumb? It sounds dumb, doesn't it?"

"Not at all. I'm proud of you. It took twenty-six years, but my baby brother is finally growing up."

"Yeah, yeah, whatever. I'm still going to annoy the shit out of you every damn chance I get."

"I expect no less. Seriously though, I'll help you in any way you need. You can come to me, or Masa, with anything." He spoke with a confidence usually reserved for his work in the family company. His support made me feel infinitely better. As if I could actually achieve some positive changes. "If you want to bulk up a bit you can come to the gym with me sometimes."

"I've seen your workouts, I'd rather not die," I deadpanned.

Theo's warm laugh filled the space around us. "I promise I'll go easy on you."

"Yeah, we'll see." I took another drink and felt myself slowly resurrect. "Oh! I know what you can tell me!"

"What's up?" Theo asked with an eagerness and adorable curiosity.

"How exactly does it work when you and Masa have sex? I mean, you're both big guys, and I can't really peg down who does what and it'd be great if—"

"Jamie, I swear to God, that better not be a serious question."

It totally was, but I knew when to push Theo and when to drop things. If I wanted him to pay for lunch and take me shopping, it would be best to drop this line of questioning and try again when he was plied with fine scotch. Yes, that plan would suffice. I smiled innocently at Theo and held my hands up in surrender, but I could tell he didn't buy my shit. I didn't blame him, though. I wouldn't buy it either.

THREE

NOVEMBER

A WEEK HAD PASSED since the Halloween party. Despite having done a lot of thinking during that time, I wasn't remotely close to having all the answers I was seeking. I was mostly thinking about all of the things I didn't want to think about, but not actually working my way through anything. I buried myself in textbooks and medical journals when I wasn't at the hospital in an effort to put off digging into the tough shit. Not to suggest that medical school wasn't tough shit, but I'd always had an aptitude for learning, and things came pretty easy to me. I didn't need to be studying as much as I was, though it served as a good distraction. Rather, it had been. For about three days. I spent the rest of my downtime high off shatter and bud and listening to my records. It was working, but I knew I couldn't hide from my problems forever. That, and Dani would have beaten my ass if she knew I was holed up in my loft, living in an ignorant cloud of smoke and junk food.

Things would have been so much fucking simpler if I could've forgotten about hunky Mario. Alas, I could not. I rolled my ass out of bed and went to the bathroom to take a piss. I deliberately avoided my reflection as I walked past the mirror. I knew what the hell I looked like and didn't need a reminder. No, what I needed was a second opinion. I ran— okay, that was a lie, I briskly walked—back to my bed and unplugged my phone from the wall charger. I fell back into my bed and kicked the blankets down. I liked to keep the temperature cranked up so I could walk around in my underwear or less. Less clothing, less laundry. Boom, life hack.

I unlocked my phone and scrolled through my recent message threads until my thumb settled on my brother's boyfriend, Masa. He and I bonded after I almost ruined our first meeting by being awkward. We got past that—much to Theo's relief—and now I considered the guy one of my best friends. And yeah, I did crush on him for like, half a second in the beginning, but it really couldn't be helped. He was hot, tall, funny, and liked a lot of the same things as me. He was born in Japan, raised in Canada, and occasionally spoke some pretty foul-mouthed French when you got him going. I never wanted him for myself, though. I loved him with Theo —he was exactly the type of person my brother needed when he was lost.

It was a Wednesday and just after noon so Masa should be on a break between classes. I sent a simple "hi" to get his attention and not lead with what was really on my mind. If he didn't answer for a few hours that would have been awko-taco. I was relieved when my phone buzzed a few seconds later. Small victories!

M: Hey, is everything ok?
J: Yes.
J: No. Yes.
J: Maybe.
M: Weirdo. What's up?

Welp, there was no use stalling.

J: What do you think of my body?

My phone started ringing, Masa's and Theo's smiling faces flashed up on my screen. I answered the call and put it on speakerphone before dropping the phone on my chest.

"What do I think of your body?" Masa asked, sounding both confused and amused.

"Mhm, and be honest with me."

"What's the context?"

"I'm wondering how guys see me. Uh, gay guys, if that wasn't clear." I'd called Masa to tell him about my new public status, and he was unyieldingly supportive and happy for me.

"Well, I can't exactly speak for all gay men, but I'd say—objectively speaking—that you shouldn't be worried about your appearance."

I folded my arms behind my head and stared up at the ceiling, momentarily inflated by Masa's words. "Okay, I know my face is good, that's never been an issue. What about, like, my body? Am I too skinny?" God, I sounded neurotic.

"You're not too skinny. You're lean, but, um… tight, I guess is an appropriate word. This is weird."

"And that's a good thing?"

"Yeah. You're built kind of twinkish. A lot of guys like that. Is this about that guy from the Halloween party you told me about before?"

"Yes and no. I've just got a lot on my mind."

Masa groaned. "I feel that. Why don't you come over on one of your nights off? I'll have Theo pick up some scotch, and I'll cook anything you want."

"Sold. You don't have to twist my arm. Does Saturday night work for you?"

"It's perfect."

"Okay, cool. Look, I won't keep you because I know you're busy being a good little scholar and all that jazz, but thank you. I do feel better now than I did before you called."

"No worries, man. You know you can call me any time."

"Same goes for you. Later, babe." I ended the call and got back out of bed. I had a shift with Dani in two hours, and I was scheduled to assist with an appendix removal, so it was time to fuckin' rock 'n' roll.

"How was your surgery?" Dani asked as she slumped into the empty space next to me on the couch in the doctors' lounge.

"No complications. The patient was only seven and pretty scared beforehand. Dr. Luna left me to calm her down before she was prepped. She apparently has a little crush on me. I told her about when I broke my arm, and she was fine."

"That's it? Damn, you really do have great bedside manner." Dani leaned further into my side and made herself comfortable.

"I maybe also promised her a kiss after the surgery." I yawned.

Dani snorted a laugh. "Of course you did."

"Just a kiss on the hand—like a princess. She beamed at the idea and promised she'd be good. Give me some credit here. You have anything exciting today?"

"I scrubbed in and observed Dr. Turner perform a nephrectomy. Watching him work is something else." Dani sounded so tired. We still had a few hours of being on call before we could go home, so using this downtime to sleep was wise, but I had to get something off my chest.

"D," I said quietly, checking to see if she was still awake.

"Yeah?"

"I want to start going to the gym. More than the couple times a month you drag me to those awful dance cardio classes."

She yawned again. "Don't knock my dance cardio. Those classes are keeping my ass nice and tight."

I laughed softly, exhausted myself. "You do have a great ass. Maybe there's something to it," I teased.

"Damn straight I do. I work hard for this ass. If you're serious about wanting to go, you're more than welcome to join me."

"I'd like that, D. Thank you."

She laughed sleepily. "Don't thank me yet. We're going four days a week. Mornings during this rotation. Meet me at my place at oh six hundred, and we'll jog there together for our warm-up."

I closed my eyes and slung my arm around Dani's shoulders. "You're going to be the death of me."

I got home just after midnight. I showered immediately then threw some leftover pizza in the oven. I was starved, but I loved myself too damn much to eat microwaved pizza whenever possible. I discovered years ago that pre-heating was for suckers. Most food would be ready by the time the oven was heated to the temperature on the box. Who had fifteen minutes just to wait for an oven to get hot? Probably me, but fuck that noise.

I sat up on the marble kitchen island and was calling Theo before I remembered how late it was. He answered on the second ring, his voice thick with sleep. "Are you okay?"

"Yeah, I am. I'm sorry to call so late. I just got home and had shit on my mind, and I forgot about the time. I'll call you back in the morning, bro."

I heard sheets stir, Theo was likely in bed. "It's okay. What's going on?"

I explained that I was going to start going to the gym with Dani and that I appreciated his offer, but it was probably a bit too much for me starting out. He agreed and said Dani would be the best gym buddy for me. Theo always had a weak spot where I was concerned. We both knew I'd complain and he'd concede and go easy on me. Despite us both being adults now, some things never changed. My big brother's desire to give me the world was one of those things.

Alternatively, Daniella would kill me, resurrect me, and then work me even harder than when I tried to quit. She could be scary, man. It was best not to disappoint her where possible. My charm always had zero effect on her, which vexed me when we'd first met and I thought us dating was what needed to happen. Ah, yes. Tender times, truly.

Like me, Theo wasn't big on cooking. Before he had Masa he did his own meal prep, and I thought it would be a good idea to ask him about what I should be eating during this hellish ordeal. Dani and Masa were basically chefs so anything they could tell me would be borderline useless to someone as kitchen-impaired as myself. Theo, though? He knew my limitations and could definitely float me a few ideas. Also, I had a feeling he really wanted to help me, and that's something I would never deny my brother.

My theory was confirmed when his reply to my ask for his help came out in a slightly higher, excited voice. I could tell he was smiling but sitting there stoically, trying to school his features. It was late, and we both had early mornings—Lord, give me strength—so we called it a night. Theo said he would email me some quick, easy meal ideas and even show me how to prepare some of the more difficult ones. I thanked him, and we said our goodbyes.

The alert on the oven sounded when I hung up the call, and I thought to myself, goddamn, things are starting to look up. Small victories for the fucking win.

I was wrong; things were *not* starting to look up. Nope, not at all. The jog to the gym fucking sucked, and I blew chunks in a garbage can. Not once, but twice. And to add insult to injury, Dani roared with laughter both times. I felt like I was already dead when we got to the damn gym. I managed to recoup a bit while we stretched more and waited for a class to start. It was one of those dance-shit things.

As people started filing into the room, I noticed an alarming number of women. In fact, I was the only guy present. I was about to ask Dani what the fuck was going on when a group of three guys around our age came in. I won't lie and say their presence didn't make me feel instantly better, because it definitely did.

Everything clicked when the instructor walked in. There wasn't an appropriate way to describe him other than cover model gorgeous. Piercing green eyes, short styled blond hair, a bright smile, and a body carved from fucking marble. He was wearing black leggings and a matching tank, and the outfit left absolutely nothing to the imagination. Everyone in the room had their full attention on him, and I groaned loud enough for Dani to hear and elbow me in my side.

That bright, handsome bastard put on some loud-ass club music and away we went. Correction: away everyone else went. The false relief I felt when I saw the other guys walk in vanished when I realized they were regulars and coordinated as fuck. I was a mess. Tripping over my own damn feet and falling behind with all of the steps. That dance-cardio shit was a lot harder than it looked on infomercials. The hot instructor ended up spending most of the hour-long class helping me with the steps, and I guess my form was bad too. By the end, I was a sweaty, panting heap of sore muscles. My hair was stuck to my forehead and the back of my neck, and it was fucking disgusting. The one positive was that nearly everyone in the class was shooting me dirty looks for monopolizing the instructor's attention.

Dani stood above me and nudged me in the hip to get my attention. I opened my eyes and looked into hers. "How're you feeling?"

"Is that a joke? Because if it was, you need better material."

"Come on"—she motioned with her head toward the door—"let's go do weights for a bit."

"Now I know you're joking because that's fucking hilarious."

She shifted her weight and placed a hand on her hip. "I'm not going to say it again, James."

Ugh, James. I dragged myself to my feet, which was really fucking hard when you feel like you weigh a metric ton. "I'm up, I'm up. Fuck me, that was excruciating."

Dani slapped me on the back, and an evil smile spread across her face, all the way to her eyes. "Get used to it, rich boy. This class is three times a week and we're always doing weights or more cardio after. The fourth day will be a surprise for you every week." She slapped my back again, and I winced. I watched her walk out of the room and could physically feel my soul leaving my body. RIP, me. It was fun while it lasted.

FOUR

FEBRUARY

Waking up after binge drinking was never a fun time. I was coming off a two-day bender and feeling every bit like the walking dead. Overindulgence was always one of my faults, whether it was booze, girls, smoking, or excessive spending. If it was an exploitable vice, you know damn well I was going to exploit the shit out of it. Although this time I had a good excuse; in fact, I had two.

Scotty and Pat had birthdays just two days apart at the end of January and beginning of February. Since we've been friends, we've always celebrated them together and went straight through into the next day without stopping. That alone would have been enough to warrant me needing a liver transplant. We had something else to celebrate too; the thirty-first of January also marked the last day of rotations for any of us. We get wild on a normal night out. Last night we were straight-up flossy as fuck.

The past few months had been a serious motherfucking grind, and we all needed last night. My final rotation was in emergency medicine and demanded more of my time to be on call. Working the emergency room patients was draining in every sense of the word, but also pretty damn cool. I got to assist on an abdominal stab wound and was a righteous bloody mess after. I missed the patient connection from the other rotations, though emergency was hands down the most thrilling. The lows were hella *low*, though. It was mind-boggling how many people got things that did not belong in the human body lodged in various orifices. Mind-boggling, impressive, disgusting, and mildly arousing.

I did my USMLE exams in December and started interviews for residency in January. I still had a few interviews left, and then I'd be free until the start of residency at the beginning of July. Assuming I matched. If I didn't match to a program, then I'd have a whole lot of free time on my hands. Honestly, not matching was a nonissue. I had impeccable grades, exceptional on-the-job skills in all of my rotations, and had wonderful relationships with all of the doctors I'd worked with. I had raving letters of recommendation from all of them. So yeah, there wasn't a doubt in my mind that I wouldn't match. I limited my applications to Chicago area hospitals and clinics for the same reason I went to school in–state. I didn't want to leave. I had acceptance letters from the Ivy League schools but was more than content going to UIC. Dad was cross with me enough over not wanting to go into commerce and work at the family business, Rey Financial. He had Theo to fulfill that requirement of dutiful son. Me refusing to go to a fancy-ass expensive university really irked him. He even threatened to cut off my allowance—Mom wouldn't have it. The threat was mostly empty anyway, I had a trust fund that I've had access to since I was twenty-five, so while my allowance was supremely appreciated, it wasn't a necessity. In fact, I really didn't have to work at all if I didn't want to.

We all still had an elective to fulfill, except for Pat. That overachieving bastard did his in Peru over the summer.

Nonetheless, we celebrated! Andrew came out with us in a show of support, which I thought was super cool of him. I know he scored major points with Dani for stepping outside of his comfort zone and partying with us, but he definitely overdid it. At one point I thought he might actually have been dead. Whoops. Andrew had passed out cold in a booth on the way to the bathroom. Even after I personally checked his pulse, I wasn't convinced that we hadn't actually killed him. Then again, perhaps I wasn't in the best state to be checking anyone's vitals. Double whoops. We put our libations on a brief hold while we saw to him getting home and tucked in. Dani came back out with us, and things got even wilder. We ended up at a gay bar in Boystown as our last stop. I came out to my mom and all of my friends about a week after I told Dani and they all took it like champs. Mom cried and asked me if I had a boyfriend. After seeing the shit show that ensued when Theo came out, we decided it would be best to hold off on telling Dad for a while. I felt like a fucking pussy for it, and like I owed it to Theo, to be honest. He agreed with Mom. Scotty had scooped me up in a hug and kissed me. No, it wasn't chaste. That crazy bastard tongued me, and I fucking burned red like a schoolgirl. I've been teased for my reaction ever since, and now Scotty was convinced that I was in love with him. Not the case, but I'd never live my reaction down.

We'd gone drinking in Boystown a few times since I came out. I assured my crew that nothing needed to change, but they were determined to make sure I explored my bisexuality to the fullest. I appreciated their support and efforts, even if it still felt strange to me. I flirted and danced with several guys, and even made out with a few, though it never went beyond that. Hunky Mario often drifted into my thoughts, and I'd be lying if I said I didn't use that encounter in my spank bank. Shit, I used it often. I continued to sleep with women because it was what I was used to—and yeah, less scary—and I convinced myself I was too swamped to deal with trying to date guys. Now that things were beginning to wind down, I promised myself I would make more of an effort.

I groaned at the prospect of having to haul my sorry ass out of bed and go to the gym. I'd kept up with my commitment to go with Dani, and even went occasionally with Theo and Masa. I had trouble sometimes keeping up with the intensity of Theo's workouts, but I was a goddamn superstar compared to what I was capable of when I first started. Theo's diet advice really made a huge impact on my progress. I had abs coming in now and some definition in my arms and chest. It wasn't a full-blown six-pack—more like an occasional four-pack—but I looked hot as hell, and I felt it too. I even lost some of my baby face. Dani told me that I looked like Theo more than ever now. My confidence was restored and then some. I drove my brother and Dani crazy with it, but what could I say? I was the bomb-dot-com even more than I was before, and people had a right to know it. I could have achieved more, though I didn't have the discipline Theo did and, frankly, I liked tasty, greasy food too much to cut it out entirely.

That was the kind of food I needed as I lay in bed, sweating out the poison from last night. I rolled over to check the time on my phone and saw that it was entirely too early for me to properly function after such a brutal night. I knew good and well that Dani would be up and ready to go to our class at the gym. I said a silent prayer to whoever was listening, and thumbed out a quick text confirming that we were to meet in just under an hour. She replied immediately —damn her—so I dragged my ass out of bed, and started the shower.

The class was rough as fuck. Despite wanting to hurl the entire time, I managed to keep it under control until I was in the safety of the locker room. Dani crushed my hopes of having a light day, and pushed us all class. She'd said we'd sweat out the alcohol and feel better. Personally, I felt like that was a crock of shit, but I wasn't about to say no to her. I loved myself a bit too much to do something ludicrous like that. In spite of the state I was in, I still had a nominal amount of fun. I knew all of the steps at this point and these hips did not lie. Like, not ever. I stopped feeling like a fool after I noticed that those dumb classes made me better at fucking. Then it was game on, and I threw myself into it with all of my effort. My skills in the boudoir were pretty damn solid—not bragging, just the conclusion I'd come to based on a lot of field research. I was unsure of how that would translate to guys—I hadn't even seriously considered which position I'd take. That was an issue for when I found the right guy. The right guy, jeez, listen to me. I assured myself it would all work out okay and left it at that.

After my shower, I felt heaps better. Still far from one hundred, but maybe, like, a solid sixty-two percent. Dani cranked me up to seventy percent with three beautiful words, "Wanna get breakfast?"

"You're a goddess," I replied with sincere gratitude.

Dani giggled, clasping her hand over her mouth in an attempt to hold it in. She hated giggling, so I, of course, took every opportunity I could to make it happen. "Come on. We'll take the train to that diner by your place."

"Yaaaas, except we're taking an Uber. You know I hate the train."

"It's a waste of money, Jamie."

I rolled my eyes and sighed. We'd had this discussion many times in the past. "The trains are confusing. Too many colors."

"That's a weak-as-shit excuse since you can read and you're not colorblind."

"Can we please just take an Uber? I'm so hungry, D. I promise I'll take the train next time."

Dani mimicked my eye roll from moments ago, but didn't protest. "Fine, you're paying, rich boy."

Breakfast was everything. They had the Brazilian dark roast coffee that Dani liked, and they made their drinks with real shaved chocolate. I preferred hot chocolate to anything with caffeine, but I often drank café mochas when I needed an extra boost. It was definitely an extra boost kind of day. Our drinks were brought out to us super-fast. Maybe it was because we looked like shit and the cute server felt bad. Who was to say? The smell of Dani's coffee hit me before I saw the server on his way back to our table. It was a smell I associated with her and could always pick out. It tasted like every other batch of vile, black water to me, but it smelled rich and like Dani.

The first few sips of my café mocha made me feel insta-better. I forgot to ask for extra whipped cream, but it was there anyway. That was a serious win. The three-egg bacon and sausage omelet with a side of strawberry pancakes I ordered also helped. I mowed through my food at record speed while Dani enjoyed her eggs benny at a far more socially acceptable pace. My phone sounded off with a text from my pocket, but I was too damn hungry to check it.

I finished my food and ordered a hot chocolate while Dani smirked at me and continued to work on her breakfast. When the server left with my second order, I stretched back in the antique hardback chair and yawned. "Do you mind if I check my messages?"

Dani shook her head while she chewed. "Go ahead."

With her okay, I pulled my phone out and saw it was

Masa who had messaged me. "I thought it might be Roz or the guys complaining, but it's Masa."

"Oh, try to keep your composure," she teased.

"I never should have told you about that."

Dani laughed, low and evil. "What's going on with him?"

"It seems that my dear brother is going on an out-of-town business trip for a couple of days. Masa wants to hang out and get proper lit."

"Lord help the patrons of whatever place you two end up in."

I snorted a laugh and shrugged. "I won't break any tables this time." Dani shook her head and went back to her food. I definitely wanted to hang with Masa.

J: Count me in, man!

J: Where at?

M: There's a pizza place I really like in Boystown. I'm sure we can find something entertaining to do after that.

J: This isn't some ploy you and my brother came up with to hook me up with a dude, right?

I really wouldn't put that kind of scheming past those two.

M: Haha, I promise I have no ulterior motives.

J: Aiighty. When were you thinking?

We hashed out a night a couple of days later that worked for both of us, and I pocketed my phone again after discreetly ordering an Uber to take us back to my place. It was only a couple blocks away, but it was February, I was full, and I just really didn't want to walk. Fight me.

Back at my place, Dani used her key to let us in, and we

piled into my king-sized bed to sleep. Things like this were what made my relationship with Andrew strained in the beginning, and understandably so. He'd since grown to realize that Dani was safe around me and that even if I did try something with her, she'd break my fucking jaw. So, yeah, our sleepovers and naps were able to continue. And thank God for it because Gallo snuggles were the absolute best.

I DID NOT EVER BREAK my promises. If I promised someone something, whether it was at work or in my personal life, I did everything in my power to keep my word. That type of integrity was heaps important to me. I'd sacrifice my own convenience and happiness to keep a promise. That was how I ended up on the damn red line train, on my way out to Boystown to meet Masa. He gave me directions from the Addison stop that were fairly straightforward. I was feeling hella confident that I wouldn't fuck it up. I'd be able to rub it in Dani's face that I *could* take the train, I just chose not to.

I wanted to text Masa to tell him which stop I was so he'd have an ETA for me. I looked out the window as the train rolled to a halt and saw something mildly alarming. I was staring at signs to the red line, which was running parallel to whatever fucking train I was on. I unlocked my phone and called Masa. I was not about to let my pride get in the way of asking for help.

"Hey, don't worry, you're not late. I'm still on my way over."

"I NEED HELP," I said louder than I'd intended to. A few people turned and scowled at me—fuck 'em.

"Whoa, whoa, what's going on?"

"I think I'm on the wrong train. Google said to take the

red line, and I thought I did, but I'm looking out the fucking window at the damn red line right now!"

That bastard had the audacity to laugh at me. It was muffled, but I fucking heard it. "It's okay, Jamie. Is the train you're on running alongside the red line?"

"Yes."

"All right, that's not bad. It sounds like you're on the brown line. Give me a sec." It sounded like he moved the phone away from his ear and I heard faint tapping on the screen. "Get off at the Belmont stop. It's going to be a bit more walking for you, but it isn't that far."

I nodded my head before I realized he couldn't see me. "Belmont. Got it. Thanks."

"I'll see you in about half an hour."

"Wait! Please don't tell Dani about this. She and the others have enough ammo against me as is." I cringed a bit at how desperate I sounded.

"I promise I won't say a thing. Scout's honor."

"Do they even have the Scouts in Canada?" I questioned, suspicious and maybe a bit paranoid. God, I was wigging out over a damn train.

Masa scoffed. "Of course there are Boy Scouts in Canada, *crisse d'épais.*"

Cheeky French bastard. "You know, one of these days I'm going to figure out what you're calling me when you say that."

I got off the train and checked the map app on my phone. To my dismay, I was a fifteen-minute walk from where I was supposed to be. Oh well, at least I'd remembered to wear a scarf. It was pretty chilly out, but not snowing, and for that I was thankful. I wore sneakers like I always did, and while they're comfortable and suit my fashion choices, they're not all that warm in deep snow or slush. Looking around, I saw that most of the people walking by were wearing sensible boots; all but one person. A pair of black and red Nikes approached, which caught my attention because they were like the pair I had about four years ago. I scanned my gaze up the rest of the stranger's body, past strong, thick thighs clad in dark denim, past a baggy black unbranded hoodie, and into the brown eyes of someone I never expected to see again. I'd hoped I would, but I hadn't been holding my breath. Okay, maybe I was a little bit.

The memory of Halloween came rushing back to me in vivid detail, and I saw the fireworks all over again. My steps faltered, and I looked down at my feet while I regained my balance. When I looked up again, he was gone. I spun around quickly and breathed a sigh of sweet relief when he was just a few steps away from me. He was wearing another snapback and had a black bag slung over his shoulder, and if I had to take a stab at it, I'd say it was a gym bag. He still looked fit as fuck. I stood there and watched him get further away while I debated what to do. I didn't know anything about him, and he clearly did not want to stick around on Halloween. I'd thought about him so many times since that night, so fuck it. If he didn't want to see me, he could tell me to fuck off. I was not going to be the kind of guy who lived with regrets.

I ran after him—no joke, dude was almost a block away, so I fucking booked it—and grabbed his shoulder when I caught up to him. "Wait… up," I panted. Yeah, this was starting out well.

He shook my hand off his shoulder and turned toward me, face unreadable. He remained silent and adjusted his grip on the strap in his hand, so I took it upon myself to carry on. "I'm sorry if I startled you. Um, you probably don't remember me, but we met at a party a few months ago and, ah, I'm not sure where I'm going with this."

He cocked his head, and I saw the moment his features relaxed as recognition took over. "Beetlejuice, right?"

"Slutty Beetlejuice, but close enough." God, someone needed to gag me. Preferably *him*.

"That's right," he said with a single nod. "Look, I'm sorry about the way I bailed after… It was shitty to do."

"You can start making it up to me by telling me your name."

His shoulders tensed, which only made him look bigger and hotter. "I don't think that's a good idea, kid."

"First off, I'm not a kid. Second, I'm taking meeting you again as divine-motherfucking-intervention, and I'm a persistent shit; I'm not leaving until I get your name." I looked him in the eye with all the swagger and confidence I could muster.

"You've got quite the mouth on you," he said with a small grin.

"You've got no idea," I replied. I was allowed to bluff if it meant getting what I wanted.

He chewed his bottom lip for a few moments before nodding again. "Name's Gus." Gus. Of course it was Gus. A masculine, one syllable porn name. Fuck, he was sexy. "Well, are you going to tell me yours?"

Whoops, I zoned out again. "Jamie. I'm being weird, my bad. I'll be honest with you, I'm kinda nervous. I don't know how this"—I motioned between us—"works. What I do know is that I'd like to see you again—just to talk."

"Jamie, I—"

"Nope. Don't even try to give me the brush-off again. I told you I was persistent, well I'm actually persistent as fuck."

Gus sighed, but I saw his gorgeous lips twist into a smile. "Okay. I'm busy right now though."

I did an internal happy dance. "No worries, I am too, actually. Give me your number, and I'll text you."

"How about you meet me somewhere for coffee?"

I was so happy that we were making plans that I didn't even think to ask why he wouldn't give me his number. "I can do that. It looks like you live in the area, so pick a time and place. I'm pretty free until next week." My elective started next week, but all I had were gym commitments and interview prep this week.

"Um, how about Peet's around the corner on Clark? Tomorrow at eleven?"

Yaaaaaaaaas! "I'll be there. Uh, I guess I'll let you get on your way." I smiled at Gus and hoped he'd think the flush on my cheeks was from the cold and not an indication of how giddy I was feeling.

"See you tomorrow, Jamie," he replied and turned and walked away.

I did the same, but turned back after a couple steps. "You better not stand me up!" I shouted loud enough for his retreating figure to hear. His answer came in the form of a peace sign held up as he kept walking. I wanted to break out into dance then and there, though I decided I'd save it for Masa. I ran the remainder of the distance to get to him feeling as if I could take flight.

FIVE

I COULDN'T FUCKING BELIEVE IT. I'd been pacing around my living room all damn morning watching the hands tick on my wall clock. I had a date with *him*—with Gus. I woke up that morning super early of my own volition. Actually, I'd been restless and anxious all night. I figured getting up and having a smoke would take the edge off, then I nixed that idea. I wanted to be fully lucid when I saw him. Well, as lucid as I could be.

Masa and I got in around one in the morning and had had a blast. He whooped my ass in countless games of pool before I managed to snag a W on the last match. At that point, it really wasn't all that fair though. He was hammered and speaking more French than English, which amused me to no end. It was also hot as hell, though I tried not to think about that.

I didn't have to try too hard last night. Gus occupied all of my waking thoughts. The bastard reappeared in my damn dreams too. The dream was what woke me up. It was Halloween again, and everything played out the same, except he stayed. That was when I woke up, which was two hours ago. I'd been pacing around ever since. I still had more than an hour to kill before I had to leave, but I was going to drive myself mad if I didn't do something.

Nearly everyone I knew would be at work or asleep right now, so I couldn't distract myself that way. I knew Dani would be up, but it was a Sunday, and Andrew had Sundays off, so I wanted to leave her alone. I texted everyone last night to tell them about Gus, and they all wanted to come with me and "just watch from a safe distance." Safe distance, my ass. I deliberately didn't tell anyone where Gus and I were meeting so no one could drop by unannounced. No, it would be very fucking announced if any one of 'em showed up. Masa could be discreet enough, but he was too damn good-looking not to get noticed. A tall, hot, Japanese guy with long black hair and hazel eyes? Get the fuck out. So, no, none of those lovely motherfuckers I called friends got any info other than I was meeting Gus today.

I glanced at the clock again—great, three minutes had passed. I couldn't bear it any longer. I would just go to Peet's early, have some hot chocolate, and wait. I hopped in the shower and decided to rub one out to calm my nerves and eat up some more time. It definitely helped with my nerves, not so much with the extra time. Ahem. I was super anxious, and when I got anxious, I got horny. I wasn't sure if anxiety boners were a thing for other people, but they were with me.

I ate up more time than anticipated choosing what to wear. Did it matter? Was this a date? What if he dressed up and I didn't? Oh, God. No, no, no. I breathed in and out in deep, measured breaths and replayed my brother's voice in my head, snapping at me to cut my shit out and get back on track. It worked alarmingly well.

I decided to wear a pair of dark wash distressed jeans and white V-neck under a burgundy cotton jacket Dani got me for Christmas. I topped the outfit off with my siren-blue-faced NOMOS watch Theo got me and all black Yeezys—because fuck the train and walking, I was taking an Uber—and I looked fresh as fuck. I grabbed my wallet and went out when my driver messaged me.

I ended up being only twenty minutes early after all that drama, so it turned out to be a good thing that I was panicky and started getting ready super early. I ordered a hot chocolate and sipped on it slowly while pretending to look at my phone. I was actually scanning the windows, looking for Gus. I told myself that I needed to relax. Even so, I couldn't shake the unease simmering in my gut. What if he didn't show up? I'd never been stood up before, but I'd also never had someone agree to meet me, and not give me their number. Fuck, why didn't I get his damn number? Right, I asked him for it, and he deflected. Ugh.

It was nearly eleven by the time I finished my drink. I was freaking the hell out. I couldn't place why I was so fuckin' rattled, but I was. Why seemed irrelevant at the time. I closed my eyes and mumbled to myself to chill the fuck out. When that didn't work, I hummed one of my favorite songs that never failed to mellow me out.

"'Letting the Cables Sleep,'" a deep, familiar voice said to me from above.

I jumped in the damn chair as my eyes shot open. Gus stood next to the empty chair across from me. He had on black, worn jeans, and a dark brown knit sweater under a black leather jacket. He smiled tentatively at me and all my anxiety dissolved. "Yeah, it is. Sit, please." I motioned to the chair across from me and felt like an idiot. Where the fuck else was he going to sit? Fuck my life.

"I hope you haven't been waiting long." His gaze drifted to my empty cup.

"Oh, yeah, I came early. I was driving myself batshit

crazy at home and couldn't stand it anymore. It's actually a good thing I came early. I'm pretty notorious for my tardiness. It's not really my fault, though. Shit happens that we can't always control and—" I cut myself off when I noticed that Gus was smiling at me. "What? Did I say something funny?"

"You don't have to be nervous."

"What? I'm not nervous." I was totally nervous. How could he tell? Was I sweating? Oh God, I hoped I wasn't sweating.

"Mhm," he hummed with a smile.

"Fine, I'm a teensy bit nervous. It's your fault." I crossed my arms, pouting.

Gus sighed and leaned forward with his elbows on the table. "Look, Jamie, I'm sorry about how I acted at the party. I had some stuff going on and really wasn't looking for more than a hook-up, but that was an asshole move."

He looked legitimately sorry, so I had trouble holding a grudge. "It's okay. It rattled me a wee bit, but everything worked out fine. Better than fine, actually. Things are pretty damn great," I said honestly.

"I'm glad to hear it. You look really good, even better than I remember."

Oh, fuck. What did I say to that? Before I could think of something sexy to say, my mind went straight to self-depreciation. "Not exactly skinny anymore, am I right?"

Gus didn't laugh. Of course, he didn't fucking laugh. He winced, which was not my intended reaction. "I'm sorry about that. I didn't mean anything bad by that. You weren't the usual type of guy I went for, but you were just too damn cute. The eyeshadow really made your eyes pop."

"Oh God, you remember that I was wearing makeup." It wasn't a fucking question.

"I remember everything about that night," Gus replied in a low voice.

"*Damn*, that's hot," I blurted out. When I realized that I'd said that aloud, I cupped my hand over my mouth and gasped at my stupid mouth's betrayal.

Gus just laughed, which was a gorgeous sound, deep and rumbling. Fuck, it was a gorgeous sight too. Seeing him in the light of day made me catch a few things about him I'd missed before. He had a horizontal scar about half an inch long through the end of his left eyebrow, and another small one on his right cheekbone. It was kinda shaped like a thin, upside-down obtuse triangle. I dug it. His beard was trimmed down to a couple days' worth of growth—shorter than it was last night —and when I looked closely, I noticed a few stray freckles on the bridge of his nose and cheeks. His eyelashes were also really thick. His lashes and the freckles made his rugged good looks somewhat softer. It made him cute, in a way.

The server came back and greeted Gus. I was too trans-fixed by the way his jaw moved when he responded that I missed his order. Gus turned his attention to me with a questioning look on his face, and then I noticed the server was watching me too.

"Oh. Sorry, what?" I asked.

The server smiled at me and, damn, she was cute too. I somehow missed that earlier when I was worried about whether or not Gus would show. I returned the smile and regained control of myself. "I'll take another hot chocolate, please."

"Extra whipped cream this time as well?"

"Ah, yes, thanks, hon." She nodded and walked away.

Gus eyed me quizzically throughout the exchange, though remained silent until the server was out of earshot. "So, Jamie, what is it that you want from me?"

That was a good question. I knew I wanted to see him again, though I hadn't stopped to ask myself why. It was a feeling I had more than anything I could logically explain, and that unsettled me a bit. I decided honesty was the best way to answer him. "I don't know that I exactly want something from you. I haven't really thought that far ahead. I…" I trailed off, looking for the right words. "I am kind of new to being with guys, and I'm still a bit confused."

"Confused about whether you like guys or not?"

"Oh, no, no. I've known that for a long time. I just haven't started exploring that part of myself until fairly recently. In fact, you were the first guy I've ever… well, done anything with." I bit my lip and looked up at Gus, unsure of how he'd take what I'd just revealed.

Gus started lightly tapping his fingers on the table—a nervous tick perhaps. Was I making him nervous too?

"Are you gay, Jamie?" Gus asked.

"Uh, no? Are you?" Ugh, stupid mouth.

"I am. Let me ask you again, what is it you want from me? I don't mean to be abrupt or rude, but I'm not going to be a confused guy's sexual guinea pig."

My eyes went wide when I realized what he was saying and what my lack of clarity insinuated. "I'm sorry. I do this sometimes… I'm really bad at explaining things when I'm nervous, and, dude, you seriously throw me off-kilter. I'm confused about a lot of things, but my attraction to guys isn't one of them. Neither is my attraction to you. Believe me when I say I think you're a mega babe. Like, Instagram hot in the flesh." Gus snorted a laugh and stilled his restless fingers. I instantly relaxed. "What I'm confused about is what I'm supposed to do about it. I want to get to know you better and see where this can go, but I don't really know how."

"You don't know a thing about me. Looks aside, why bother?" Gus asked genuinely.

I shrugged and waved my hand in a circle in front of me. "It's just a feeling I have. I've had it since I laid eyes on you at that party. I just want to know you. Who knows, maybe you're a dick, and I'll want to smother you in a snow bank when we're done here. I'm really hoping you won't want to do the same because I value my life too much, and it wouldn't be a fair fight."

He laughed in earnest that time, and I felt the tension between us finally settle. "All right. I can't promise that you'll like me, but I'm interested in knowing more about you too. I just needed to make sure you knew why you were here."

"What I told you is as much as I know. That, and I thought about you constantly for almost an entire month. I'm not going to go all *Single White Female* on you, so don't worry." I winked at him because dammit, I was a charmer.

He shook his head with a smile that I couldn't help but return. "Jesus, you're funny. You don't seem to hold anything back, which is a bit terrifying, but I think I like it."

"Wunderbar, because we'd have a real problem on our hands if you didn't think I was a riot. Seriously, though, I am clueless. I don't date much. I mean, I get mine, don't worry about that, but sitting down and getting to know someone? New territory for me."

Gus bowed his head and sighed. "I get that. I don't date all that much anymore. Though, as you know, I'm no saint." He quirked an eyebrow at me, and I felt my dick stir in my jeans.

"Lucky for me you're not." The cute server came back with our drinks and was gone just as quickly. A familiar scent reached my nose, but it was hard to nail down with all the fucking coffee… in the café. Yeah, okay, of course, it would smell like coffee. The flirty mood was gone, but things didn't feel awkward anymore, so I launched my inquisition. "So, how old are you? Is it rude to ask a guy that?"

"Not at all. I'm thirty-two. And yourself?"

"Twenty-six—not a kid."

"You don't look twenty-six, can you blame me?"

"You don't look thirty-two," I countered. "Or maybe you do. You're the same age as my brother. I guess you look about his age. Have any siblings?"

He took a sip of his coffee and nodded with a small grin on his face. "I have a kid sister. She's a handful, but I love her. My turn, what do you like to do for fun?"

"I've a pretty solid group of friends and we over-indulge in adult beverages as often as our schedules will allow. I also really like just chillin' at home and listening to music or watching movies. I'm not really a racket-ball-on-Thursdays kind of guy. And yourself?"

"When I'm not at work I'm either at the gym or occasionally at a bar in Boystown." Gus took another drink, and I stared at the movement in his throat, suddenly feeling parched.

"And the odd house party in Lincoln Park," I added.

Gus grunted in amusement. It turned out that was another sound that spurred my cock on. "I don't normally go to that part of town. I was actually there to meet someone."

"Oh. *Oh*," I repeated as realization dawned. "Who were you supposed to meet?"

"Some guy named Trent. I guess it was his party. I ditched that idea when I laid eyes on you." I wasn't entirely sure, but I thought Gus was giving me flirty bedroom eyes. Yeah, he absolutely fucking was.

"Trent Baxter is gay?" My eyes bugged out of my head for a second before I remembered we were talking about something way more important than that dudebro's sexuality. "You know what, never mind. I'm super glad you bailed on him. I mean, you kind of ruined me that night, but it was totally worth it." Gus laughed again. Yeah, that was a sound I could easily become hooked on. "I'm serious, dude. Everyone I've been with since then has paled in comparison. At this point, I'm not even sure how much is a memory and what's fantasy."

"I'd love to show you again sometime—just to rectify that memory issue for you."

"Fuck, dude," I groaned. I shifted in my chair to adjust my growing erection. "You can't say shit like that to me in public." I looked down at my lap then back up at Gus.

"I feel like I should apologize, though I'd be lying if I said I was sorry. I'm not in the habit of being untruthful. Guarded, yes. Dishonest? Never." Gus started tapping his fingers on the side of his coffee cup. Was he feeling uneasy after disclosing that?

"I don't want you to apologize. There's plenty I want from you right now, but an apology isn't on the list." I sounded ragged, which Gus seemed to notice. His nostrils flared, and his fingers squeezed around the cup, just like they had done once before around my cock.

"Think you can handle me?" Gus replied teasingly.

I scanned my eyes up and down his torso and broad shoulders, and bit my lip against a grin. "Honestly? I don't know. I'd sure as hell like to find out."

Gus didn't reply to me. He didn't have to. The look in his eyes screamed his reply loud and clear; he wanted me as much as I wanted him. I cleared my throat and was about to ask him if he lived close by, but the server came back and startled me. I jumped in my chair at her pleasant voice.

"Does anyone need a top up?"

My mouth didn't work. Gus looked at me, grinned crookedly, and then answered. "I think we're doing just fine. Thank you." He sipped his coffee again as the server smiled and walked away.

Then it hit me. What I smelled earlier was Dani's coffee.

Gus was drinking Dani's blend. It was dumb and shouldn't have made me like him more, but it did. I guess you could say I had a Pavlovian response to the smell; a smell that represented love, comfort, and all-around badassery.

"What are you thinking about?" Gus asked.

I blinked at him blankly and decided to lay it all out. "I want to see you again."

He smiled, tapping the side of the cup again. "I guess that means we're going to behave today?"

"I'm a man of class. I won't jump you until I've bought you dinner. Or you buy me dinner. However that works, but that's not the point. Can I see you again?"

Gus leaned back in his chair, never taking his eyes off mine. His brow was lightly furrowed and his jaw was tight. He was clearly thinking about my proposal, though he was taking longer than I was comfortable with. I wouldn't take no for an answer last night, but—after a kinda rough start—I thought we were getting along well now. If I saw him again, I wanted it to be because he wanted to see me, not because I didn't like hearing "no" to anything. I wanted to say something to break the silence, but it was important to let him decide. The worst he could say was no, right? If that happened, I'd be hella bummed and probably go on a bender, but I'd get over it. I always did.

"Okay. I want to see you again too," Gus said quietly.

I raised an eyebrow, and my knee started to bounce absently. "Are you sure about that? You took an awfully long time to answer. I think I actually died and was reincarnated."

Gus grunted, his lips curling into a small grin. "You've got a smart mouth. My hesitancy in replying has nothing to do with you. I like you. I'm just a bit of a mess right now."

"But I'm irresistible, so you said yes anyway."

"Yeah, something like that."

I leaned back in my chair and exhaled the biggest fucking

sigh of relief before picking up my hot chocolate and breathing in the sweet fragrance. "Now, back to business. How do you feel about long walks on the beach?"

We talked and laughed for about another hour. I told him I was a student at UIC and that I was working in my field of study as part of my degree. Not exactly a lie, but I wanted to save the med school bomb. I found out that he loved nineties movies and music—Bush turned out to be one of his favorite bands—and used to play the piano. He'd stopped when he got to high school because "it wasn't cool." My mind drifted to the Steinway grand piano sitting in that weird second sitting room at home that I was never allowed in when I was a kid. Rude. That piano hadn't been played in years, but Mom kept it… what did you do to a piano? Tuned? Serviced? Whatever. A dude named Gautier came out to the house and took care of it.

My brother learned to play while I was hopeless in the lessons. I wanted to hear Gus play. He swore he wasn't any good, but I wanted to hear it all the same. I wanted to watch his strong fingers glide over the keys and finger them with the same practiced hands that played my body. The thought ensured that I spent the entire date with a serious case of blue balls.

The lunch crowd filled up the café, so we decided to call it a day. Gus had some errands to run, and I had a serious need to bust a nut ASAP. Outside, Gus waited with me while I pulled out my phone to order an Uber.

"So, are you ready to give me your number yet?" I tapped away and got my confirmation that a driver would be there in just a few minutes.

"How about we meet again?" Gus asked. He sounded hopeful and not guarded like before, so I didn't push.

"Okay. When are you free?"

"I can do Tuesday or Wednesday after seven," Gus replied.

"Works for me. Um"—I tapped my thumb on my locked phone screen—"how about we meet here Wednesday at seven thirty?"

"Okay," Gus said with a shy smile on his face. I imagine I wore one that mirrored his.

"Okay," I echoed. I rocked on my heels and bit my lip while we awkwardly stood there looking at each other. "Gus, I don't really kno—"

His warm lips silenced mine, and thank fucking God for it. He kissed me chastely; just a soft graze of our lips, but it was *everything*. It was a stark contrast to the first time he kissed me. This new kiss seemed better though. It was sort of our first kiss. I kissed him at the party—a loooooot—when he was a gorgeous stranger, but this was my first time kissing *Gus*. And I loved it. I tried to touch him, but I couldn't move my arms. Only then did I notice his firm grip, holding me still. He pulled back when I tried to deepen the kiss and rested his forehead on mine.

"Your ride is here."

"Fuck it, it can wait." I tried to reach for him again. His grip held me. Fuck, he was strong. "Come on, kiss me again."

He chuckled, and I felt the vibrations where his nose touched mine. Gus released my arms and pressed another soft kiss to my forehead before stepping back. "I'll see you on Wednesday."

My stomach flipped. I felt like I was going to be sick—in a good way? I wanted to kiss him again, but I managed a weak nod, and my feet started toward the waiting car. I opened the door and turned back to Gus. "I'll see you on Wednesday," I repeated. I got in the car and shut the door.

Fuck me, I was in trouble.

SIX

I SPENT A GOOD PORTION of the day after the date jerking off until I thought my dick was going to fall off. A phone call from Mom spared my spent junk, and then I went over to the house for dinner. Mom was pleasant and eager to hear about my interviews. Dad was… well, he was Dad. He didn't pay much attention to me unless I was royally fucking something up. I tried not to come around when he was home, but sometimes it just couldn't be avoided. He banned Theo from the family home after he came out, and I hated him for it. Theo insisted that I should still be civil to Dad, though it was fucking hard.

When I got home my mood lifted, and my thoughts drifted back to Gus. I'd been about to tell him I didn't know if it would be weird for us to kiss when he took the decision out of my hands. I hadn't ever been kissed like that before, and it left me pretty shaken. In a good way, like a martini.

I poured myself a drink because it seemed like a damn good idea after that thought popped into my head. And by poured myself a drink, I mean I took a bottle of Johnnie Walker Blue into the living room with me to enjoy while I played video games. Life-hack: if you drank from the bottle, you wouldn't have dishes to do. Without dishes and laundry, I got to spend my precious time doing what was important, which at the time was *Tekken 3*. Classics never died.

I was still in the fucking clouds the next day when I met up with Dani and Masa at the gym. It was a pretty miserable day out with snow and an overabundance of ice-cold wind sweeping off the fucking lake. Masa had taken the bus and was coated in a layer of ice and snow and pretty pissed about it. I caught him cursing to himself under his breath while we got changed and tried—and failed—not to laugh. He'd been under some stress of his own with his dissertation, and we all noticed. He was handling it like a champ, but he deserved a break. Lucky for him, Theo came to me for help with Masa's Valentine's Day gift last month, and I suggested a trip somewhere hot and sweaty. They could thank me later. Andrew was keen on five-star dining and jewelry so I was certain Dani would be getting some ice.

It was pretty busy when we got into the machine area, but we managed to snag three treadmills in a row. I might have sweet-talked a girl into giving hers up early. I didn't think she minded. Dani and Theo often teased me about my hair being too long, but girls dug this shit. It wasn't like I was an eighties rocker or anything, it wasn't nearly long enough to tie back. Fuck all the haters.

I was feeling a bit rough from overindulgence the night before, and I wanted to walk. Dani and Masa insisted we run. So we ran. It was only half an hour, and I was thankful when we shifted into walking for a cooldown. We never talked much while running. I was a hand-talker, and I got distracted easily. I might have tripped and fallen off the treadmill once or twice. Definitely not thrice. Nope.

With tall-ass Masa between Dani and me, it was easier to

look ahead at the mirrored wall to talk to them both at once. "So, someone ask me about how yesterday went."

Masa grinned and brushed some stray bangs behind his ears. His shoulder-length hair was tied back, but there always seemed to be strays. "Jamie, how was your date yesterday?" He spoke in an all too proper, mildly patronizing tone that he sometimes used on me to poke fun. I liked to refer to it as his sexy prof voice.

"Don't encourage him, he can tell us on his own," Dani muttered.

"Too late! Since you asked, the date was, in a word, awesome. I was awed and then some, for sure."

Dani rolled her eyes and sighed, but Masa's shoulders shook with contained laughter, and a smile lit up his features. "For real, tell us about it," Masa said.

"What I said before was totally true. I kind of almost fucked it up in the beginning, like when I met both of you, but by the end, it was going great."

"Did he say why he bailed on Halloween?" Dani asked with a raised eyebrow.

"Ah, not really. He apologized several times, and he sounded sincere and remorseful. I'm not really concerned about that. We've all got shit going on, ya know? He did tell me that he went there specifically to hook up with someone else, so maybe he wanted to leave before he saw him? I dunno, and I don't really care."

"You should care."

Masa glanced over at Dani and whispered something I didn't catch over the sound of our moving feet. He faced forward again and looked at me in the mirror. "We're happy for you, don't question that. Dani is just worried and wants to baby you to death. Her beloved *fratellino* is growing up and going out with boys now. It's stressful stuff," he teased.

Dani shot him an evil glare and probably would have

whacked him had we not been on the treadmills. "Shut up. My concerns are valid. Did he at least give you his number this time?"

My face twisted while I tried to find the right words. "Um, not exactly. We're going to meet at the coffee place again on Wednesday night." I watched my reflection as an involuntary smile appeared. Jeez, I needed to get a handle on this.

"Jamie, what the hell? That's shady as fuck. He's hiding something." Dani huffed. I didn't need to be right next to her to feel the anger radiating from her body. In fact, I was glad I wasn't right beside her. I'd said it before and it was still true: Dani could be scary.

"That is a bit weird," Masa agreed. "Maybe try for something a bit more casual next time, like his Instagram or something."

"Yeah, I'll try that. I know how it sounds, but you guys weren't there. We were connecting in this way I'm not used to. He was definitely holding back. Then again, so was I, so I can't knock a man for having secrets." Another pesky smile formed on my face. "He kissed me while we were outside waiting for my ride," I said in a lowered voice.

Masa beamed, and a grin cracked through Dani's worried features. "And?" Masa asked eagerly.

"It was just a short peck, no tongue, no getting handsy. It was so sweet; I didn't know what the fuck to do with myself. I tried to kiss him back once I got a fucking clue, but he, like, was holding me in place by my arms and I couldn't move. I demanded another kiss, and he kissed my forehead before I left."

"That's fucking adorable," Masa practically swooned. "I still catch my breath when Theo does cute stuff like that."

"If it was anything like what happened yesterday, I get

why. I always thought y'all were lovesick fools, but I'm starting to get it."

Dani switched her machine off and dismounted. Masa and I followed suit. She wiped her face with her towel then threw it over her shoulder. "That does sound pretty damn sweet. Look, I'm not trying to piss all over your happiness, okay? I just want you to make sure you really get to know this guy before you get too attached." She clapped Masa on the shoulder and knocked her knuckles lightly against my chest. "Come on, let's go get some lunch and hear about what led up to that kiss, yeah?"

"You know I'm never going to say no to food," I replied.

"And the chance to talk about yourself," Masa mumbled with a grin. He and Dani both laughed, so I flipped them off with double-fisted middle fingers and strode off to the showers.

I WAS EARLY AGAIN on Wednesday. Only by ten or so minutes, so that was progress. I scanned the patrons inside to check for Gus. He hadn't yet arrived. I'd worn sensible maroon leather boots this time, so my feet wouldn't get cold and wet. Based on my plans for us, I dressed in my faux-paint-splatter jeans—Roz said they hugged my ass "just right"—and a super soft, light blue button-up with a patterned lining. When I rolled my sleeves up, printed brass knuckles would be displayed. It was a fucking dope shirt. I tossed a navy blue jacket over it—D always said blue was my color—grabbed my watch, and that was a wrap. I contemplated a tie, but I didn't want to be too fancy, and honestly, I tried to avoid wearing them whenever possible. If I were going to be choked all day, I'd at least like to be naked while it happened.

Gus came into view, coming from the same direction on Belmont that he was when I walked past him last week. Perhaps he lived *very* close. I ordered an Uber then walked up the street to meet Gus. He had on dark wash jeans and his boots and jacket from the last time I saw him. His jacket was zipped up, so I couldn't yet see his shirt.

"Hey," I said with a smile.

"Hi. Sorry if I'm late."

"Not at all, you're a bit early. Walk with me. An Uber is coming to pick us up"—I pointed down the street to Peet's —"down there."

Gus cocked his head to the side ever so slightly, which was adorable. "Where are we going?"

"Ah, that is for me to know and you to discover."

"Cryptic, but I'll bite."

"How hard?" I blurted out. "Ah, sorry. My filter is occasionally out of order. Fuck, it breaks a lot."

Gus laughed and stepped into my space. I met his gaze and raised an eyebrow in an unspoken question. He answered by pressing his lips to mine and stroking his thumb along my jaw. I was prepared that time and slid my tongue tentatively along his lips. I felt him smile and open for me, so I stood up on my toes and grabbed his jacket collar for leverage while I massaged his tongue with mine. Gus pulled back first, and I let go of his collar and sank back down off my toes.

"I've been looking forward to seeing you again," Gus said, just loud enough for me to hear.

"Me too. I thought about you a lot. Like, probably more than what's acceptable, really." Gus kissed me again and nipped my bottom lip before he pulled back. "Okay, point taken. If I want you to kiss me, I just have to talk too much. Or go off on tangents, perhaps. I think both would probably work just fine. Maybe one would be more effe—"

Gus kissed me again in a rush of nips and swipes from his hot tongue. He tasted like peppermint and smelled like the fucking forest after a rainstorm. It suited him. My dick seemed to like it too. There was another scent on him that I couldn't quite place, but it worked well with the sexy foresty thing he had going on. He nipped at my lip one last time, and then took a step back.

"I'll shut up for now. But I'm counting this as a win for me."

"I think it's a win for both of us, Jamie," he drawled.

"Ouu, say that again."

"What?"

"Say my name again, like you just did."

Gus snorted a laugh and shook his head. "Jamie, you're being silly. Come on, let's start walking." Gus waggled his prominent, yet maintained eyebrows at me, and walked away.

"Uuuf, Daddy," I mumbled under my breath.

"I heard that," Gus called over his shoulder.

"Tch, who says I didn't want you to hear it?" I totally didn't mean for him to hear it, and I was pretty sure we both knew it.

The car I ordered pulled up about twenty meters from where we were so we jogged to catch it. The heat from the car felt great on limbs I hadn't realized were nearly frozen. My stomach roared as the car drove away and the realization that I hadn't eaten dinner and was taking Gus to a place that didn't serve food hit me like an on-season linebacker.

"Um, have you eaten yet?" I asked Gus.

"No. I wasn't sure if we were going to get more coffee or order some food."

"Ah, shit." Gus eyed me with a raised eyebrow and a questioning look. "No, I've got this." I unbuckled my seatbelt and leaned up between the seats. "My man," I said to the driver, "do you mind doing me a solid and swinging by Arturo's at twenty-oh-one North Western?" I lowered my voice so Gus wouldn't hear. "There's a c-note in it for ya if you can help me out." The driver nodded his agreement, and I sat back and fastened my seatbelt feeling all kinds of self-satisfied.

"What was that about?" Gus asked.

"Last-minute dinner arrangements. I hope you like tacos."

"Who doesn't like tacos?"

"Crazy people who can't be trusted… and perhaps the gluten-free crowd."

"Is there a difference?" Gus asked without missing a beat.

I huffed out a laugh and leaned my head back against the seat. I looked over at Gus to find him watching me through heavy-lidded eyes. "Not at all."

Tacos were definitely a great idea. We wolfed them down —and a few shots of tequila, laaawd help me—and were back in the car in about ten minutes. The drive over to the bar only took another ten, and I felt warm and buzzy during it. I discreetly slipped the driver the aforementioned one hundred dollar bill as well as an additional one, just for being the night's MVP. Way to be, dude.

It was around half past eight when we arrived at the bar I chose in Logan Square. It was a great spot with virtually no outdoor signage. Gus didn't seem like a flashy guy so somewhere super fancy and pretentious seemed like an ill-advised idea. This place had cool live music, so I figured he might like it. It was also pretty damn close to my place. I didn't want to be presumptuous and say we'd end up going back there, but I'd hoped it might happen. Fuck, I'd hoped a lot. I'd even had a cleaner come. It looked a bit too staged after that, so I rolled through and messed a few things up after they'd left. Who in their right mind would believe that I would fold the beginning of my toilet paper roll? Yeah, no one.

We didn't have to wait to get in, as it was pretty early on a Wednesday night. The Whistler was rather tiny and got packed really fast closer to nine thirty when the live music started. Due to its size, seating was, uh, very limited. There were a few high chairs at the bar and a long table along an industrial brick wall. The place was long and narrow, and could maybe squeeze fifty people on a busy night. And I meant *squeeeeeze*. I met a really cool girl there a few months ago at a jazz show. She was practically standing on top of my toes the whole night, but the night ended in a way that I really have no business complaining about.

I was motherfucking pumped when we walked in, and I saw available chairs at the bar. We made our way to the end of the bar closest to the small stage and swiped those chairs. I pulled Gus's chair out for him without thinking, and he chuckled warmly while he sat down. I didn't know if that was a weird thing to do or not but fuck it. I was going to do this date thing the only way I fucking knew how. I took the adjacent chair on the corner of the bar, instead of the one right beside him on the right with the idea that I'd be able to talk to Gus easier if I were facing him. And because he was damn nice to look at, sue me.

Gus craned his neck and looked around the room. There were probably small groups of hipsters and young professionals laughing and sipping after-work cocktails, but I didn't notice. All of my attention was on the babe before me. "This is a cute place. How did you find it? I didn't see a sign outside."

"I stumbled across it one day a couple years ago when I was wandering around. I actually live a few blocks away. To be honest, I was high as fuck and the art display in the front window caught my eye. I stood out there looking at it for probably a good twenty minutes before I noticed the door and came in. They were having a Cards Against Humanity Night, and I was sold."

Gus barked out a laugh. He licked his lips, tilting his head back. "From what I know about you, that sounds spot on. You live in Logan Square?"

"Mhm. I like the area. Lots of bars, never a dull moment. Fuck, it's toasty in here." I ripped my jacket off and hung it sloppily on the back of my chair.

"It is, but I like it. It's quaint in a way… intimate. You're right about the coat, though—it has to go." Gus unzipped his jacket and spun around to hang it over the back of his chair. He had on a black button-up that fit him very nicely. When he turned back to me, I zeroed in on his black skinny tie.

"You're wearing a tie."

He looked down at his chest and ran a hand over it. "Is it too dressy?"

"No."

"Does it look bad?" Gus sounded uncertain, which, once again, was my fault for not being clear.

"Oh, no. You look hot. Really hot. I actually considered wearing a tie, because, duh, date, but I don't wear them often and didn't want to feel all choky." I motioned to my neck and made a face, which could only be described as "ew."

Gus chuckled softly and loosened his shoulders. "What's wrong with a little choking once in a while?"

Oh, that smooth fucker.

"Although, I will say that it's more fun when clothes aren't involved," he continued with a wink.

My thoughts exactly. "I can't believe I'm saying this, but you need to behave. These jeans are way too tight for me to be sporting wood all night."

Gus leaned closer to me and brushed his lips against my neck. His scruff scraped my neck in a way that was completely foreign to me, but *fuck* was it ever good. The close proximity brought his divine scent back to my attention, and I moaned, louder than I intended to. He overwhelmed my senses completely, and I forgot where the fuck I was. In that moment nothing mattered except for his touch and his smell driving me crazy. Gus nipped my earlobe, the pain grounding me back in my body. His tongue soothed the bite, and I felt his hot breath on my ear before I heard his gravelly voice.

"I wouldn't make you wait all night, Jamie," he said. I whimpered. I fucking whimpered. Gus pulled back and scooted back to a close, yet socially acceptable distance from me. "But, I will be fair and stop torturing you while we're in public." He opened the drink menu and perused it for a moment before looking back to me. I was still in a fucking daze and just stared at him with wide eyes. "What's good here?" He asked oh so casually.

Oh, I was going to get him back. "Um, ah, the drinks change daily." I shifted in my chair and adjusted the very uncomfortable hard-on I was now sporting. "Fuck me, you're evil." Gus chuckled, the rich sound reaching me in waves. "No, I'm serious. You're positively evil. You might actually be Satan. Tempting me with your sexy as fuck mysterious vibe and whatever the fuck you just did to my neck and ear." I narrowed my eyes at Gus in an over-the-top display. "I'm onto you."

"I wish you would be," Gus said casually.

"Ugh, be nice."

I was saved from Gus's verbal torture by the bartender. He came over sporting a friendly smile. "What can I get for you tonight?"

Gus was still scanning the menu, so I ordered first. "I'll

have the Prime Meridian, please." Because there was scotch in it and I was a hoe for scotch.

"Ah, the Pieholden, please," Gus said. The bartender nodded and slid away to take a few more orders.

I crossed my arms and eyed Gus with intrigue. That drink had apple rum and cinnamon in it. "So, you like sweet drinks. I wouldn't have pegged you with liking sweets."

"There's a lot you haven't pegged me with yet. But I love sweets. Probably too much."

"From what I can see, I don't think you have a problem."

"Thank you. You look great tonight too." Gus eyed me appreciatively, which did not help the situation in my jeans. "Blue is definitely your color."

"Aw, jeez, you're gonna make me blush. Oh! I was at the gym with some friends the other day and they asked about you. I realized that I don't know what you do. Care to enlighten me?" I asked.

"What do you think I do?"

"I actually do have a theory. I'd say you're a boxer. Or you used to be."

Gus quirked his eyebrows. "A boxer, huh? What makes you say that?"

"A couple things. You're tall, pretty jacked, and those scars on your cheek and eyebrow. They're sexy as hell—typically the kind you'd see on fighters."

"I'm glad you didn't say it was because I'm Italian."

"You're Italian?"

"Indeed, I am. My grandparents immigrated here from Brescia.

"So, I guess that's not an artificial tan you're sporting?"

Gus snorted a laugh and shook his head. "No, it's not. You're not entirely wrong about the boxing either. I've never boxed professionally, though I do it as part of my workout routine. As for the scars"—Gus motioned toward his face —"those are from my misspent youth."

"I'm not glad someone socked you in the face, but I kind of am because it's really working for you. Sorry, not sorry." Gus laughed and tugged on his tie, loosening it. "What're you doing?"

"It is warm in here. And I feel like a waiter with this tie on," Gus replied as he pulled the tie off and stuffed it into his jacket pocket. He unbuttoned the top two buttons on his shirt, revealing a hint of his chest hair.

"One more button."

"Excuse me?"

"Oh Jesus, I said that out loud." I closed my eyes and cringed.

"As much as I'd love to give you a show, I don't want to look like an escort or stripper," Gus said with a smirk. "So you'll have to make do with two buttons."

"Ugh, I'm awful. What were we talking about before my brain short-circuited? Right, misspent youth. Did you grow up in Chicago?"

"Sure did. Did you?"

"Yeppers. I love it here. I've traveled a fair bit, but this is my city. I couldn't imagine living anywhere else. I've never been to Italy though," I said with a wink.

"I haven't been in about a decade. It's a beautiful country. I've moved away from Chicago a couple times, but I always seem to end up back here." The bartender came over with our drinks, and we nodded our thanks.

I took a sip of mine and perched my feet up on the rungs of the chair. "Where have you lived?"

"Boston, Newark, Queens, and Fort Lauderdale."

"Which was your favorite?"

Gus shrugged and grunted. "They were all pretty terrible

experiences, but at least Fort Lauderdale had nice weather. Hot guys too. They were crazy, but no one is perfect."

"I dunno, I'm pretty damn close," I said teasingly.

"We'll see about that. My turn. You said you always knew you liked guys. Why start exploring that now?"

I should have expected a question like that. It was a damn good one to ask. I felt like I should answer as truthfully as possible, even if it was kinda lame. "I always thought liking guys would make my dad go ballistic and overcomplicate my uncomplicated way of life. So I was kind of like, miss me with that bullshit, and just dated girls because I liked them too. It sounds bad, but I really don't like drama. As I got older, I thought about it more and more, and then my brother came out. I was so fucking happy for him. I wanted to tell him then and there how I'd been feeling, but I didn't want to take away from what that moment meant to him and make it about me, ya know? I mean, I make nearly everything else about me, but that was important."

"I don't think any of that sounds bad. There isn't any set way to come out. You did what worked for you, and there's nothing wrong with that. How did your dad end up handling it?" Gus asked before sipping on his drink.

"Yeah, about that. He's the only person in my life who doesn't know. He took it extremely awful when my brother came out. I wanted to tell him as a 'fuck you,' and to show my brother that I was on his side and not Dad's, but he and Mom thought it might be a good idea to hold off on that until I graduate. I get it, though it kinda sucks. I try not to let it get me down. What about you? When did you know you were into guys?"

Gus licked his lips as they curved into a grin. The serious turn in conversation killed my boner but seeing that action almost brought it back. Almost. "I always knew. I waited until after graduation to tell my family. They all took it fine.

The idea of family is really important to us, so Pop was angry that I lied to *la famiglia*, but he didn't have a problem with my sexuality. None of my friends knew, though. They weren't the kind of people who would have taken it well."

"More misspent youth?" I asked. Gus nodded in reply. "Have you had any serious boyfriends?"

Gus leaned an elbow on the bar and lightly drummed his fingers on his glass. Yeah, I'd bet money that that was a nervous tick. "You're really just goin' right in, huh?"

"I have even less second date experience than I do with first dates. I might have browsed around and found a Cosmo article about important questions you should ask guys on dates. Don't judge me."

Gus's fingers stilled, and he snorted a short laugh. "I would never. I think it's cute that you've come prepared." He took a moment and his brow furrowed like he was contemplating something. "I came prepared too," he drawled.

Was he talking about sex? I thought he was talking about sex. I guess I wasn't alone in hoping something more might happen. It sounds like he brought some condoms. What else did guys need to have sex? Oh, right, lube. Shit, I didn't have much of that left. I wasn't sure how much I'd need, but the more the merrier seemed appropriate considering nothing had ever been in my ass. The thought was… daunting.

"Preparation is, uh, very important," I said lamely because I was a clueless idiot.

"You have no idea." Gus laughed quietly, seemingly to himself, and took another drink. "To answer your question though, I've had two relationships I'd classify as serious. One when I was eighteen and one a couple years ago."

"Why didn't they work?" I was genuinely curious.

"Well, the first guy was a lot older than me, and he decided he wanted to be with his wife. I didn't know he was married and was pretty devastated. That was why I moved out of Boston. The other one didn't work out because he wasn't honest with what he wanted. He was bisexual and in the closet. I never pressured him to come out, but after a couple years of dating, he told me he wanted to marry a girl and give his parents some grandkids." The tapping started again, despite Gus trying his best to give me a reassured smile. It didn't quite reach his eyes. "After that, I decided to stick to casual encounters with no expectations."

I grabbed Gus's hand and stilled his fingers. Gus's body tensed as his eyes shot to mine wildly. I saw a flash of that defensive attitude from when I grabbed him on the street unannounced, kind of like a cornered animal. I didn't flinch. "I'm really sorry about those assholes, Gus." He bowed his head then looked up at me with a small, honest smile that made me want to stand up and hug him. I let go of his hand, gently sliding my thumb over his fingertips as my hand slipped away.

"Ah, thanks," Gus said in a voice so slight, I'd have lost it to the commotion around us if I weren't watching him say it.

"For what it's worth, the bastards you dated didn't deserve to be with you. I'm not perfect, but they weren't worth shit. I've sure as hell never led anyone I was involved with on. That's all kinds of shady and that's not what I'm about.

"I understand your reluctance to give me your deets before, and your more recent hesitancy to go out with me. You've been burned; I get it, but I really don't want that to color what's going on here." I motioned between us and smiled. "I like spending time with you, Gus. I'm not promising anything heavy, but I'd like to keep going with this and see what happens."

Gus cleared his throat and ran his fingernails through his scruff. "I appreciate your honesty. You sure you're only twenty-six?"

"Wanna see my birth certificate?" I joked.

"You could have just offered your driver's license. Don't gotta go straight for birth records."

"One, I'm extra as fuck, and you're just going to have to accept it, and two, I don't actually have a license. I've driven a car before, but yeah, no license."

Gus grunted and sat up straighter like he was before we launched into ex-talk. "Kids these days," he said before finishing his drink.

"Oh, don't start with that kid shit again."

"Thank you, Jamie. I feel the same way." We'd switched gears again, but I just knew he was talking about what I said about spending time together. I knocked my knee into his and smiled shyly, my heart thumping in my chest.

We ended up staying until the bar closed at two. Gus was reluctant to keep drinking, though I managed to convince him that we'd have a good time and ordered another round. The rounds after that came much easier. He really liked the band that played. They were mellow rock, yet kinda jazzy and had a great vibe. We didn't get to talk too much more before the band started and it got really loud, but just being with him and enjoying the drinks and music was enough. When Gus wasn't paying attention, I'd slipped the bartender two hundreds with a wink. I was used to paying on dates, and since I was the one who brought Gus here, I figured I should pay. I had a feeling he would've protested, so I just went ahead and did it. By the time we were ready to leave, paying the bill wasn't remotely on his mind, judging by the way his hand curled around my thigh.

Perhaps I'd enjoyed the night a little too much. I stumbled out of the bar, but Gus caught me and stopped me from falling on my pretty face. The cold wind slammed into me and burned my lungs on the first deep inhale. My jacket looked dope, though it really wasn't all that warm. Gus pulled me up to my feet and asked if I was okay with a kind smile. I nodded in response and urged him to walk with me. We set off toward my place in silence, just taking in the sounds of the city at night. There were a few other people on the streets, too many cars still on the road, and the classic, sirens in the distance. I'd probably have been alarmed if I didn't fucking hear sirens.

We stopped at a red light, and I felt like I was being watched. I turned my head toward Gus and he was indeed watching me. His brow was furrowed, his jaw twitching like he was clenching and unclenching his teeth. His features finally relaxed and he licked his lips.

"Jamie," Gus started, shakily, "do you mind if I hold your hand?"

If I could have swooned to death, I'd have died right there on the concrete. I pulled my hand out of my pocket and grabbed Gus's, squeezing it gently. His hands were bigger than mine, so it felt different, but it was a good kind of different. I pulled him close to me by our connected hands and kissed him once his face was within my reach. It was just a short kiss, but the heat it sent through my body kept me warm until we reached my building.

I stopped walking rather abruptly, and Gus eyed me questioningly. "Ah, this is my building."

"Okay," Gus said. He kept his gaze on me, and I could just tell he wanted me to invite him up. At least I think he did. I doubted myself and didn't want to ruin things by making the wrong assumption either way. I knew I was over-thinking things, but I couldn't shake it off and sort out what I wanted to say. Cursed alcohol, my catalyst, and my downfall.

"You look like you're conflicted about something," Gus said. He watched me closely then grinned knowingly. "On second thought, I do want to see your birth certificate, Jamie. I'd really like that."

I nodded my head, then squeezed Gus's hand tighter and led him into the building.

As soon as the door closed and the lock clicked, Gus was on me, pinning me to the door. My back was to him, and I could feel him getting hard through our jeans. Holy shit. I turned my face toward him, and he peppered my jaw with pecks and nips until our lips met. Gus grabbed my hips and turned me around to face him. He looked me in the eye appreciatively, and a slow smile spread across his face, making him even more attractive.

"God, you're irresistible," he whispered to me between ragged breaths.

Me? Irresistible? Before I could think of what to say, Gus stroked his thumb over my bottom lip and crashed his lips to mine again. He tasted like cinnamon, spice, and Gus—like fucking perfection. Unwilling to be a passive participant for a second fucking time, I pushed myself off the door and into Gus, making him stumble backward. I continued to push until he hit the island in my kitchen. I reached up and pulled Gus into a kiss, but I didn't keep my hands still this time. I went for his jacket, pulled the zipper down at lightning speed, and ripped it off his shoulders and down his arms. I fumbled with the buttons on his shirt and pulled away from the kiss to look at what I was doing. My hands were shaking.

"Get this fucking thing off. Now," I demanded. Gus growled and made quick work of the buttons, then whipped the shirt entirely off, exposing his strong, hairy chest. I ran my hands over his firm pecs and up his neck to pull at his short, wavy, dark brown hair. Gus winced then growled again and roughly grabbed at my hips. I'd never been so manhandled in my life, but goddamn, it was *hot.* Gus wasn't going easy on me, which eased my trepidation in how I should touch him in return. I skimmed my hands down past his shoulders and over his sides. He had a spattering of hair over his abs, which disappeared under the waist of his now in-the-fucking-way jeans. My hands were still unsteady, and I fumbled with the button on Gus's pants. I cursed under my breath and felt the heavy pressure of hands leave my hips. When the touch returned, Gus was holding my hands still.

"Relax, Jamie. We don't have to rush this. You're probably nervous as hell—"

"I'm horny as hell. Take your goddamn pants off before I reach for a paring knife and make a fucking mess." I wrenched my hands free from Gus's grip and got the button on his pants undone. I made easy work of the zipper and slipped my hand over his boxers. He inhaled sharply when I squeezed his balls over the thin fabric. The sound turned into a moan when I massaged them, just how I liked it done to me. I worried about the pressure for about half a second until I saw Gus's parted lips and dark fuck-me eyes. It was the same look he'd given me at the party, the one that compelled me to follow after him. With just the slightest bit of pressure, I grazed my thumb along the side of his dick before I was bold enough to take it in hand. Baby steps, ya dig?

Gus shuddered, his dick twitching against my hand. I kissed him again as I worked his balls around the palm of my hand. His hands found purchase in my hair and cupping my ass over my jeans. He moaned into my mouth, which was honestly the sexiest thing. Gus's thigh wedged between my legs and the friction along with the way he felt in my hand and the sounds he was making was nearly enough to make me cream in my pants.

I pulled back from the kiss and bit Gus's bottom lip hard

enough to make it swollen and pink. He winced then growled again, so I did the same thing to his neck. Gus spun us around and grabbed both of my wrists, holding them behind my back. He kissed my neck up to my ear and nibbled on the lobe like he had earlier.

"Where's your room?" Gus rasped in my ear.

My skin prickled into goose bumps down the side of my neck and arm, though I felt the jolt all the way down to my cock. I needed to get my fucking jeans off STAT. "Right here. Right here is good."

Gus stopped his assault of kisses and bites, but kept hold of my wrists. "Where is your room?" His voice was dangerously low and gravelly.

I jerked my head to the left and said, "Around the corner, first door on the left."

"Walk," Gus demanded. I apparently didn't move fast enough for his liking. I felt his arms wrap around my waist, and then my world tilted. That motherfucker had me in a fireman's carry. I kicked and wriggled and heard a loud crack before I felt the stinging on my bare ass.

"Did you just pull my pants down and *spank* me?"

Gus grunted. "You were acting like a brat."

I grumbled under my breath because I couldn't deny it— but still. Gus tossed me onto my bed, momentarily knocking the wind out of me. I sat up and watched him toe out of his shoes and socks. "Are you going to get naked now? Because I'd really like to see that."

"Whatever you want." I had to stop myself from doing a happy seal clap. I grabbed my dick and gave it a few firm squeezes, watching as Gus slid his jeans down his sculpted, hairy legs. He had another tattoo on his right shin, but I couldn't bring myself to look at it for longer than a second. Not when Gus's barely concealed cock was at eye level. I was wrong before. Gus wasn't wearing boxers. Nope, he had on black briefs with red piping—fuck me dead—and they were fucking hot. His erection was straining against the fabric, and I could already tell he was fucking huge. Way bigger than me. Fuck, was that going to matter? I figured it didn't since Gus had already fondled the shit out of my dick and was now stripping off in my bedroom for me. Rock 'n' roll.

Gus looked down and stuck his thumbs under the waistband of his briefs. I held my breath and waited for the drop, but he just looked back up at me and teased by pulling one side down, then back up, almost giving me a peek of the base of his cock. It was *killing me*. I squeezed my length again and watched as Gus continued to tease me with a smile on his face that was equal parts evil and sexy. Maybe a little bit sexier. He rubbed a hand along his chest and teased a nipple to attention. No, that smile was definitely evil.

"Gus, please." He smiled wider at me then pushed both sides of his briefs down. His hard cock sprang free and bobbed in front of me, like the lewdest fucking diving board I've ever seen. I gasped. I was fucking speechless. His cock was thick, long, uncut, and oh, did I mention it was fucking thick? He was going to tear me apart, and the thought terrified me.

"Are you okay? You're just kind of staring at my dick."

I barked out a dry, panicked laugh. "Have you seen it? It's fucking huge. I need a level-one dick to get used to the game. You've got a final boss dick, and I'm gonna die, and it's gonna be game over before I even had a chance to really play!"

Gus laughed—at me! The nerve!—and kneeled on the bed in front of me. "It's all right. We'll take it slow." Gus leaned down and kissed me, and I let him push me backward. He sat up and ran a hand down my leg and tapped my foot. I was still wearing my fucking shoes for Chrissake. "It's your turn to lose some clothes." Gus didn't wait for an answer. He pulled my shoes and socks off and tossed them aside. He made quick work of my jeans and left my boxers on. I unbuttoned my shirt, but he took it off me. He ran his hands up from bent knees, over my thighs and stomach, and brushed his thumb over my nipple. I inhaled sharply. He did it again. "Jesus, you're sensitive. Tell me what you want."

I wanted everything, but I knew I wasn't ready. "I'm not ready to fuck just yet. I mean, I've done anal before with girls, but that's different. For various poking-me-in-the-thigh reasons." Gus laughed, the rich sound settling my nerves enough for me to continue. "Swap spots with me. I want to see you."

Gus rolled onto his back, and I flicked the bedside lamp on before quickly discarding my boxers and carefully straddling his legs.

"Sit back and rest your weight on me." I did as Gus instructed and shuddered as our cocks bumped. I looked down at the man beneath me and couldn't believe what was happening. Gus was a god, and right then he was *mine*.

"Fuck, you're even more attractive naked," I said appreciatively.

Gus snorted a laugh and crossed his hands behind his head. Oh, God. Was it weird that I thought his hairy pits were sexy? Fuck it; I'd just be a weirdo. "I'm glad you think so. Part of me was worried seeing me naked might turn you off."

"Are you fucking kidding me?" I grabbed the base of my hard cock and slapped it against Gus's groin for effect. "Do you not see how hard I am? I feel like I'm gonna blow and you've barely touched me."

"Get down here, and I'll fix that."

I leaned down and took Gus's mouth in a claiming kiss, complete with the occasional nip of his lip and tongue. I propped myself up on one elbow and explored Gus's body with the other. It was time to stop fucking around and start *fucking around*. I leaned back so I could have a clear line of sight, and took Gus's hard cock in hand. I couldn't close my fingers around him, but I held him firm and started slowly stroking him from root to tip. His dick was so different from mine, and it intrigued me to no end. His foreskin was soft and slid easily over his shaft, creating the kind of smooth friction I could only dream of.

"Oh fuck, that feels good," Gus moaned. I continued my slow, even strokes, tightening my grip. Gus moaned more and bit down on one of his index fingers.

"Put your hands back up behind your head. I want to hear every sound you make." I barely recognized how desperate and demanding my voice sounded, but it had the desired effect, as Gus did as he was told.

The tip of my cock was pretty sensitive, but I remembered I'd read that it was way more intense for uncut guys, and I wanted to check that out. I slid Gus's foreskin back and held the base of his cock. I licked my other hand and cupped it over the tip, rotating it in a slow circular motion. Gus cried out and nearly bucked me off of him. I gripped his hips with my thighs and kept on working on his cock.

"I'm gonna come if you don't stop," Gus said breathlessly. I sped up my motions and stroked him up and down as well. His sighing and breathing came in a crescendo, clearly indicating when he was about to come. Gus's cock pulsed against my grip, and I felt his hot cum against my palm while his sexy moaning filled my ears. It was intoxicating, and I couldn't wait to see him enjoy his post-orgasm high before I had my cum-slicked hand stroking my own cock. I was so close from touching Gus. Watching him. Hearing him. But I couldn't quite get myself there.

Gus stilled my hand with his and pushed it aside. With his other hand, he wiped up some of his cum and took me in hand. I thrust into his hand and closed my eyes as my body took over. *This* I knew how to do. A warm hand touched the back of my neck and guided me down to connect with soft lips in a bruising kiss. I fucked faster, and Gus squeezed me tighter. The wet slick sound was so loud in my ears, only serving to drive my desire higher. I was so fucking close and starting to pant.

"Come for me, Jamie," Gus ground out.

And I fucking did. I came with a loud shout as my balls emptied between us and my body shook in a fit of spasms. The fireworks I felt at that party had nothing on how Gus made me feel in my bed. We kissed until my cum got cold between us, then I rolled onto my back beside Gus. Our breathing leveled out, and I started laughing.

"Care to share?" Gus asked playfully.

"I wanna do that again. Fuck, when are you gonna be hard again?"

Gus groaned and laughed resulting in a sweet, tortured sound. "Give me fifteen more minutes."

"I don't know if I can wait that long."

"Please try," Gus said wryly.

I rolled onto my stomach, closer to Gus, and rested my chin on his arm. "When can we do this again?"

"About fourteen more minutes," Gus deadpanned.

I bit him because he deserved it. He yelped, and I internally did a song and dance. "Don't be a dick. When am I going to see you again?"

"Um, I'm free Saturday and Sunday until about six in the evening if you want to do something during the day. Or any weeknight after seven next week."

"Dibs on Sunday morning! You ready to fork over your digits yet and stop living in nineteen-eighty-five? Texting is super convenient, you know."

Gus smiled and leaned in to kiss my forehead. "I know it's asking a lot, but can you please meet me again?"

I was in too great a mood to push and risk fighting, so I conceded. "All right. Only because you're so damn hot, though. Nine at Peet's. But inside this time 'cause I'm gonna need the caffeine."

"It's a date," Gus said with a smile.

"Is it?" I asked. "Because I really hope it is."

"Yeah, it is."

Gus kissed me while he crawled on top of me. His rough hands set fire to every inch of skin they touched, and I relished in the burn. We explored each other's bodies with our hands several more times—each better than the last—before sleep took us, and twice again in the morning before Gus left me with a kiss at my door.

Yep. I was definitely in trouble.

SEVEN

"Y OU WERE RIGHT ABOUT A TRIP," Theo said with a smile he just couldn't hide. "Masa was so excited that I thought he was going to tackle-hug me again."

"Of course I was right, bro. Where are you taking him?" Valentine's Day for my brother was a smash. It would have been regardless of my input, but I didn't mind sharing in the glory.

"Japan in April. I figured it would be nice for him to see where he came from. Also, it'll be cherry blossom season."

"I never thought I'd see the day when you turned into such a romantic sap," I teased. I took a drink of the beer in front of me and took extra pleasure in it. My six weeks with Northwestern Memorial were starting on Monday morning, so I was going to enjoy day drinking while I could. You know, and weekly lunches with my brother. We'd have to switch to dinner or something.

"Love changes you," Theo said with an easy shrug. "What about you? Masa told me you had a second date with that Gus guy."

That Gus guy. Oh, Theo. "Sure did. We saw some live

music, went home and made some sticky memories. Gus used to play piano and, lemme tell you, he's got magic hands." I waggled my eyebrows.

Theo's face wrinkled, and he shook his head. "Ew, that's not what I want to hear about, Jay. Masa said he and Dani had some concerns about whether this guy is being truthful."

"He's not a secret spy, if that's where you're going with this. He's a little mysterious, yeah, but I think I found out why last night. He's been burned pretty bad in some relationships and is guarded because of it. I think he really likes me though," I said hopefully. Just the thought of Gus made me smile like a damn fool. It was probably a good thing that I didn't have his number because I'd be harassing him all the time. Sexually, if I needed to be specific. I was quite fond of taking gorgeous dick pics and sending them to willing recipients. And Dani. It ruined her day whenever she opened a Snap and saw my junk in some weird display. Scotty took screenshots every time.

"That's good. You seem happy about it, but Dani and Masa aren't worried for no reason. Especially not Dani."

"Y'all are just overprotective. It's endearing but unnecessary."

"I have every right to be overprotective," Theo grumbled.

"You never cared about what girls I was seeing," I countered.

"It's different—"

"It's not."

"He's too old for you."

"Whoa, whoa. Do you hear that ringing?" I held up my hand to my ear. "It's the Pot calling. Oh, it's for you, Kettle. The gap between you and Masa is bigger, so don't even." Theo muttered something under his breath I didn't catch and silently started rage eating his lunch. He never handled defeat well, and it was always some sort of entertaining. It was adorable sulking this time around, and I was okay with that.

"Are you ready for your interview today?" Theo asked, wisely changing course.

I shrugged and shoveled a few bites of my aloo palak into me before answering. "I'm always ready, dude. Look at me; I'm wearing a boring suit for Chrissake—although I look dapper as fuck. I'll lay the charm on thick, and they'll love it."

"I'd call you a cocky son of a bitch, but I don't doubt that it'll go exactly like that. I'm proud of you for doing your own thing, Jay."

"Thanks, man," I replied. He got me all warm and fuzzy feeling when he started saying sentimental shit to me.

"Any idea what you want to specialize in yet?" Theo cut a piece off his chicken tikka and popped it in his mouth. It looked delicious, and I was totally going to snag a piece when he wasn't looking.

"I'm still undecided. I'm thinking pediatrics or oncology, though. Definitely surgery. I really liked working the emerge at Mercy, but I like people, you know? I want to know the person whose life I'm saving. I wanna hear their story. I think it'll be good for me."

"I have to agree. You'd be great in Emergency, though your people skills would be wasted. Kids love you to pieces and, well, we both know how much cancer takes out of people. You'd do wonders interacting with those people. You'd be good at anything you applied yourself to. I firmly believe that."

My cheeks heated. I was used to praise—I fucking thrived off it—but hearing it from Theo always disarmed me. "Okay, okay. Don't get me all fucked up before my interview."

Theo snorted a laugh. "You're drinking beer before your interview. Me being nice isn't going to fuck you up."

"It's light beer," I countered. Theo laughed, and I asked how work was going with Dad. He said it was more of the same small, petty behavior, and that it wasn't anything he couldn't handle. Dad was the head of the mergers and acquisitions department Theo worked in, so avoiding him entirely was impossible. I knew Theo could handle it, but he shouldn't have had to.

"He called a last-minute meeting on Valentine's Day and drew it out as long as he possibly could. I was annoyed, though I mainly felt bad for the rest of the team."

"That sucks. I'm assuming Masa forgave you for being late."

Theo's cheeks reddened as his eyes darted around the restaurant. There were plenty of people present, but no one would have been able to hear me over the hum of the lunch crowd. This place was small and owned by the parents of a girl I knew from my undergrad. It was always busy, but we luckily didn't have to wait long to get a table.

"He did," Theo replied in a hushed voice. I could see by the dumb look on his face that he was probably replaying the evening's events, and I snickered. My brother in love was such a curious thing.

"I have a serious question. What are the cheat notes for what I need to know about sex between two dudes? I mean, I've seen some porn, but porn is so grossly unrealistic—who even looks like those guys? Well, actually Gus totally does." I stroked my chin and pondered Gus doing porn. Gus and me making videos—*fuuuuuck yaaaaaaas.*

"Jesus, Jay." Theo looked around us again. "It's neither the time nor the place to talk about that."

"*That*?" I teased. "Are you even capable of saying the word 'sex'? My, my, I didn't realize you were such a prude."

"I am not a prude. This is something we can discuss at home."

"We're both here now. I'd like to know sooner rather than later. I'm seeing Gus in a few days, and I wanna be ready." I dramatically pounded my fist on the table, rattling the glasses and garnering a few looks from other patrons. "Sorry!" I announced to anyone still looking.

Theo huffed, but it was the good kind—the kind that meant he was going to give me what I wanted. "Ready for what, exactly?"

I shrugged easily. "Whatever Gus is up for, I guess. I chickened out of sex last night." I waved my hand in a circle in front of me, searching for the right words. "Like, fucking-sex."

"Penetration," Theo said dryly.

I snapped my fingers and pointed at him. "Yes. There we go. He was really cool about it and didn't even try to push it at all. He just laughed when I said I didn't want to and we… proceeded to do other adult activities."

"And you're sure you want to bottom? You don't have to just because you think you're expected to."

"I'm intrigued, though not super keen on the idea. It's different than what I'm used to—clearly. Different isn't necessarily bad… It's just daunting," I said in a lowered voice.

"Take it slow. Don't rush into it before you're ready."

"Okay, but what can I expect?" I was genuinely curious; I was also hoping to get the lowdown on the dynamic with Masa. I'd tried to let it go—couldn't do it.

Theo chewed his bottom lip then sighed. "It's going to hurt at first. Maybe a lot, depending on how relaxed and stretched you are, and how big he is."

"He's pretty fucking huge."

Theo nodded. "Then make sure he spends a decent

amount of time on the prep. You set the pace. Have him go slow and use a lot of lube. More than you think is necessary. Don't hold your breath either. You're going to want to, but you'll tense up if you do. Try to breathe steadily and stay relaxed. It gets easier after the initial resistance, then the feeling changes. It'll burn at first, then it'll be a sort of pressure and fullness. The more you do it, the more you'll get used to it, and it won't hurt as much and for as long."

I nodded pensively while screaming internally. I licked my lips and tried for nonchalance. "Are we speaking from experience here?" Theo nodded, and I tried my best not to react. I couldn't stop my nostrils from flaring and my eyes from going wide for a moment, though. My lip may have even twitched. Damn involuntary reactions.

"I commend your attempt at restraint, but you're doing a piss-poor job of it. Come on, let it out."

"Ah! I've been absolutely *dying* to know. Is that weird? Dani said it's weird. She also said you'd be the bottom. I really wasn't sure. Maybe I'll get better at being able to tell."

"Calm down. Top and bottom are just rigid labels. Not everyone subscribes to them, and people can be more fluid than what the label suggests."

"You mean, like ambidextrous. Oh! Ambisextrous."

Theo groaned. "Versatility, yes. You also don't have to have penetrative sex. There isn't a rulebook on being queer. Just do what feels right, Jay."

"Damn, sound advice. Thanks, bro." I held up my fist, and he bumped it begrudgingly.

"Um, there's something else you should be aware of," Theo said.

"Oh?"

"Anal takes some preparation."

"Yeah, you were saying. Stretching and all that jazz." I threw up jazz hands. Because all that jazz, am I right?

Theo scoffed and shook his head. "I don't mean that prep. I'm talking about before."

"Before?"

"Ah, hygiene."

"Ooooh," I drew out.

Theo cleared his throat and scanned the room again. "Yes. A shower can be enough if you have a good grasp on your, uh, schedule. But"—Theo dropped his voice and leaned in closer—"douching is a safer bet. It'll be one less thing to worry about when you're trying to relax and… stuff."

I nodded and finished my beer. I peeled the corner of the orange label while Theo returned to his meal. I had the rest of the day free until my evening gym date with D, so I figured I might as well hit up a sex shop on the way home and pick up some goodies. "I can't get over you. I thought I knew everything about you. You wild."

"I hope this doesn't change how you see me," Theo said, just loud enough to reach me.

"Oh, it totally does." Theo's face fell as soon as the words left my mouth. I sucked my teeth and kicked him under the table, hard enough for him to grunt. "Don't start that shit. I think I like you better now than I did ten minutes ago."

Theo huffed out a laugh, and picked his knife and fork back up. "Did Masa really not tell you?"

"I swear to fucking God, he didn't say a thing. I've been trying to get it out of him for, like, a year." Theo hummed to himself and smirked. "You might as well have just said he was gonna get some ass tonight. That little happy sigh and the dopey-happy look on your face are screaming it." I rolled my eyes.

Theo hummed again and quirked his brows. "Tact, Jay. You'll learn it one of these days."

Interviews didn't usually make me nervous, but I felt different than I did the day before. I felt exposed and raw, and I felt like the panel could see it. I knew that was silly. I wasn't wearing some scarlet letter G—or B, in my case—that people could now see. Sure, I felt different, but not all of that was because I was with a guy a few hours before the interview; it was because I was with Gus.

We had a great fucking time, and I wanted to do it again long before Sunday morning. I was disappointed with myself for chickening out of letting him fuck me, though I liked that he didn't make a big deal out of it. I also wanted to take him out and talk with him and laugh with him more. I wanted to spend time with him, and that mindset was new. I didn't catch feelings, especially not after seeing someone twice.

It was like my brother said about love, it does change you. I wasn't absurd enough to think I loved Gus already, but deep down I thought I *could.* No, I was pretty fucking confident I could. And with that on my mind, I wasn't as "on" for the Kindred panel as I should have been. I was more annoyed at myself than anything else. I only applied to Kindred because it was in Logan Square and would be a short commute. My last interview was with Northwestern Memorial on Monday morning, during the beginning of my first day there for my elective. Northwestern would be a better fit for my career, so that was the interview I really needed to crush. I wasn't about to dwell on the hiccup with Kindred. Not when Siri found me a sex shop just a couple miles away. Rock 'n' roll, leggo.

"Can I help you find something today?" I tore my attention away from the walls plastered with various sex toys and books to the slender clerk in front of me. He was cute, in a spunky kind of way. He was short with black hair and a lip ring. I could dig it.

"Yes, I suppose so. I'm looking for a douche, I guess?"

"Is that a question?" he asked teasingly.

I smiled and shook my head. "I need a douche and anything else a professional such as you can recommend for an anal sex newb." He grinned at me from ear to ear, and we started with glass butt plugs.

I ended up buying more than I'd intended to, but what else was new. I left the store with not one, but three douches —all different styles, a small, blue glass plug, and what might as well have been a gallon-sized jug of lube with a pump top. Eager to get started, I headed straight for the bathroom when I got home and decided to try the bulb-style douche with the narrowest tip.

I rinsed it out and filled it with warm water. Dude from the store said it was best to douche standing for a quick clean. Something about preventing water from going too far up and triggering a mess. So yeah, standing up it was. I was supposed to hold the water in and jostle it around, so I jumped in place a few times and felt like an idiot. I released the water in the toilet like instructed and repeated the process three more times until the water came out clear. Dude said this plus an external clean would be more than enough for regular anal play, but if I wanted someone to "rearrange my guts" I'd have to opt for a thorough clean, which could take up to an hour sometimes and cause cramping. Awesomesauce.

With the cleanest ass on the block, I put a Kid Cudi record on and grabbed one of my rigs from the underneath storage of the table that held my modern record player. A pleasant crackle sounded before Frequency sounded through my Bluetooth speakers. I set the rig on the table in front of the couch and ran into my room to grab some shatter from my dresser. The bed was a righteous mess. My poor black and white constellation duvet cover took the brunt of the damage, but I should probably wash the sheets too. Or change them altogether. Black sheets were pretty unforgiving when it came to cum stains.

Oh well. I shrugged the task off for later—or possibly the next day, fuck it—and went back out to the couch for some Cudi, dabs, and games.

GUS WAS EARLY and already seated when I arrived at Peet's on Sunday morning. He was wearing another snapback—black this time—and a white henley with a couple of buttons undone under his leather jacket. I was into it. A lot. He stood and hugged me when I got close to the table, and I thought I was gonna die. Gus gave me a quick kiss before releasing me, and then I knew without a doubt that I was fucking dead. He told me he missed me and I leaned up, wrapped a hand around the back of his neck, and kissed him again. My head bumped his hat, but neither of us seemed to give a shit. We broke apart, sat down at the small square table, and made light conversation about our weeks. Gus didn't have much to say about himself, though he didn't have a shortage of questions for me. I, uh, left out the part about me having gone to a sex shop and trying out douching. I also left out that I did it again this morning, just in case.

When we finished with our breakfast, I checked the time to see we'd been there for about an hour. In deciding what we should do today, I Googled Chicago winter date ideas and settled on skating at the Maggie Daley ribbon downtown. I hadn't been on a pair of ice skates since I was a kid, and even then I was terrible. It would be hella entertaining if Gus couldn't skate either. Meh, I'd find out soon enough.

"We're going skating?" Gus asked, his voice climbing higher toward the end of the question. We stood at the end of the rather long rental skate line, but I was already on the lookout for a way around it.

"Indeed we are! Although I can't skate for shit, so I hope you can."

"I can," Gus simply said. I gave him my best side-eye and waited for more of an explanation. "Pond hockey in Boston. The older guy I dated there was really into the Bruins." Gus rolled his shoulders and shivered as a gust of wind rolled past us. "He taught me how to skate."

I reached up under Gus's jacket and rubbed his lower back while I gave him a reassuring smile. "We're going to have fun today, I promise. You don't know me all that well yet, but do know I'm a confident shit who doesn't make promises he can't keep. I'm kind of like a Lannister."

Gus cracked a smile that reached his eyes. "I don't think that's quite how that saying goes."

"You know what, it's close enough." I spotted what I was looking for and turned back to Gus. I dressed in a warmer jacket than I normally would and even had a scarf since I knew we'd be outside. I took off my scarf and wrapped it around Gus's neck, pulling him down for a quick peck. "Stay here. I'll be right back." Gus nodded, and I briskly headed toward the info center inside.

I purchased the ninety-dollar package for two, giving us rental skates, lockers, skip-the-line rights, and best of all, hot chocolate! I returned to Gus with the passes and a grin, and we made our way to the front of the rental line. We stowed our shoes in our assigned lockers and were on the ice in minutes. Let me amend that, Gus was on the ice. I was still securely on the non-slippery ice, looking out at said ice like it was lava trying to kill me. Gus waited for me along the edge of the entrance. I wanted to tell him to go ahead and do a warm-up lap while I figured my shit out, but he laughed and said he'd wait for me.

He held his hand out for me, and I took it instantly. He slowly slid backward, farther onto the ice. I didn't let go of his hand, so I stepped out to follow him. He told me to grab the side rail with my free hand until I found my balance, and I clung to it for dear life. I was probably squeezing the fuck out of his hand too, but he never complained.

Gus gave me some pointers on balance and how to move my feet, but I was still skeptical. We managed to skate—at the slowest pace known to man—several yards while I held his hand and the railing. He convinced me I was ready to let go of the railing, so I reluctantly did. I only faltered for a moment before things went back to relatively smooth. We skated halfway around the windy ribbon before Gus suggested I try it on my own. At that point, I was so inflated that I was liable to float away, so I instantly agreed. I released his hand and missed his warmth immediately. I made it a few more yards with Gus cheering me on before I wiped the fuck out and landed on my fucking ass. Better than my face, so gahbless.

Gus slid to a stop in front of me and kneeled down. "Are you okay, Jamie?" He sounded worried, and I swooned a little bit. *Fucking swooned.*

"I'm okay. My ass hurts, but I mainly just feel like an idiot. So many people saw that." I cringed and looked around. Yep, the place was packed and based on the looks of concern and occasional smiles, I'd say quite a few people got an eyeful.

"Come on, let's get you off the ice."

"Nah, I'm good to keep going. I haven't seen enough of your mad skills yet."

"All right," Gus said. He stood and held his hand out for

me, which I took. I was pulled to my feet by his unwavering strength, though he didn't drop my hand once I was upright. Gus held my hand up then bent down and gently kissed the inside of my exposed wrist. He gave me a warm smile then switched my hand to his other so he could hold it while we skated. He didn't let go until we left the ice an hour later to enjoy our hot chocolate. Even the heat coming from the drink paled compared to what I'd felt when Gus had been holding my hand.

Gus didn't object when I suggested we go back to my place to continue our date. He didn't rush me the second we got through the door, which I was a little bummed over. Gus looked around seemingly taking everything in while I took off my coat and boots. I tossed the coat on the kitchen island. "Um, so this is my place. I know you've been here before but it was dark, and we were… busy."

"It's really nice," Gus said as he ran his hand over the grey quartz countertop of the island. Gus looked around again. "Are your roommates home?"

I shook my head. "I don't have any roommates, dude." I motioned around the open-concept kitchen with all glass cabinets and modern stainless steel appliances. "This is my place. Granted, I didn't work for it. My parents bought it for me when I started my undergrad." I rounded the island, slid my arm around Gus's waist. "Want the grand tour?"

"Sure."

"Good. Now, I think tours are boring, so we're going to make this one fun. Take off your coat and boots and stay a while, yeah?" I released Gus, and he unzipped his jacket and hung it on the edge of one of the high stools at the island. He hung my scarf up as well while he toed out of his boots.

"I'm ready." He looked at me expectantly.

"I don't have a lot of rooms, so for every space we enter

you're going to remove an article of clothing. The jacket and boots don't count." I motioned around us. "This space counts as two rooms. Kitchen and entryway. Get naked," I said teasingly.

"Easy there, I'm not wearing a lot of clothes, but I'm still going to make you wait for the main attraction." Gus bent down and pulled off each sock, tossing them aside. I looked down at his bare feet and smirked.

"You're lucky you've got some sexy feet. Come on, then." I guided Gus past the framed posters and record sleeves mounted on the exposed brick walls leading to the wide-open main space. We stopped in front of the opening leading to my bedroom, and I raised an expectant brow at Gus. He got the hint and took off his shirt, and lucky for me, he wasn't wearing an undershirt. Gus was definitely a snack, but what drew my attention were his tattoos. It was too dark last time for me to make them out clearly, and in the morning I couldn't have been expected to be observant while I was getting jerked off. Someone could have robbed me, and all I'd have cared about was Gus's hands on my body. I was starting to get a semi just thinking about that prospect again.

Gus's tattoos were just like the rest of him—gorgeous. On his upper bicep, he had a skull with flowers coming out of the eyes, nose, and mouth. It was super pretty. I didn't know flowers for shit, but they were blue, purple, and white. On the back of his arm, he had a vicious-looking anchor with, like, washed-out, watercolor red splotches by the bottom and behind the hooky part. It was rugged yet pretty and artsy. On the top of his forearm, there was a minimalist olive tree with geometric roots, and the last one I noticed was a badass, super-realistic wolf tattoo on the back of his forearm.

"I really like your tattoos. The wolf in particular—it suits you."

"Thank you. I have one more."

"Where is it?" I asked.

"You'll have to continue the tour and get my pants off to have a look." The rest of the tour was super quick. I was hard in my jeans and wanted them off. Gus took off his belt and tossed it onto the red leather couch. I merely pointed to the other side of the room where my bookshelves and records were and pulled Gus past the living room, toward the only white painted wall in the loft, toward my bedroom. I heard a zipper and looked behind me to see Gus shimmying out of his jeans, revealing his other tattoo: a DNA strand with piano keys as the base pairs and bonds located on his shin.

I signaled with my head toward the right and said, "Bathroom's there, walk-through shower, blue and grey tiles, you'll see it later." I pulled Gus into my room and flung him onto my bed. I crawled on top of him, pleased to feel that he was just as hard as I was. He was wearing briefs again—all black this time, and damn, they suited him.

I worked my way up his body, taking in all the sights and marveling at how good his skin felt under my palms. That delicious scent was there again too, all fresh and wild, with a hint of musk that was unique to him. I touched every inch of his exposed skin I could as I made my way up his body. He gently writhed beneath me, so I kept going, getting bolder with my exploration. As I slid my hands up Gus's chest, I squeezed his firm pecs. His dick twitched against me, so I tried circling his nipple with my thumb. Gus's whole body jerked in response, and he sucked in a sharp breath. His hands were fisting the sheets, as I continued to toy with his nipple until it was hard and pointed. I leaned down and closed my mouth around the hard nub, alternating between sucking and circling it with my tongue. Gus went fucking wild. He fisted both hands in my hair and ground his cock into mine. I whimpered at the too light touch and abruptly pushed up off Gus.

He looked at me questioningly, but my brain was too fried to consider explaining that my pants were public enemy number one at the moment. I ripped my shirt over my head and flopped onto my back to shuck off my jeans and underwear in one go.

Butt-ass naked, I climbed back in Gus's lap and shivered when he ran his hands over the front and backs of my thighs. With his eyes locked on mine, Gus slid his rough hands up my body and pulled me down to him by a firm grip on the back of my neck. He stopped just shy of his lips and waited. I closed the distance between our lips and drew his bottom lip between my teeth in a gentle tug. Gus smiled and leaned up to kiss me, his hands on the back and side of my neck. I teased his nipple with one hand and just held myself up with the other.

"What do you want, Jamie?" Gus rasped against my lips. "God, I want to touch you."

"Touch me then. Do whatever you want." Gus took my words to heart and flipped us over. He pressed his body flush against mine and held me down with his weight while he kissed behind my ear and down my neck. His soft lips soothed the scratchiness from his short beard, creating a sensation that I craved.

I ground up against Gus, desperate for any sort of friction on my aching cock. The contact drove me crazy, but it wasn't enough. "I need more," I panted.

Gus groaned and dragged his body down mine, leaving kisses in his wake. He made a point to stop and tease both of my nipples to attention before continuing his descent down my torso. Gus stopped and hovered just above my cock, close enough that I could feel his hot breath on my sensitive skin. It was too-fucking-much.

"Gus, please," I pleaded.

"Please what?"

"Suck me," I begged. "Please."

Gus nuzzled into the crease between my thigh and groin, and I jumped when his beard tickled my balls. He held me down by my hips and continued to rub, occasionally grazing my taint and balls, driving me wild. I tried to squirm and seek out more friction, but Gus's grip held me still. I threw my head back in frustration and cried out when my cock was enveloped in the warm, wet heat of Gus's mouth. Scratch that, I fucking screamed. He swallowed me down all the way without a hint of warning, nearly ripping my orgasm from me. Gus swallowed around my cock twice more before pulling off and letting it slide free from his lush, kiss-swollen lips. He twirled his tongue around my tip and looked up at me with heavy-lidded eyes.

"Holy shit, you look all kinds of lewd right now," I said. Gus took me in his mouth again and hummed, sending shivers through my whole body. I wanted to move my hips and fuck his mouth, but his grip didn't let up. He was damn good at sucking dick and seemed to be enjoying it as much as I was, which only turned me on more.

I was close to coming again when Gus pulled off entirely and kissed down the underside of my cock, toying with the sensitive nerves. He didn't stop when he reached the base and tongued my balls before sucking one into his mouth and massaging it with his tongue. The other got the same thorough treatment, which was fan-fucking-tastic.

Gus gave my cock one more lick from root to tip, then slid one hand over from my hip and stroked me, oh so slowly. "Fuck me, that feels so good," I said breathlessly.

"You've got a gorgeous cock; I could suck it all day."

"Fuck, no protesting here," I moaned. Gus laughed and swiped his thumb over the pre-cum spilling from my tip. He drew his thumb into his mouth and sucked on it in a way that made my cock jealous. All that came out was a frustrated whimper.

"Is there anything else you want to try? I'll do whatever you want," Gus ground out as he resumed stroking me. I put my hands on his to stop him.

"Dude, I can't think straight when you're jerking me off."

"Nice phrasing."

I snorted. "Shut up. There *is* something I want to try. Rather, something I'd like you to do to me. Ah, you don't have to though, if you don't want to." Ugh, I was a rambling mess again.

"Well?"

"Wanna toss my salad?" I cringed as soon as the words left my stupid mouth.

Gus barked out a laugh, so I'd say he was pretty damn amused. "You want me to rim you?" He asked, much more tactfully than I had.

"Yes. I know it's like, my ass and stuff, but I, uh, took care of it earlier." Gus licked his lips and raised a brow at me. "I douched earlier, okay? God. I'm embarrassed." I threw my arms over my face as if I could hide from Gus. Kinda hard to do while my cock was still in his hand.

Strong hands pried my arms to my sides, and the first thing I saw was Gus's warm smile. "Don't be embarrassed. Being prepared is good." He leaned down and bit my earlobe. "It's also hot that you did that for me. Now turn over and spread your legs." Gus pushed up and sat back, massaging his cock through his briefs. I flipped onto my stomach as fast as I could and opened my legs about shoulder width apart. "More," Gus said, so I did. "Good. You've got a cute ass, Jamie. It's really too bad."

What was too bad? I couldn't even think about it before Gus's big hands cupped my ass and spread my cheeks wide.

There's feeling naked, and then there's feeling *exposed*. This was definitely the latter. My dick twitched beneath me, despite me being sure I was as red as a baboon's ass after getting spanked. I was tense as fuck and jumped out of shock when Gus's beard scraped over my hole. "Jesus Christ," I hissed.

Gus let go of my ass and massaged the backs of my thighs. "Relax, Jamie. I'll stop if you don't like it. But I need you to relax." I hummed my reply and took deep breaths to calm the fuck down. The next contact was a kiss to each of the globes of my ass, followed by soft bites and more soothing kisses. Gus spread me wide again and slowly licked from my balls to the top of my crack.

"Oh," I said with wide eyes. Gus hummed and swept his tongue across my hole, then again in tight circles. "*Oh*." Gus chuckled and then continued to tongue my ass and massage my cheeks until I was moaning and grinding against the bed.

"Turn over. I want you to come in my mouth."

"Fuuuuck, you're so hot," I moaned while I ungracefully flopped onto my back. Gus took me to the back of his throat and swallowed. He came up fast, circled the tip, and sank back down, letting his throat muscles do the work. I came with an unrestrained shout and shot my kids down Gus's throat—sorry, guys. I felt completely boneless when my body stopped its spasms. "Fuckfuckfuck! I think you just sucked my soul out through my dick."

Gus laughed and rubbed the tops of my thighs. "I'm glad you liked it."

"Liked it? You just blew my fucking mind. I need a second here, and then I wanna try blowing you, that okay?"

"Well, I'm not going to say no," Gus replied lightly.

"Fuck me. I legit think you stole some of my life-force there. Okay, I'm ready." I sat up and clapped my hands together. "Do you mind sitting on the edge of the bed? I dunno if I can hold myself up right now. My bones are seriously jelly."

Gus smiled and nodded, then scooted over to the edge of the bed. I got up and kneeled between his legs and eagerly pulled his briefs down and all the way off. I could have sworn his fucking dick got bigger.

His foreskin was partially retracted, exposing the ultrasensitive, brown tip of Gus's cock. I licked my lips and went in for it, taking him a couple of inches into my mouth. Gus sighed when his cock passed my lips. He was thicker than I thought and I had to work to relax my jaw, but it wasn't bad. Gus's reactions spurred me on to try more, so I took a few more inches, pulling back and coughing when I'd inadvertently gone too far. Damn, he made this look easier than it was.

"You okay?" Gus asked, sounding concerned despite how thick his voice was.

"I'm good. Got a little greedy. You made it look easy."

"You'll get there. Just don't force it."

I chewed my bottom lip and thought for a moment before I looked up into Gus's heavy-lidded eyes. "Can you help me? I really want to make you come. I can play around and figure it out later." Gus's bottom lip twitched, and he nodded. He slipped a hand behind my head and gripped my hair.

"Tap on my thigh twice if it's too much," he drawled. I quirked my brows and smirked up at him, then licked his tip before he guided my head forward. "Hold the base so you don't go down too far." I did as instructed and kept my jaw as relaxed as possible as Gus guided my head to his liking. I wanted him to be rougher, to take his pleasure from my mouth, but I appreciated the restraint he was showing by going slow and not giving me the brutal throat-fucking we both knew I couldn't yet handle.

Gus's scent was stronger in his crotch, and it was fucking hot. I wanted to bury my face in his pubes and just breathe it in, but that would have to wait. Humming had felt really good when Gus did it, so I tried humming around his cock and was not disappointed. The fingers in my hair tightened, and Gus got a little rougher. His breathing came out harsher and faster, a tell-tale sign he was going to come soon. I considered my options and decided that I was going to taste him. I really wanted to.

He let go of my head and gave me a warning that he was going to come, but I released my hold on his thick base and tried taking him down further. It was the strangest thing; I felt Gus's cock pulse in my mouth just before he shot his load down the back of my throat. His grip on my hair was painfully tight, but I liked it. I kept sucking to get more moans out of him until he pulled me off and collapsed backward on the bed.

"I didn't mean to come in your mouth," Gus said through labored breaths.

I climbed up and lay next to Gus with my head resting in my palm. "I wanted to know what you tasted like." I made a show of licking my lips obnoxiously. "Hmm, it's bitterer than I was expecting, but I didn't actually get much in my mouth. Next time I'll have to time it better so I get the whole load and not just swallow it right away."

"You're something else," Gus said with a smile.

"I'm something good."

"You're something wild. Unpredictable," Gus replied.

"I'd be pretty boring if I were predictable." I leaned down to kiss Gus and stopped just short of his lips. "Ah, do you want me to go hit the mouthwash or something? Last couple girls I've… whatever with didn't particularly enjoy kissing after mouths were on… body parts." You'd think I wasn't about to graduate medical school, what with my firm grasp on anatomy. Ugh.

"Good thing I'm not one of the girls you were fucking." Gus leaned up the rest of the way to meet my lips and kissed me. Tongue and all.

We spent as long as we could enjoying each other's bodies until Gus had to leave for work. I asked him again for his number and got the same response as before. I wanted nothing more than to talk about why he wouldn't give it to me, but it wasn't the right time. Fighting with him before he had to go to work would have been the type of shitty behavior I'd drop a chick over. So, I held my tongue and asked him to meet me at a restaurant not far from my place next Friday at seven for dinner. I'd get my answers then.

EIGHT

I WAS RIDING A HIGH FROM seeing Gus, and I fucking demolished the Northwestern interview. The panel members were charmed and impressed, but with my credentials, knowledge, skill, and charisma, I wasn't the least bit surprised. The rest of my first day went well too. It was weird not having D or one of the guys around, though it was something I'd adjust to quickly once I threw myself into the work. I was a pretty frivolous guy most of the time, but my work was something I took very seriously. I liked to have fun with it where possible, though I strived for excellence with my job.

Crushing my last and biggest interview was a huge deal. Everyone in my group finished theirs last week and were also relieved to have them over. For a change of pace, I offered to play host to my friends for a low-key celebration at my place that night. We all had early mornings and going out always resulted in overindulgence.

I ordered some pizzas and garlic fingers and stocked the fridge with beer and some cider because it was Roz's preferred drink. I was so wired and restless waiting for them to show up that I had to crack the window and smoke a J to calm down. I was going to tell them more about Gus, which both excited and unnerved me. Dani would likely still be cautious because that's just who she was, but I wanted to convince her that everything would be all right.

A knock at the door stole my attention, and I cracked my neck on the way to the door and opened it. Patrick greeted me with a half grin and a curt nod. Dressed in one of his signature dress shirts, he tried to snake past me, but I hauled that adorable bastard into a bear hug and ruffled his hair. He was taller and older than me, but I'd never *not* treat him like an adorable child.

"Nice to see you too, Jamie," Patrick deadpanned and walked around me.

"Grab a beer and go sit. Pizza should be here soon," I called after him. I left the door unlocked and headed into my bedroom to grab some shatter in case Scotty and Roz wanted to indulge. Patrick never smoked with us. Dani did on occasion, though never on a school or work night. She was responsible and shit like that.

Roz showed up next, followed shortly by Scotty. Roz wore a grey oversized knit sweater, which fell off one bare shoulder, and black skinny jeans styled with rips in the knees. Scotty came straight from his shift and was still wearing scrubs. He claimed the outfit made him sexier, and he got his driver's private number, so I guess it worked. We were congregated in the kitchen—because that's where the pizza boxes were—with Roz and me sitting up on the island and counter respectively, and Scotty and Pat standing close. We were talking and enjoying our drinks when the sound of keys in the door lock reached my ears.

"It's open, D," I called out. The door opened, and Dani walked in carrying several canvas grocery bags.

"Sorry I'm late, guys. There was some drama at the restaurant. Also, I figured Jamie wouldn't have anything with any real nutritional value, so I stopped to pick up a few things." And she was right.

I slid off the counter and kissed Dani on the cheek while I relieved her of the bags. "What did you bring for Daddy?" I asked in a playful tone.

"Greek salad, some grapes, strawberries, and garbanzo salad."

I gasped. "Did you make the garbanzo?" Dani smiled, and I squealed. It was one of my favorites from *Ciao Bella*. "I love strawberries, but why them?"

"You've got Dom in your crisper, don't you? We're celebrating, so bubbly and strawberries are a must."

"Jamie always has Dom in the crisper," Roz said.

"If you mean those champagne shelves at the bottom of the fridge, then yes, I most certainly do." It was a staple at my place. I had it on hand at all times because it was tasty and flossy as fuck.

We got some food plated out, and mugs filled with bubbly and sat down in the living room. The couch sat three comfortably and the chair, just one, but Dani and I squeezed into it in a tangle of limbs. She'd probably shift into my lap or sit on the arm when we were done eating. She'd always declined when I'd offered her the chair to sit in solo, so I stopped.

I put on a Spotify playlist instead of my vinyl because there was no way in hell I was touching them with greasy-ass pizza fingers. It was also more convenient because Scotty always had a weird request that would otherwise have me constantly switching out records. We ate and recapped our weeks and how we were feeling about our elective placements, then switched on a basketball game on mute so Scotty and Pat could keep up with the score.

"So, what are you even doing all day since you don't have any reqs left?" Roz asked Pat.

"It's actually quite boring. I considered traveling again, but I'd rather stay here until Match Day. I'll probably book something after that. Somewhere far away from my mother," Pat groaned.

"You're lucky. I'd kill to be that bored. My supervising physician has a hate-on for me already." Roz brushed her short hair to the side. It had grown out a couple of inches, but she kept it dyed blonde. "I don't think she likes my nose ring," she added.

"You should probably not let her see your nipples then," Scotty said with a smile.

"I'm going to be a good fucking doctor. I don't need her shit because of some archaic prejudice about how a proper woman should be. It's exhausting."

I laughed under my breath, as did the others. "Roz, love. You're the second most privileged person here—me being the first," I said.

Roz looked around and sighed. "Fair point. I'll stop complaining."

"You don't have to stop. It's super cute when you get mad. Your little nose scrunches right up," Scotty said as he poked Roz on said nose. She bit him while he was laughing. "Ow, fuckin' piranha. *Oyinbo*, what's up with you and that guy? Get plowed yet?"

"Jesus, Ade," Dani said. Adeoye was *technically* Scotty's real name, but I preferred Scotty.

"What? We're all dying to know. Don't act like you're not." Dani huffed, but didn't deny it. She'd shifted onto the chair's arm and had her legs resting over my lap.

I took a liberal swig of my drink and followed it with an overly enthusiastic "ahh." "Things have escalated, but we haven't fucked yet."

Scotty leaned forward and rested on his hands. "Come on, spill."

"Well, I now know what cum tastes like and how fan-fucking-tastic getting my ass eaten feels." I flashed Dani an apologetic smile. "Sorry, D."

Scotty and Roz were ecstatic with big smiles and hollers of congratulations. Scotty held up his fist, and I waggled my brows at him and bumped it. Dani rubbed her toes against my stomach, and I looked up at her to see her smiling at me.

"I'm still suspicious of him, but I'm damn happy for you, *fratellino*."

"Thanks, D," I replied.

"When do we get to meet him?" Roz asked.

"Yeah! I wanna meet the guy hot enough to turn you off pussy," Scotty said with a toothy grin. Roz whacked his arm, though he wasn't deterred.

I shook my head and snorted. "I'm not 'turned off pussy,' as you so delicately put it—"

"You're one to talk about delicacy," Pat mumbled.

"Shush, Pattycakes," I said to Pat, before focusing back on Scotty. "So, I still love women just as much as I did before, I just really like Gus too. Well, not just Gus. I find a lot of guys attractive, but it's more than that with Gus."

Roz gasped while her eyes went wide. "Shit, you're sweet on him."

I wasn't sure how to answer since I was still trying to sort out my feelings—ugh, my feelings—but I didn't feel right outright denying it. "I don't know yet. I like spending time with him. I don't get to see him enough, though. I'd like to at least be able to talk to him on days I can't see him."

"Oh my God." Scotty shot to his feet excitedly and pointed at me. "You're dick-whipped. I never thought I'd see the day where a chick did this to you, let alone a dude. But you're happy—it looks good on you, man." I started to protest, but Dani cupped her hand over my mouth and shook her head. Shit. Maybe I was.

Roz whacked Scotty again and said, "That means the same thing as what I said, you dumbass. Sit down before you hurt yourself." Scotty complied obediently, his perma-grin never faltered.

Dani removed her hand from my mouth and ruffled my hair as Pat and Scotty got distracted by the game and booed at the silent TV. Scotty booed. Pat manically chuckled at Scotty's frustration over his team losing.

We called it a night after another round of pizza and drinks, like the responsible adults we were so soon going to become. Once I was alone, I lit another J and waited for my hammering heart to calm itself. I'd been on edge ever since Roz and Scotty called me out. Dani stopping me from blurting out any sort of knee-jerk denial kinda sealed it for me. She knew it was true, even if I hadn't figured it out or put a label on how I felt.

I'd tried not to think about it while my friends were over, but it was always in the back of my mind. After they'd left, there was nothing to keep the thoughts at bay. So, there I was, smoking by the open window in the living room and avoiding thinking about tough shit. No, not even tough shit. Scary shit. I didn't like how twisted up I felt and would for sure talk to Gus about it on Friday. We hadn't even discussed what we were—were we even *anything*? We'd gone on a few really great dates, but did that amount to anything? I hoped it did, though I needed to hear it from Gus. Soon enough I would.

I HAD to call in a favor to get a table on Friday night. It wasn't a super upscale place, but the food was orgasmic and the weekends were always booked in advance. I showed up early and was led through a sea of cream-clothed square tables adorned with fresh tuberoses in tall black vases. It was simple and clean, which wasn't my usual scene, but, again, the food was a slam dunk. The perimeter walls were restored brick, like so many older buildings in Chicago. I was seated at my table, and ice water was brought immediately.

I was nervous as hell and reached to loosen my collar, even though it was already unbuttoned. I wore a dark blue button-up with all-over print off-white stars on it tucked into khaki-colored, belted chinos. In an attempt to look like a real adult, I left my sneakers at home and opted for brown leather chukka boots. I probably should have gone for a plain shirt, but I needed *something* to feel like standard me, while still impressing Gus.

My water was gone in a matter of seconds. I was a nervous drinker, which usually resulted in pain and what felt like endless suffering. Water was harmless, so I wasn't worried about it, although I would have to piss somethin' fierce later, but that was an issue for later.

The tables around me buzzed with chatter between couples and friends. I'd been waiting for what felt like a while, and a check at my watch confirmed that Gus was running late. It was just a few minutes after seven—no big deal. I pulled out my phone to scroll through some gossip rags and browse Instagram to keep myself occupied. It worked for about fifteen more minutes, but there was still no sign of Gus. I tried not to jump to any conclusions and be patient. He could have missed the train or got off on the wrong stop. A simple text giving me a heads-up would have been enough to put me at ease, but we didn't have each other's numbers. I didn't even know where Gus lived. If he wanted to ghost me, he had the perfect setup to do so.

No. Gus wasn't like that. I hadn't known him long, but I knew he was a good guy. He wouldn't stand me up without a damn good reason, especially if he couldn't tell me he had to cancel. I needed to chill out and be patient. I needed a fucking drink.

I waved down a blonde server dressed in head-to-toe black with a tight, high ponytail, and asked for a refill on my water and a double of Bruichladdich Black Art. She brought out both within minutes with a kind smile, which I returned. Once she was out of sight, I slammed the scotch back in one go and shook my head like a wet dog. I could remain optimistic and rational. I'd drink my water and mellow the fuck out, and Gus would show up, and we'd have a great evening.

Nearly two hours later I was drunk off my ass. The lovely server kept my drinks coming and brought out a basket of fresh bread, despite me having declined ordering any food. I'd cycled through several rounds of panicking over the possibility that something was wrong, being angry at being stood up, and being hurt and confused. I felt like such a fucking loser. I wasn't that guy. I didn't get down over shit like that—I didn't fucking put myself in situations like that. Yet, there I was, alone with a busy mind. I wanted the noise to stop, so I ordered more drinks until it slowly faded into a dull hum. After that I should have left—I should have gone sooner—but I couldn't bring myself to believe that he really wasn't coming. So I drank more and waited.

I'd nearly passed out on the table when some commotion caught my attention, though not enough for me to lift my head off the table. I was a sloppy mess, but who the fuck cared? Certainly not me. Whatever the hell was going on in the restaurant got louder. The buzz of patrons whispering was loudest in my ears, but there were arguing voices above that, one of which was deep and smooth and sounded *very* familiar. I found the strength to lift my head and saw Gus hurriedly walking toward me with my blonde server, as well as another, right behind him.

His brows were furrowed, and he sounded pretty fired up, more than I'd ever seen him. He had on a red, worn base-ball cap, dirty navy coveralls, and brown work boots. He had his gym bag slung over his shoulder. His expression softened when his eyes met mine, and my heart stammered. The servers' voices rose, and they were close enough that I could hear them clearly.

"Sir, you can't be in here dressed like that," one of them said.

Gus stopped and turned to face them, but I couldn't make out what he said. It was low; almost a growl and they took a step back from him. Gus turned back to me and closed the distance between us in a few long strides. He dropped to his knees in front of me and hung his head low.

"I'm so sorry, Jamie. I'm so fucking sorry," he said just above a whisper.

I was fuzzy as fuck from all the alcohol, and mildly confused by the situation. The servers were hovering about ten feet back, whispering to each other, and we had the attention of nearly the entire restaurant. It was a lot for me to process through the haze of the scotch, but I knew without an ounce of doubt that I was happy to see him and that I really wanted to talk to him.

"I wanna talk t'you," I slurred.

Gus nodded his head and looked around at our capti-vated audience. "We should talk. Do you mind if we go back to your place?"

"Waited for you t'night. I wanted t'see you."

Gus stood up and held his hand out for me. "Come on, Jamie. I'll take you home."

I took his warm hand and was pulled to my unsteady feet. Gus steadied me with a firm grip on my biceps, and I flashed him a toothy grin. "Oh, wait! Needa pay m'bill. Where's that cute waitress?" I dragged my eyes around the room and settled on the blonde. I stumbled over to her and pulled out my wallet. "How much I owe ya, hon?"

She looked at her colleague then opened her order pad. "I can go print off your official receipt for you—"

"Nah, s'all good, jus tell me what I owe."

"Um." She cleared her throat. "Four hundred, ninety-eight dollars and sixty-two cents, sir."

"I'm on it." I pulled my wallet out and pulled out seven Benjis and handed them to her. "Keep the change, hon. Sorry 'bout the scene." I motioned my hand around us. She nodded, and I turned back to Gus with a smile. "I'm ready to go, doll." He took hold of my hand and led me out of the restaurant.

Once we were outside, the cold air hit me hard, and I shivered almost immediately. Gus rubbed my arms, the contact making me burn. "Did we leave your coat inside?" Gus asked.

I shook my head. "Nah, didn't bring it. I took 'n Uber… Ubered?"

Gus set his bag down and unzipped it. The streetlights caught my attention, so I didn't notice that he'd taken out his leather jacket until it was draped over my shoulders. He guided each of my arms into it then zipped me up. "Can you walk? We're just a couple blocks from your place, and I think the fresh air will do you some good."

"I can walk," I said as I held my thumb up to show him I was good to go. He took my hand again, and we walked maybe ten feet before my feet stopped working and I tripped. Gus caught me before I fell, but the all-too-quick motion brought up all that top-shelf scotch I drank way too fast. I hurled on the sidewalk like some fuckin' freshman. I should have known better. If the mess in the snow was any indication, clearly I didn't. I saw Gus move in close out of the corner of my eye, but a second round of throwing up kept all of my attention. My throat burned and my eyes stung when I was finished, though I did feel better. Not quite ready to stand, I sat back on the cold sidewalk and felt the snow start to seep into my pants. Damn, I was probably gonna have to buy new chinos.

"Are you okay?" Gus asked softly.

"Better now. Just needa sit for a sec."

Gus took off his hat to run his hand through his short hair, and then put it back on. "Come on, Jamie. You can't sit on the street." Gus stood up and held his hand out for me. I took it and was pulled upright. I wavered again while protesting that I was fine to walk, and Gus just smiled. He turned around and kneeled. Looking over his shoulder at me, he grinned and said, "Hop on. It's not far." Never one to turn down a piggyback ride, I lowered myself on Gus's broad back and wrapped my arms loosely around his neck. He stood up and jostled me a bit higher, then handed me his bag, which I hung over my shoulder. Gus held the underside of my thighs and carried me home in silence.

About twenty minutes later I was unlocking the door to my loft. I headed straight for my couch, but Gus steered me into the bathroom. He tried to get me to have a shower—I vehemently refused. For no particular reason other than I was drunk and being difficult. He managed to get me to brush my teeth then stripped me down to my boxers and tucked me into my bed. Gus asked if he could use my shower and left the room after I nodded.

Lying down felt amazeballs. I thankfully didn't get the spins, and just snuggled into my pillow while my mind quieted. I distantly heard the shower turn off a few minutes later, and the floorboards creak as Gus entered my room.

"Do you mind if I crash on your couch?" he asked me.

Was that a serious question? I groaned and reached

behind me to pull the covers down. "Get in, doll," I murmured as I closed my eyes. Gus slid into bed behind me —without the wet towel—and held me in his arms. He smelled like my citrus soap, but under that he still smelled like Gus. That, along with the steady rise and fall of his warm chest against my back, comforted me until I fell asleep.

I woke up with one prevailing thought: why the fuck was the world so damn bright? I rubbed the sleep from my eyes and chanced a peek to see that my motherfucking curtains were open. Why hadn't I closed them last night? And why was I so hot? I pushed the duvet down and bumped my elbow into a hot, solid mass. *Oh.* That was right, Gus carried me home last night after I got shit-faced and puked on the fucking sidewalk. Ugh.

I turned and peeked over my shoulder, just to fact-check my shoddy memory. Gus was there, lying on his back, asleep and looking adorably worry-free. He usually held some tension in his features but looked so at peace while he was sleeping. I carefully turned over to get a better look at him, ignoring how creepy that inherently was. Gus's freckles really were cute. His hair had been trimmed recently, as it was shorter on the sides and left longer on top, which was messy from sleep. The hair on top was less than two inches long, and I wondered how he would look with a longer style if it would be as wavy as mine. I couldn't resist the urge and ran my fingers gently through his hair. He stirred but didn't wake. It was thick as hell and a bit coarser than mine—and also just long enough for grabbing.

Wanting to explore my voyeuristic side more, I pushed the blanket down a bit farther until—*oh, dayum.* Gus was naked and, um, sporting some serious morning wood. I gulped, because really, what else could I do? After one final peek, I pulled the duvet back up and rolled onto my back.

"Did you get a good look?" Gus asked, his voice thick with sleep.

I jumped at the suddenness of his voice. Also, I got caught being a letch. Whoops. "I'm not sorry, so I won't bother with formalities and say that I am."

"Fair enough." Gus paused and cleared his throat. "We need to talk about last night."

I barked out a laugh. "We need to talk about more than just last night. But I can't do that with you being all at attention at the ass crack of dawn."

Gus sighed and sat up. "It's a physiological response. It'll go away in a few minutes. You should know that, being so young."

"I dunno. I jerk off if I wake up hard. It's like my body telling me it's time. I've got whiskey dick right now though, so it ain't gonna happen."

"There's so much I want to say about that, but it's not what we need to discuss."

I sat up too, and turned so I was facing Gus. "Okay, so where do we start?"

Gus chewed his bottom lip then shrugged. "I don't know."

"How about this, where were you last night?" I asked.

"I got stuck at work. A delivery came in late, and my boss wouldn't let me leave until it was unloaded and catalogued. I tried to leave, but I need that job. So I worked as fast as I could and went straight over after I finished. I should have changed first." Gus ran his hand over his face and hair. "It's bad enough I was fucking late. Then I had to go and make a scene by showing up looking like that. I'm sorry."

"Like what?"

"In my filthy work clothes." Gus lowered his gaze from mine. "I'm sorry if I embarrassed you."

I considered what Gus was saying, though something

didn't compute. "Why would I be embarrassed? Because you were late? I tripped balls about that earlier, but I was pretty drunk by the time you got there." I crossed my legs and leaned my elbows on my knees. "I'm missing something here. I get why you were late, and I get that you're sorry because of it. But why did this have to happen at all? A simple text would have made a world of difference, and we could have rescheduled. No big deal. But I don't have your number, and I think that's kinda fucked up. I just wanna know where I stand with you." Gus tapped his fingers on the blanket over his thigh. His jaw was tense, and he wouldn't make eye contact with me. "Will you look at me? I don't want to sound like an overbearing chick or anything, but I had a great time each time I've seen you, and I don't really know if it was like that for you."

"Of course it was," Gus said quickly.

"Okay, then why be shady?"

Gus's fingers kept moving while he remained silent. His brow was furrowed, and he chewed on his bottom lip. I put my hand over his and curled my fingers around his palm. He looked up at me, and I saw the sadness in his eyes. It hurt my fucking soul to see him like that, and it hit me that I really fucking cared. Gus had all the power at that moment. He could've broken me with a few uttered words. And that realization was more frightening than anything I'd felt in a long time.

I held my breath and waited for Gus to answer me. I didn't dare speak again until he gave me a sign to see where this conversation was headed. I needed to be ready.

"I didn't give you my number because I couldn't," Gus scraped out.

I swallowed the lump in my throat. "What do you mean?"

"I don't have a phone right now."

I tilted my head as if it would help me make sense of what Gus was saying. "Okay?"

"My phone broke a couple of months ago, and I haven't been able to afford to replace it. It hasn't been an issue until I met you." Gus still wouldn't look at me.

"All right, your phone is busted; you could have just told me that," I said.

Gus shook his head. "You're not hearing me. I have a shitty job unloading pallets downtown for minimum wage. My phone is broken, and I can't afford to replace it with the cost of living and the rent I pay on my shoebox studio apartment. I'm a fucking loser, Jamie. I didn't want you to know if I could help it." He pulled his hand from mine and fisted the top sheet.

What? Was that it? "Is there more? You're not like a drug addict or a fugitive or something?"

"What? No."

"Well, what the ever-loving fuck is your problem? None of that shit you just told me matters. Had I known, we wouldn't be sitting here having this damn conversation." I huffed in frustration. "Is that really all that's been making you weird and secretive? You didn't want me to know you were broke?"

Gus winced. "It matters. Who wants to be with a guy who doesn't have his shit together? I don't—"

"Ah, shut up!" I yelled. I got out of bed and paced. "I am so motherfucking frustrated with you. I could smother you with a pillow if you didn't look so damn defeated. Gus, your financial situation really doesn't matter to me. I like you, whether you're broke or whatever. You need a phone?" I stomped over to my dresser and opened the top drawer. I replaced my phone whenever a new model came out and kept the others boxed. Why? Because they were pretty and I didn't have a reason to sell them. I grabbed the iPhone 8 Plus box and tossed it on the bed. "There's a fucking phone. Problem solved."

"I can't accept that."

I turned to Gus with my hands on my hips. "Do you want to date me? Because I do. Want to date you, I mean. I don't know what makes you different, but I want to try, Gus. If you don't want that, you need to tell me right fucking now."

Gus looked up at me for the first time in what felt like ages. He was clearly torn up, but he held my gaze as he said the words that made me soar. "I wouldn't be here if I didn't want you, Jamie."

I clapped my hands together once and threw up a double thumbs-up. "Wunderbar. This is what's gonna happen. I'm gonna go take the piss of a century while you kindly close my blinds and block out that demon-sun. When I come back you're gonna snuggle me like you did last night and we're going to sleep for"—I looked over at my bedside clock to see it was barely seven—"at least four more hours. After that, we'll get up and showered, and we can hash out the finer points of this little chat. Feel me?" Gus nodded. "Good."

It really was the piss of a century, and I felt a billion times better. My mouth was dry, so I brought two glasses of water back into my wonderfully darkened bedroom from the kitchen and handed one to Gus. He thanked me and drank half of it before setting the glass on the nightstand on his side of the bed. He turned back toward me and lay flat on his back with his arm held out. I scooted over and nestled into the crook of his arm, as so many of my exes had done to me. And I understood why—it was fucking warm and cozy as hell all tucked up under Gus's arm and against his chest. But it was the sound of Gus's heart beating that I liked best about it. Yes, I liked that very much.

NINE

W AKING UP FOR THE SECOND time that morning was much more pleasant than the first. My arms and legs were wrapped around Gus, and it was beyond cozy. He tilted his head down at me when I yawned and nuzzled into his pit. Did I think I'd be trying to burrow into a hot guy's armpit a month ago? Nope, but I'm glad I was.

"You're finally awake," Gus said quietly.

"Mhm," I hummed. "What time is it?"

"Almost one. You seemed like you needed the sleep." Gus traced small circles on my back while he spoke. It tickled a little, but it also felt really nice.

"Good call." I yawned and untangled my legs from Gus's. "I'm gonna hit the shower. I'll put on some coffee for you when I get out. Or you're welcome to have at it right now." I rolled out of bed and stretched until my spine cracked.

Gus sat up in bed with the covers pooled low in his lap. "I'll wait for you. Do you mind bringing me my bag? It's out by the front door."

"No, I think I like you just how you are," I said as I

scanned my eyes over Gus's bare chest. "I quite like it, indeed."

Gus crossed his arms behind his head and leaned back against the headboard, stretching the muscles in his abs and looking oh so tasty. "I'm flattered, but I'd rather not walk around here naked."

"Why not? I already told you I don't have any roommates."

"We're not finished talking, and it's not a conversation I think I can have with my dick out. Although I'd consider it under other circumstances." Gus grinned at me, but it was short-lived.

"Do you want the whole bag or just something in particular?" I asked.

"Just my jeans."

"Ew, no. Freeballing in jeans—however hot—is not comfy." I turned around and opened the third drawer of my dresser and dug around until I found a pair of black, cotton lounge pants. "Here"—I tossed the pants on the bed next to Gus—"those should fit you. I keep them around for when my brother crashes here. You're a bit bigger than him, but they should fit you okay. So, yeah, feel free to have a look around or watch TV or whatever. I won't be too long." Not sure what to do, I waggled my brows and saluted Gus before I left the room.

When I came back from my shower, Gus wasn't in my bed. I slipped into some lounge pants and draped my towel over my bare shoulder. Being naked would have been preferred, but Gus was probably onto something about not talking about serious shit naked. If I got cold, I could always bundle up in the quilt on my couch. I still needed to dry my hair, but I could do that after I laid eyes on Gus. I was relieved to see him sitting on the couch—also without a shirt, fuck me dead—waiting for me when I came around the corner.

"Oh, thank fuck. I wasn't sure you'd still be here," I blurted out.

"Still here," Gus replied smoothly.

I grinned like a fool and rubbed the towel back and forth through my hair as I made my way over to the kitchen. "Want some coffee?" I called out.

"Yes, please," Gus said. Please. How adorable.

Remembering that he liked the same coffee as D, I pulled out a Brazilian roast K-Cup from a drawer and popped it into the Keurig. I kept them on hand for when D visited, as well as a slew of other coffees for other guests. I took out a hot chocolate cup for me, as well as two matching white mugs, and set them next to the machine.

A few minutes later, I sat down on the couch next to Gus, two mugs in hand. I handed Gus his coffee and said, "Careful, it's hot. Um, well, I mean no shit. It's coffee, right? I'm just gonna sit here and shut up."

Gus chuckled softly and thanked me as he took the mug and brought it to his lips. "Hey, did you remember what coffee I like and how I take it?" Gus asked in surprise.

"Honestly, I didn't hear you order it because I was distracted. When I got with the program, I recognized it by the way it smelled." Gus cocked his head to the side and slightly narrowed his eyebrows, making me realize how dumb that must have sounded. "That sounds weird. I only recognized it because it's what my best friend drinks. It's a smell I've always identified with her. I assumed you took it black based off that."

"Impressive."

"Oh! Speaking of D, her name is D, by the way, I need to send a Snap." I shot up to my feet and pulled my phone out of my pocket. I opened Snapchat and pulled the waistband of my pants out while angling the phone above for a good angle.

"What are you doing?" Gus asked.

"I like to Snap dick pics to my friends. It's, like, one of my favorite things to do. The key is not to send them constantly." I snapped a pic and smiled at the screen while I chose the lucky recipients. "They have to be a surprise when they come for maximum impact." I closed the app and sat back down. "Done!" Gus shook his head and sipped his coffee; I did the same with my hot chocolate. "So, where do we start?"

Gus sighed, setting his cup down on a coaster on the table. He looked me in the eye, and I saw pain in his eyes again. "Earlier I told you why I didn't have a phone and that I had a shitty labor job. Right now, I unpack pallets downtown. Before that, I've done countless other menial general labor jobs in every city I've lived in. Brooklyn was supposed to be different. My cousin had something lined up for us, but it fell through. I stayed there as long as I could before I ended up moving back here."

"You don't sound happy about it."

"Not really, but it's all I can do." Gus picked up his coffee and held it while he rested it on his thigh.

"Why do you think that?" I grabbed the quilt behind me and draped it over my shoulders.

Gus's jaw ticked and his fingers started tapping against the mug. I wanted to hold his hand but figured I should let him say what he needed to say. "It's not just me being negative. I'm not qualified to do anything more. The highest education I have is a high school diploma." Gus dropped his gaze from mine and slumped his shoulders a bit. "It's really a miracle that I even graduated. I did well in school until tenth grade when I got in with some really bad guys in the neighborhood and did a lot of things I'm not proud of."

The tapping got faster, so I scooted closer to Gus and played with the back of his hair. With my other hand, I took the mug from him and put it on the table, then took Gus's fingers in mine. "You don't have to tell me everything right now if you don't want to." I wanted to hear it, but not if it was going to mess him up. It would drive me batshit, but I could wait.

"No, it's better if I do so you can make an informed decision. I used to be an awful person, Jamie. I stole, vandalized, assaulted people… I was a drug runner for a while for a guy named Marco. He was a few years older than me and always trying to recruit students. I'd fucking jumped at the chance to work for him. The scars on my face are from me getting jumped and robbed. It happened a few times while I was young, not so much after I started working out and bulking up."

"Why do that in the first place? It doesn't seem like you."

"My family didn't have a lot of money. I wanted to make sure my kid sister didn't miss out on anything she wanted, so I turned to the fastest way I could make money. It was stupid, but I just wanted her to be happy and have all the things I didn't. It sounds stupid, and it was. Things ended badly between Marco and me. I was being chased by the cops one day in the middle of a transport and dumped a brick of coke that I had on me. I couldn't go back to Marco and tell him I lost it while saving my own ass, so I panicked and split town." Gus sighed and rubbed his eyes. "Which probably made matters worse. Well, there it is. Now you know what a winner I am," Gus said dryly.

"Stop it. I'm glad you told me so you can cut the cryptic shit out. I'll be honest, I thought it was kind of old-fashioned and charming at first, but last night was a prime example of why it's actually archaic and frustrating as fuck." I huffed and leaned my forehead against Gus's arm.

"You seem to be missing the point of what I just said. I—"

"No," I interrupted, "*you're* missing the point, Gus. I don't care about shit that happened… fourteen years ago. You made some bad decisions with good intentions. You were a kid. Bad shit happens, and people make mistakes. I'm not gonna hold that against you; sounds like you do a fine job of kicking yourself over it enough for the both of us, anyway." I turned Gus's face toward mine and forced him to look at me. "This isn't an issue for me unless you actively make it one. Got it?"

Gus rolled his shoulders and nodded. "Yes."

"Good. Now, in the interest of full disclosure, there are a few things I've been keeping from you too." Gus blanched, and I quickly waved my hands in front of me. "No, no, it's nothing bad. I already told you I'm a student, but I'm in medical school—this is my last year actually."

"Why keep that a secret? That's a fantastic accomplishment." Gus asked with a furrowed brow.

I shrugged and sipped my hot chocolate. "People used to treat me differently when I told them before. It's a good way to see who gives a shit about me, and who just cares about my career. That leads us to a nice segue into the other thing I tend not to disclose." I set the mug down and traced stars on Gus's thigh. "My family is kind of loaded."

"I assumed you were probably decently well-off when you told me you lived here alone and were a student."

"Yeah, it's not something I'm trying to hide or flaunt, but it's more than a nice loft. My great-great-whatever-grandpa moved over from somewhere in France with an assload of cash and founded a bank, so, yeah. I'm not like in direct succession to inherit majority shares or anything—my cousins have that pleasure. But I do have shares in my name from my grandpa. Oh, and a trust fund from him as well. So, basically, I don't have to work if I don't want to. I'm really intrigued by medicine, which is why I'm doing what I'm doing. My dad doesn't really approve, but then again, there isn't much he does actually approve—"

"Jamie," Gus said.

"Oh, sorry, I was rambling again. Nerves, ya know? I never know how people are going to take that." Gus smiled at me, but it didn't come remotely close to reaching his eyes. He looked around the room then again at me. I felt more than saw his thigh muscles tense, and looked closer to see his whole body was rigid. He turned his head toward the door then looked back at me; he was going to fucking bolt.

"Oh, no, you don't," I said as I climbed in Gus's lap at the same time he tried to stand. He wasn't expecting me, so I managed to push him back onto the couch. "Where the fuck do you think you're going?"

"I'm not—"

I put my hand over Gus's mouth and groaned. Goddamn, he could be stubborn. "That was a rhetorical question. This is the last time I'm gonna say this today: all of this doesn't change anything, Gus. This"—I motioned between us—"isn't gonna work if you won't trust me. Yeah, I know, it's only been like, a month, but you have to try. Or at least want to try. This is new and scary for me, but I want to try for you," I said sincerely. Was that right? "For you? With you? No, for you. For you, but with you. Boom."

Gus chuckled, and it was the sweetest sound I could ever want to hear in that moment. He skimmed his hands up my legs and settled them on his hips, making me hyperaware of where I was sitting. I could feel my dick getting hard and knew I was about to pop an anxiety boner. Or fuck, maybe it was just an "I'm sitting in my hot boyfriend's lap" boner—which raised a pertinent question.

"So? Earlier you said you wanted to be with me. Is that still true?"

"Yes," Gus replied.

I did a happy dance, but I was pretty constricted, so it was more like shimmying side to side. Gus groaned and dug his fingers into my hips. I moved my hips again, slower, and watched as his eyes darkened behind those gorgeous thick lashes. "Does this mean I get to call you my boyfriend and be exclusive and all that shit?" I kept moving my hips as I felt Gus's cock harden against my ass. Yes, that was much better than drama.

The lustful expression on Gus's face softened, as did his hold on my hips. He looked at me—really looked at me—and kissed me slowly and deeply. Gus nipped my lip and pulled back to say, "You can have all that shit."

And that was exactly what I wanted to fucking hear. I kissed him fiercely, with more urgency than skill, and continued to grind down into his lap. "How fast can we get out of these clothes?" Not fucking fast enough.

"No need," Gus said against my lips. His scruff scraped my cheek as he moved to my ear and sucked on the lobe. I was vocal in my appreciation of Gus's efforts and ran my hands over his chest and shoulders. I could touch him all fucking day and not get bored, but I had a destination in mind. I rubbed my thumb over Gus's nipple while I palmed his dick through his pants with the other.

"Sure you don't wanna get naked with me?" I asked as I continued teasing Gus's body.

"You're catching on to gay sex pretty fast," Gus drawled.

"I've always been a fast learner. And I've got a gorgeous teacher I want to impress."

He growled when I squeezed his cock a little harder, the sound going straight to my own cock. I could feel pre-cum oozing out and dampening the front of my pants. Gus was only touching my hips and neck, and I was already so close to blowing just from touching him and experiencing his reactions.

I moaned as Gus bit down on my collarbone then soothed the spot with his tongue. He did it again higher on my neck and I almost fucking lost it. "Time for another lesson, Jamie." Gus freed my aching dick from its cotton prison and squeezed the base. More pre-cum pooled at my tip, and he swiped it with his thumb and stroked me up and down. I closed my eyes and lost coordination in my hands as Gus brushed his thumb back and forth over my frenulum.

"Oh, fuckfuckfuck. I'm gonna come soon." As soon as I said it, Gus went back to slow, long strokes. He shifted higher, moving me a couple of inches down in his lap, then his hand left me and was replaced by something hot. Something long and hot. I opened my eyes and watched with my fucking mouth hanging open as Gus took both our hard cocks in his big hand and stroked them. I was essentially just getting jerked off, but it was so much more. My dick sliding against his was so insanely dirty, and far beyond the scope of sexiness I could fucking handle.

With Gus's hot breath coming faster and faster against my neck, I knew he was close too. I leaned back so his face became visible then crashed my lips to his in a demanding kiss. I wanted all his focus on me when he came, just like mine would be on him. The kiss was sloppy as hell, but that wasn't the point. Gus moved faster with an unwavering grip that had us both panting against each other's connected mouths; the pretense of maintaining any semblance of an active kiss was shattered—about as shattered as my control over my body.

I came without warning, basically screaming in Gus's face like some crazed son of a bitch while my cock pulsed in his hand and my hot cum slid down our chests. Gus stroked us faster as his breaths came out harsher. The sensation was almost too much for me, but I held on until Gus cried out with a strangled moan and his cum mixed with mine on our chests. He got more of it than me, but it didn't really matter after I fell against him and rested my forehead on Gus's shoulder while my breathing evened out.

"That lesson line was pretty cheesy, but you're forgiven. Consider me learned." Gus's laughter rumbled through my chest and felt so damn good. The cum between us was drying, but I never wanted to move.

"Come on, get up. We're a mess," Gus said.

I groaned and nuzzled into his neck. "Mm, dun wanna." I was fucking boneless and useless.

Gus chuckled fondly and stroked his fingers through my damp hair. "Hang on, then," he said as he moved one hand under my ass and stood up. I wrapped my arms around his neck and my legs tight around his waist but didn't lift my head. I had no doubts about his manly ability to carry me at that point. "You're like a clingy spider monkey."

"You told me to hang on!"

"Yes, but you were tangled around me this morning too."

"I won't apologize," I said.

"I'd never ask you to."

Gus was radiating nervous energy the whole ride over to his place. I managed to get him to accept the phone after I showed him the drawer in my room, but he wouldn't let me find him a plan, and I didn't dare offer to pay for it. I would have, though the offer probably would have sent him flying out the door, and I really didn't want that. He promised he'd get it set up tomorrow after work and text me. I couldn't fucking wait, but tried to downplay it, since he was so on edge in the car.

He lived ridiculously close to Peet's so it was no wonder

he'd suggested meeting me there for our first date. The apartment building was older with brown carpeting and white walls in the lobby. We took the small elevator up to the eighth floor, and I followed Gus to his unit, taking note of the number on the door. He stalled after he put the key in the lock, and I seriously had zero chill. I grabbed Gus's ass and leaned up on my toes to whisper in his ear from behind him. "I'm going to grope you in the hall if you don't open the door and let us in." Would I actually grope him in the hall? Maybe. Did he doubt me? Nope. Gus inhaled sharply, opened the door, and stood aside for me to enter first. What a gentleman.

He warned me that the unit was small—and it was. Since it was a studio, it was wide open with the kitchen off to the immediate left with a small fridge, microwave, and oven. Counter space was nearly nonexistent, but the area was free of clutter. Oak-colored fake wood cabinets, light laminate countertop, and a single sink left much to be desired in the kitchen area, though the main space had a ceiling fan and a massive window on the wall across from the entrance. The window had thin brown curtains that were probably there when Gus moved in, but I could fix that. There was a doorway next to the fridge, which I assumed led to a closet and bathroom. A queen-sized bed with a nightstand sat in the far right corner with a radiator and wall mounted TV and a small stand under it on the opposite wall. There wasn't much in the way of decorating, just some dumbbells lined against a wall, and sneakers and boots neatly paired by the door—but that wasn't *really* decorating. The bed was made, which stood out to me since I never made my bed. It was just as small as Gus said, but it was super cute and clean. It was minimalist, but then again, Gus wasn't a flashy dude. It suited him.

"I like it. We're gonna need to get some blackout curtains

if I'm gonna be sleeping over though," I said as I turned to him with a smile.

Gus scratched the back of his head as he closed and locked the door. I was sure he'd be doing that finger-tappy thing if he was holding something. "You don't have to say that. I know it's nothing compared to your place."

I knocked the back of my hand against Gus's chest, and then again for good measure. "I wouldn't have said it if I didn't mean it, dude."

"You know, you called me doll last night," Gus said with a raised eyebrow.

My eyes went wide. Yeah, I liked to give people nick-names and pet names, but I'd been careful not to say anything emasculating to Gus, and my drunk ass went and called him *doll*. Whoops. "Ah, sorry about that."

"It's okay. I actually liked it. No one has called me that before." Gus smiled shyly, and ohmyGod, he was so cute. Doll really was fitting—good on drunk me.

"Oh, thank God. I'm partial to nicknames, and I'd have slipped up eventually. I don't know what the fuck it is about people's names, but I just can't do it. You were actually hunky Mario to me until you told me your name. Do you have any idea how it feels to jerk off to the memory of a dude you identified as hunky Mario? I haven't been able to play Smash since!"

Gus laughed and finally relaxed. "I haven't played in years and don't have a Nintendo"—he looked down then bit his lip and looked up at me—"but if you want to smash, I'm avail-able whenever you're ready."

"Goddamn." I stood there gaping at Gus like a lunatic while his smile grew wider. "I can't process how hot that was right now." I kicked off my shoes, walked over to Gus's bed, and collapsed face-first. *Fuck*, it smelled just like him in all the best ways. I could've rolled in the sheets like a dog had I been alone. Instead, I nuzzled my cheek against the blanket and involuntarily moaned.

"Having a good time down there?" Gus said above me.

"Get down here and watch a movie with me."

"I figured you'd be hungry."

"Get your ass in this bed. It's a nonnegotiable." I rolled onto my back and added, "Pizza with extra sausage, tomatoes, and green peppers is also a nonnegotiable."

Gus lay down and rested his head on my chest. I put my arm around him like he did for me the other times we'd cuddled. It was the position in bed I was used to, and it felt really nice to hold him. He was kinda heavy in a way I wasn't used to, but I didn't mind getting used to it.

"Pizza can be arranged. Movies are a bit limited. I don't have Wi-Fi, so we're stuck with what's on my PlayStation hard drive."

I poked my head up and looked at the stand I saw earlier. Yep. There was a PS3 on it—and a case for NBA 2K18 next to it. So my man liked basketball. Noted. Oh, how I couldn't wait to fuck him up in literally any game. I cracked an evil grin, but quickly schooled my expression before Gus saw. "I'm not picky with movies. Anyway, I'm more excited about getting to spend the afternoon in bed with you than I am about watching any movie."

Gus hummed against my chest and wrapped an arm around my waist. I couldn't see his face, but if he was a fraction as happy as I was in that moment, I knew he'd be smiling.

TEN

MARCH

T HE NEXT FEW WEEKS WERE fan-fucking-tastic. Like, everything was perfect. Gus texted me right after he got his phone set up like he promised, and we texted and talked on the phone every day. We were both pretty busy during working hours, but mornings and evenings were fair game. Being able to reach him whenever I wanted was a luxury I was not going to squander. So, yeah, I spammed the shit out of him every chance I could get. I made Gus download Snapchat with the promise that he'd be added to my dick pic recipient list. He tried to act disinterested, but I knew he was full of shit. I sent him the first Snap while we were eating dinner at my kitchen island, and he dropped his fork in surprise. He was pretty sold on using it after that. I haven't been able to get him to send me nudes yet, but I got to have the real thing, so was there really a loser in that situation? I'd think not.

Having a way to contact Gus also meant we ended up seeing each other more. We spent a couple of nights during the week staying over at each other's places. What I'd learned was that our dates hadn't been a fluke and we genuinely got along and had fun doing anything. Whether it was video games, sitting and listening to music—and making out, because I'm not a priest—or cooking, everything was fun. Cooking was the biggest shock for me. I warned Gus that I was culinarily challenged, but he was dead set on teaching me. He said I wasted too much money on eating out, which was probably right. He was impressed with the few things Theo showed me how to make, but he said I could do better. It turned out he was a fucking wizard in the kitchen. Who knew? Unfortunately, his skills didn't transfer to me through dick-to-mouth osmosis. I ruined enough pots and pans that I needed to buy a new set a week ago. Whoopsie.

Another thing I learned was that I was pretty insatiable. I always liked sex and had plenty of it, but things were different with Gus. Then again, everything was. I wanted Gus at all times, whether I was dead from a long day at the hospital, had just been worked to the bone at the gym, or if he'd made me come moments before. I couldn't get enough of him, but I was sure enjoying trying to get my fill. If Gus's actions were anything to go by, he shared my problem—if you could even call it a problem.

My dick-sucking skills had come a long way, but I was still not even close to the wonders Gus could do with his tongue and throat. I was determined to get there, though. Rey men were a stubborn lot, and I was no exception there. As much fun as we were having with sex, I was equally happy and confused about why Gus hadn't been pushing to fuck me. It was something I'd been thinking about more and wanting to try, and I was glad Gus wasn't pressuring me for it, but I was also left wondering why it seemed like he just didn't want to. Yeah, I knew that I was a brat about it, trying to have my cake and eat it too. Or cock in this case. Gus not giving me any signs that he wanted more—outside of when he'd joke—made me too nervous to ask for it, and I hated that about myself. As chill and comfortable as I felt around him, I was hung up on that one damn thing, and it boiled down to fear. I was afraid to put myself out there and have him turn me down. It was irrational to think that way since Gus had never told me no, but I couldn't help it.

After a usually long morning at work, I'd decided that I'd push for sex soon, perhaps after Match Day, which happened to fall on the last day of my stint at Northwestern. I only had the rest of the week left, and then I was home free. It was only Monday, but it was a big day. In about an hour I'd log in to R3 and find out if I matched or not. I wouldn't find out where until Friday. But I wasn't stressed about it.

I grabbed my phone from my locker and saw a missed call from D, along with several texts, texts from friends, junk emails, and a text from my bro. I checked Theo's message first since he never texted me out of sheer boredom. It was a simple enough request, asking me to call him when I could. I tapped his name then the call button.

"Theo Rey speaking."

"Really? I don't even get a 'hi'?"

I heard him sigh. That guy worked too damn hard. "Sorry, Jay. I didn't check the display before answering. It's been a hell of a morning."

"I feel ya, bro. I just got out of a surgery that went way longer than anticipated. You should see the sutures I did, though; my deep-dermals were a thing a beauty."

"That sounds interesting at least. I'm glad to hear you're doing well." Theo sounded lighter now.

"Thanks, bro. What've you been up to this morning? Dad being a dick again?"

"That, and I'm prepping reports for a big potential client I'm meeting within a couple of weeks. The meeting was supposed to be in a month, but they asked to bump it up, and I wasn't in a position to say no."

"I have no doubts that you'll pull it together and wow them. You and me, we're fuckin' rockstars."

Theo barked out a laugh. "You might be. I'm tired."

"Whatever, dude. Anyway, what did you need me for?"

"Think you can make it for dinner tonight?" Theo asked. Gus was coming over later, and I reeeeaaaaally didn't want to bail on him. I guess I took too long to answer because Theo added, "Masa is making *tourtiere*."

"Fuuuuck me. Yes. I'll be there." I knew he was hiding something, but I couldn't say no to fresh French Canadian meat pie. Ever. "Now I'm hungry. You going out for lunch today?"

"No, I'm pretty busy. I'll probably have something al desko."

"Um, that's a little racist."

"What are you—no, never mind. Feel free to bring Gus with you if he's free. We'd love to meet him," Theo said, trying, and failing, to sound casual.

"I'll see what he's up to."

"Perfect. I need to get back to work, Jay. Come by around eight, okay?"

"See ya then." I disconnected the call after Theo said his goodbye then thumbed out a text to Gus with the invite. I tossed my phone back in the locker, then headed upstairs to the staff room to scoff down the pork loin tortellini Gus made last night. The guy was basically a five-star chef, gahbless.

I didn't mind that I'd have to wait until the end of the shift for his reply. I already knew he was going to decline politely. Shortly after we became official boyfriends—that term in relation to me still makes me want to break out into dance—I was having one of my excited rants and mentioned wanting him to meet my brother and Masa and all my friends, and I think I spooked him.

Gus ended up sitting me down and saying that he thought we should wait longer before he met my family and friends. He'd said it would be a good idea to wait until I was sure about everything since all this shit was hella new to me. That sounded valid at the time, but the more I'd thought about it, the more I leaned toward Gus being the one who needed the time to be sure about what we were doing. I hadn't broached the subject of his exes since our second date, but I'd bet my left nut that he was still pretty messed up over it, which I understood. I'd probably be wary about guys who weren't certain about what they wanted. I still had a lot to figure out and adjust to, though I never questioned how much I liked Gus. It was just everything else that I was still figuring out. I hoped Gus knew that and that I was able to convey it nonverbally; through snuggles and sex. Okay, I could probably do better and use my damn words like a real adult. And I would. Soon.

I knocked on Theo's door around quarter after eight. Alone, like I knew I would be. Gus answered my text earlier saying he didn't think it was time to meet my brother yet, and I wasn't surprised. It was the answer I was expecting to hear, so I wasn't overly disappointed. Mildly disappointed? Fuck yes, but nothing some tasty food couldn't fix.

With the promise of sexual favors, I convinced Gus to come over after work. He'd showed up just after six, and I made good on my promise of sexual favors as soon as the door closed behind him. He kindly returned the service and made a compelling argument for me to skip dinner. Oh, so compelling. But my bro wanted to see me, and I'd never bail on him. I made Gus promise me he'd stay over so we could have more fun when I got home, and he agreed without a fuss.

The door opened while I was standing there, grinning

like an idiot at the very fresh memory of Gus on his knees. Me on my knees. Uuf, be still, my dick. Luckily, it was Masa who answered, his long hair messily tied back, leaving his hazel eyes unobscured. He looked his stylishly casual self in a loose crew neck black sweater and charcoal drop-crotch pants. He was barefoot too and, damn, did he always have sexy feet? He probably did. And I shouldn't have been looking.

"Hey, congrats, man," he said as he pulled me into a full hug, which I returned. Because fuck that half-hug bro shit. "Just a heads-up, I didn't know what he was planning, I swear."

I released him and eyed him curiously. "Whaddya mean?"

"Is he finally here?" a familiar feminine voice called out. Shit. Masa smiled at me apologetically then walked back into the modern kitchen and—I shit you not—pretended to busy himself by fussing with *everything* in sight. I'd seen Masa cook enough to know he wasn't one to meander and fumble around a kitchen, so it was clear he was trying not to engage in whatever Theo and Dani had planned in the living room. Theo's condo was a lot smaller than my loft, so I could clearly hear when Dani and Theo ceased their whispered conversation about how they'd talk to me. I sighed and made my way inside after toeing out of my sneakers.

Theo was sitting on the end of the dark grey couch closest to the kitchen, which wasn't unusual. He liked to be close to Masa and I'm sure he'd have been sitting on one of the stools up at the bar or on the counter had they not had company. Similar to how I pestered Gus when he was cooking, I supposed. Okay, maybe less annoying than me.

Unlike Theo, Dani was pacing in front of the sliding glass balcony doors. She stopped when she saw me and pointed at me with her index and middle fingers. "You're late. And where is Gus?"

I quickly looked to Theo for an explanation, but the bastard wouldn't make eye contact with me. Oh, I would remember this. I turned my attention back to Dani and tried for casual, despite how anxious I suddenly felt. "Sorry, D. I got tied up." Not exactly. But my hands *were* held behind my back at one point. "And Gus couldn't make it tonight. He had—"

"Bullshit," Dani snapped.

"Goddammit! It's not fair that you're a human lie detector machine," I whined.

She shrugged then closed the distance between us and pulled me over to the couch. Theo got up and posted up next to Dani while she urged me to sit. There wasn't any point in being difficult, so I sat and looked up at them, feeling like a kid about to get tag-teamed by Mom and Dad over how much they disapproved of my boyfriend. Bring it.

"We're not here to grill you, Jay," Theo said, sounding more than a little guilty.

"We just want to know what the hell is going on with Gus. Why hasn't he been around?"

"Is there even *tourtiere*? Or have I been ultimately deceived?" I asked.

Theo sighed sympathetically and Dani side-eyed him. "I wouldn't lie about that," he said.

Satisfied with that, I cracked my neck and decided to answer candidly. "Gus and I have talked about him meeting you guys, but he doesn't think it's time yet. He said he wants me to be sure it's—that we're—what I truly want before family and friends get dragged into it."

"Are you unsure about him? Has he hurt you?" Theo asked with clear worry in his voice.

Before I could reassure him that wasn't the case, Masa

spoke up from the kitchen. "*Nounours*, Jamie is fine. I don't think that's what the issue is here. Relax and let him finish." Theo exhaled and visibly relaxed at Masa's words.

"Yo, Masa's right; I'm fine. Gus has been anything but rough with me. Well, except—"

"Jamie," Theo and Dani said in creepy unison.

"Right, sorry. Focus. Look, I think he's just scared I'm going to turn around and change my mind about liking dick. He's had some past experiences with douchey guys who broke his heart. He's just being cautious. Once I convince him I'm not like that, I'm sure he'd be happy to meet you guys. He's barely even talked about his family, but that's just how he is. He kinda reminds me of you, Theo. Very much the strong, silent type who takes on the weight of the world, and has a heart of gold." Dani crossed her arms and huffed. Theo furrowed his brow and looked down.

Masa came around the bar and wrapped an arm around Theo's lower back. He leaned in close and whispered something in his ear before kissing his temple. "Food's ready, guys."

"Peeerfect, I'm fucking starved." I turned my attention to Dani. "D, wanna skip the arm and go right for my lap?" Theo and Masa only had the one couch, which was a pretty tight fit with three dudes on it. There were two stools at the bar, but that was work.

Dani shook her head as Theo sat down next to me and Masa went back to the kitchen. "No, I'm not staying. Andrew is expecting me for dinner tonight."

"Does he know why you're late?" I asked. She nodded. She was very honest with him about the nature of our relationship. It was too late for us to change, and neither of us wanted to. Dani liked to fuss over me, and I liked that she did. "Dammit. Indy will never like me if he thinks I'm monopolizing all your time and attention."

"He likes you just fine now," Dani replied.

"He'd like you more if you stopped calling him Indy," Theo added.

I shook my head vehemently. "Absolutely not."

Dani rolled her eyes and uncrossed her arms. She stroked her fingers through my hair then sighed. "If Gus really is like Theo, you have to be persistent."

"Yeah, don't take no for an answer. Force him to listen to you," Masa added.

I looked at my brother, and he just shrugged and nodded. "I can sometimes. Like when he's pissed me off. I'll talk to him about it again after Match. Shit, speaking of, congrats, D."

"Thanks, you too. It's a bigger relief than I was expecting. I do have to go, though. Call me tomorrow, *fratellino*." Dani turned to Theo and nodded. "Next time, T." Dani hugged Masa goodbye on her way out then the place fell into dead silence. I wasn't awko-taco or anything. Absolutely not.

Theo and I both turned our heads at the sound of dishes clattering. "*Crisse!* Sorry!" Masa called out. After seeing that all was okay, I returned my attention to the wall in front of me, next to the dark TV. From the corner of my eye I could see Theo still looking in my direction.

"I'm sorry we surprised you like that."

"It's really okay. You did it because you care and keeping Gus more or less a secret isn't like me. I get why you guys are worried. Also, this plan has D written all over it, so you don't have to apologize for that." I scooted closer to Theo and rested my head on his arm. "I'm glad you guys care so much about me."

"I love you more than anything in the world, Jay." Theo peered over my shoulder then back at me. "Just don't tell Masa."

"Too late; I heard, and I wouldn't want it otherwise,"

Masa said as he walked over balancing three plates of that which I loved. I made grabby hands for my plate as soon as he was close enough for me to. Masa giggled and stepped so I could take a plate. "Is beer okay?" Masa asked as he set the other two plates on the table in front of the couch. "Or do we want wine?"

"Beer, please," I replied around my first bite of the savory deliciousness in my lap. Masa disappeared for a hot minute and reappeared with three open bottles of Budweiser. "Still rocking the Bud? Get with the craft beer scene, dude," I teased.

Masa set the bottles on the table and retied his hair, catching the stray pieces that slipped free. "Hey, I'm a simple guy. All that fancy beer is good, but so is Bud." He leaned down and kissed Theo chastely before taking a seat.

"Jesus, you guys are forever going to be couples goals for me."

A faint flush colored Theo's cheeks as he cleared his throat and tried his best to hide behind his beer bottle. Masa waggled his brows and smirked. "I'm not worried about you, Jamie. You'll make someone really happy if they let you."

I smiled in return and sincerely hoped Masa was right. Mainly, I hoped that someone would be Gus. He was the kind of trouble I wanted.

I got home a little later than I'd anticipated, but I wasn't expecting to walk into the place completely dark. I flicked on a light in the entryway and breathed a sigh of relief when I saw Gus's work boots and shoes. I called out for him while I tossed my keys and jacket onto the island, and made my way into my room when I heard him answer.

The bedroom was dark when I entered, and I tripped on a pile of what were likely my damn clothes. Gus's snickering came from behind me, and I reflexively turned around to face the origin of the sound. "Where are you?"

"Sit down on the bed and turn on the lamp." Okaaaay. I did as instructed, squinting while my eyes adjusted to the light, then saw Gus leaning against the doorframe dressed in the black lounge pants I let him borrow, a loose white tank— with a dangerously deep neckline, heeeeeello hairy chest— and the red snapback he wore on Halloween. He looked fucking hot.

"I thought you'd gone to bed without me. Why are you slinking around in the dark?"

"I have a surprise for you," Gus said as he pushed off the door and walked toward me. No, he fucking stalked. He eyed me like I was his prey, making me squirm under his gaze. "I wanted to congratulate you for matching, but I couldn't decide what to get for you." Gus stopped in front of me and ran his hands up the tops of my thighs, making me gulp like a goddamn cartoon character. He leaned down and whispered in my ear, making my skin break out in goose bumps. "What I came up with is something I hope is another first for you." Gus pushed off my thighs and pulled his phone out of his pocket. He must have already been connected to the Bluetooth speakers in the room because music started playing just before he tossed the phone on the far side of the bed. Not just any music, no. He put on some sexy-ass fucking music. The opening notes of Massive Attack's "Angel" filled the room while Gus just smirked down at me. "Keep your hands on the bed, do you understand?"

"Yes," I ground out. I wasn't sure what was happening, but I knew that I liked it. Bossy Gus was damn sexy.

A slow, dirty smile pulled at the corners of Gus's lush lips, and he started to move to the pulsing beat. His hips swayed fluidly while his hands began an exploration of his body that made me feel breathless. The shadows playing across his skin were alluring, creating beautiful patterns in the dips of his muscles, placing emphasis on Gus's masculine form. The more he moved, the more I wanted to reach out and touch him. The urge was almost overwhelming, so I white-knuckled the duvet beneath me to occupy my hands.

He gave me teasing glimpses of his abs at work by occasionally lifting the hem of his shirt, then pulling it back down. His wolf tattoo stared back at me when he lifted his shirt, somehow making the whole experience hotter. As the song picked up, Gus slowly pulled his shirt off, over his hat, and tossed it at me. I let it hit me in the face, and groaned as the smell of him filled my nostrils. The familiarity of Gus's scent made me warm all over, and my already semi-hard cock became fully erect—painfully so in my jeans. I took one more whiff of Gus's shirt before draping it over my shoulder and reaching for the button on my jeans.

"Nah uh," Gus said almost musically. "No touching yourself either." He rubbed his hands over the expanse of his bare chest, teasing his brown nipples to tight nubs that I wanted to taste. I whimpered and gripped the sides of my thighs while I watched Gus move. I tried to ignore my aching cock, but it was increasingly difficult the more Gus danced and enticed me. He maintained eye contact with me as he tossed his hat behind me then gave me the filthiest "come-fuck-me" eyes I'd ever seen. And, fuck me, I wanted to. I wanted to throw him down on the bed and make him scream my name. I wanted to make him feel so good that he forgot who he was. I wanted to draw out every last bit of pleasure he had and greedily mine for more. I wanted to see him wrecked and debauched. I wanted—no, needed—those things at that moment.

I sucked in a sharp breath when Gus inched the waist of his pants down his rolling hips. He glided closer to me and took hold of my hands while I watched on in a lust-filled daze. Gus led my hands over his skin with a grin on his face. I tried to move of my own accord, but he set the pace and guided where I could and couldn't touch. I stopped trying to take control and let him lead me, and was rewarded when he stepped closer and pushed my hands down the back of his pants.

My fingers passed the band of his underwear—then there was *nothing*. Fuuuck. I bit my bottom lip and squeezed the globes of Gus's firm, round ass. He moaned in response, deep and low, then pushed free of my reach. I was about to beg when he turned around and hooked his thumbs into the waistline of the pants, dragging them down over that gorgeous ass. My breath caught when I saw the red jock strap he wore, and I nearly died when he spun around and climbed into my lap. Holyfuckingshit.

I fought hard not to hyperventilate and jizz in my fucking pants as Gus straddled me. He raised himself, grinding against my stomach and chest. He rubbed my face against his chest, and into his intoxicating scent. Wrapping his arms around my neck, he licked and nipped my jaw, leading back to my ear.

"Undo your pants," he rasped in my ear. I did just that and shimmied out of them, kicking the pant legs off. Gus rubbed his hands through my hair, squeezing and tugging to draw my head back so he could kiss my neck. I lost my motherfucking mind when he sank into my lap and ground against my cock. I still had my trunks on, but the sensation was overwhelming after being deprived of relief. Gus was sure making up for having me wait, though. He held my neck with his fingers laced at my nape and stared longingly into my eyes while he continued the slow, tortuous rotation of his hips.

My resolve broke, and I grabbed Gus's hip and leg, running my hands over his ass and the back of his thigh. I held him tight as he tore me apart. I tried to hold it back, but the look in Gus's eyes did me in. I dug my blunt nails into his leg and back and shuddered through my orgasm, gasping as Gus leaned down and claimed my mouth in a slow, deep kiss. I moaned into his mouth and desperately clung to his body as I rode out the aftershocks.

"You okay, *caro*?" Gus asked as he brushed the hair back from my face.

I eased my tight grip and skimmed my hands over the areas I scratched, hopefully soothing any pain. "I'm better than okay. Are you? I didn't mean to go all feral cat on you."

Gus smiled warmly at me while continuing to play with my hair. "I'm fine. I'm just glad you liked it."

"I creamed my fucking drawers; I think saying I enjoyed it is putting things mildly." I moved my hands to Gus's front, gliding over his thighs and resting on his hips. "A jock strap, huh? Last time I wore one, I don't recall it being quite this hot." I pulled at the elastic with one finger and let it snap back with a loud slap. Gus growled at me and narrowed his eyes, but I felt his cock twitch against my stomach, so I ventured a guess and said he liked it. "*Please* tell me you have more of these?"

Gus shrugged with a look on his face that said pure amusement. "Maybe I do. What are you going to do to earn the privilege of seeing them?"

Oh, he wanted to be sassy. I leaned back, pulling Gus down with me, then flipped up over so I ended up on top. I slid back, off the bed and pulled Gus's jock strap down past his knees and left it hanging on one foot. He propped himself up on his elbows and watched as I licked him from root to tip then took him to the back of my throat in one practiced motion, relaxing my throat and resisting the urge to choke. His eyes rolled back, and he groaned in pleasure, spurring me on as I felt tears stinging my eyes. I hadn't decided if this was going to be a punishment or a thank-you. Maybe I'd figure it out after making Gus come a few times. Maybe I wouldn't—there were no losers in this game.

MATCH DAY WAS a huge motherfucking success. I logged in to R3 and was stoked to see I would be doing my general medicine residency at Northwestern. I called Dani and the others to get their results and was relieved to hear that everyone got accepted into their top two picks. Scotty would be going to Mercy, Roz and Pat to different states, and Dani would be going to Northwestern with me. Sitting in the lounge after the calls was very bittersweet. I was elated for Roz and Pat, yet the selfish bastard in me didn't want to see them go. But that was all part of growing up, wasn't it? School and my family's wealth had more or less kept me shielded from the hardships of adulthood. Or maybe stunted was a more appropriate term. I hadn't lost anyone in my life I cared about since my brother's best friend died two years ago. And that was the *only* time something terrible like that happened. Roz and Pat leaving would probably depress the hell out of me, but at the core, I was happy for them and extremely proud.

Feeling like a fucking sap, I opened up our group text and proposed celebrations that night. With many adult beverages, and even more poor decisions. Everyone replied in agreement, with Roz even inquiring about Gus and if he'd be coming too. I replied that I'd try my best to entice him into coming, then switched over to my chat with Gus. I was set to go over to his place after work, and probably should have talked to him before making plans. Goddammit, I was doing this wrong. In the text, I briefly mentioned the good news and plans to get sloppy tonight. I said that I'd still come over before going out, and would come over after if he wanted me to. After that, I thumbed out quick messages to Theo, Masa, and Mom to let them know that presents were in order soon. And cake. Always cake.

I arrived at Gus's apartment building just before seven. I wasn't due out for drinks until ten, so we had plenty of time for… whatever we ended up doing. Gus didn't answer my text from earlier, so I assumed he'd still be expecting me. I didn't dwell on why he didn't answer—coulda been any number of things, and I didn't want to get all riled up about it without the facts. He buzzed me up and left the door unlocked for me, which I took as good signs.

I found him shirtless by the sink, washing a few dishes, and wearing some deliciously low-hanging sweats. Gus turned to me with a smile when I closed the door. "Hey."

I closed the distance between us and snaked my arms around his waist. "Hey, doll," I said before peppering his neck and shoulder with soft kisses. "Did you get my text earlier?"

He shut the water off, leaving several dishes in the sink, and turned to face me. "I did. I saw it on the train. Sorry I didn't reply, today was crazy."

"That's okay. Wanna talk about it?"

Gus shook his head and sighed. "It wasn't anything important, just another late shipment that needed to be dealt with before the end of the day. It came in earlier than the last time, so I was able to get done. I skipped my breaks though, and I'm famished."

"Jesus. That sounds rough. Wanna order in? My treat," I offered, hoping to take the stress of cooking out of the equation. I'd have offered to cook, but Gus probably would have laughed and cooked anyway.

"I'm fully capable of buying dinner."

"Yeah. I know you are. It was my idea, so I offered to pay. No biggie if you don't want to."

Gus sighed again and leaned his weight against my embrace. He looked so damn tired. "I'm sorry. I didn't mean to snap at you."

"It's okay, doll. Come on." I pulled him toward the bed and lay down first. I held out my arms and wrapped him up against my chest. "I'm sorry you had a bad day. I won't bug you to come out tonight if you really don't want to. I can stay in too if you want."

"No, I want you to go out and celebrate with your friends. You guys deserve it."

"Can I apologize in advance for being an annoying drunk later? Also, I give you permission to ravage me later."

Gus cocked his head back and wrinkled his brows at me. "Do you mean ravish?"

"Nah, man. You can fucking wreck me later if I'm in a handsy mood. It'll knock me right out."

"I wouldn't do that to you unless you were coherent enough to fully enjoy it. And remember it."

I hummed and traced little stars on Gus's back. I'd scratched him up pretty good the other night, but those marks were lower and I was careful to avoid them. "Kinda like I am right now?"

Gus snorted a dry laugh. "Yes, *caro*, like you are now. But this"—he held me tighter and sighed—"this is good too."

"Yes. Yes it is."

ELEVEN

A WEEK AFTER I FOUND out Gus was motherfucking Magic Mike I got a call from my mom, inviting me to dinner. I was bored as all get-out during the days and started spending more time at the gym in an attempt to combat it. Between picking up shifts at the restaurant and, you know, her actual boyfriend, Dani was pretty busy. Under different circumstances, I'd have taken a trip until graduation and got a killer tan. But my lovesick ass didn't want to go away without Gus, and he couldn't take that much time off work and afford to go.

When Mom called I was playing *Crash Bandicoot: Warped* because it's the best one, duh. It was a rare evening where I was home alone. Gus and I had been spending a lot of time together, but there were still the occasional days where I didn't see him at all. I knew that was normal, but I wanted to be around him constantly like the clingy spider monkey he claimed I was. Again, lovesick fool in the house.

I showed up for dinner the next night dressed in a light grey button-up and dark blue chinos. It went unsaid that Dad always expected a certain level of attire for family gatherings, no matter how informal or impromptu. Dad was always worried about appearances. I walked in without knocking and startled Mom in the kitchen. She never used to cook much, but she found it to be an immersive hobby in the last year. More than a few times she'd used me as a delivery boy to take Theo home-cooked meals she was proud of.

"Hey, Mom," I said with a smile.

She startled only for a moment before spinning around from the counter and wheeling over to me. "Jamie, darling." I leaned down to hug her, and she stroked the back of my hair like she always did. "How have you been, dear?"

"Really great, Mom. "I peered into the main sitting room and lowered my voice. "I have something to tell you after dinner. Something really great." She nodded and cradled my cheek in her hand like only a mother could. I asked if there was anything I could help with and was promptly shooed from the kitchen. Mom had wheeled over my toes before when I wouldn't listen, so I didn't need to be told twice.

She hadn't always been in a wheelchair. When I was twelve she was involved in a bad hit-and-run that left her paralyzed from the waist down. It had happened only a few blocks from the house in the middle of the fucking day. Since then, I made it an effort to make myself useful to her, though I never treated her any different or tiptoed around her.

Football season ended a month ago, so I wasn't surprised to find Dad on the couch watching baseball. He was wearing a suit without the jacket, probably the same one he'd worn to work that day. His wavy dark brown hair was greying at the temples, and the creases in his forehead made him look the part of the serious man that he was. He looked a lot like Theo—shockingly so. I got the wavy hair and blue eyes from him, but my rounder nose was definitely all Mom. My lack of ability to grow a full beard probably also came from her side of the family as well.

I sat down at the other end of the couch and noticed a tumbler of amber liquid on a coaster on the table. My appreciation of whiskey and scotch came from him. Usually, I'd have poured myself a drink before I sat down and silently watched the game with him, but I wasn't in the mood. Fully expecting the night to go like all the others did, I wasn't surprised when he didn't speak to me.

Twenty minutes later the three of us were seated at the table and plating up the roast Mom made. I felt my brother's absence, as much as I'm sure Mom did, as I looked across the table at the empty place setting where he'd usually sit. I wanted to scream in my father's face that I was bi, just to see if he'd have a meltdown. Only Theo was ever able to crack Dad's cool composure, though I'd sure like to fucking try. The prick didn't even seem to notice that I was shooting daggers at him throughout dinner. Mom did, of course, and tried her best to lighten my mood by congratulating me and asking me what I would do until residency. She and I had a great conversation, and she asked me to watch the house for a week while they took a trip in a few weeks. It was a business trip that Mom forced Dad to extend as a mini getaway. Throughout dinner, Dad silently ate his food then excused himself to his office without so much as an acknowledgment of me graduating from fucking medical school. I knew he didn't agree with my choice, but I'd be lying if I said that him completely ignoring the accomplishment didn't sting.

"I'm sorry about your father," Mom said quietly as she brushed my hair behind my ear.

"It's fine. He's not what I wanted to talk to you about." I looked in the direction of Dad's office and listened for any sound. I heard none. "Come on. I'll tell you about it in the sitting room." I got up and wheeled Mom to the room in question. She could handle her chair on her own, but I liked pushing it for her when I could. I also liked rolling through the house at top speed whenever I was on housesitting duty over the years. And if I could convince Gus to stay over with me? Boom.

I closed the door behind us and engaged the break on the chair. Helping Mom out of her chair had become infinitely easier for me since I started regularly working out. I could carry her now if I had to, which made me feel like a right-eous superhero. I mean, I probably wouldn't get far, but it was more than I was capable of before.

Once we were both situated on the couch, I couldn't keep it in any longer. "Mom, I have a boyfriend."

"Oh, honey, that's great. What's his name?" Mom asked excitedly.

"Gus." I paused and realized I didn't know his last name. I wasn't sure if I'd told him mine either. Whatever. "He's thirty-two and oddly adorable."

"Why is that odd?"

"Well, he's, like, really manly-hot and muscly and tall. But he's also super-cute and likes to cuddle. He comes off as a little gruff at first, then he's a big softy," I said with a smile.

"You really like him. You didn't smile like that about any of the girls you dated."

"I do. It hasn't been long, but I do. Is that weird? I don't really have anything to go off as a standard."

Mom shook her head and smiled at me reassuringly. "It's not weird if it's how you feel, honey. Has Theo met him?"

"Not yet. I'm still working on that. Hopefully, you'll both get to meet him soon." She was satisfied enough with that answer and continued asking questions about Gus and what my residency would entail. We ended up talking for over an hour—Mom talked, I gushed—before she booted me out of the house in favor of going to bed.

I wanted to see Gus, but it was a work night for him, and one of the couple nights a week we spent apart. Instead of inviting myself over, I sent him a goodnight text and ordered an Uber to take me home. Gus was coming over the next day. I could be patient until then. At least I'd hoped I could.

I WAS SO ready for Gus to arrive. I was pacing and finger drumming on crossed forearms while I burned a hole through the wall clock. It was nearly a quarter after six and Gus should have arrived at any moment. I sat down on one of the kitchen stools and tried to relax. I wanted to have sex with Gus tonight and from what I read online, being tense and nervous wasn't going to be conducive to me being able to enjoy it.

I wasn't kidding when I said I was ready. I spent nearly an hour douching and showering to make sure I was squeaky clean for Gus. Was it a bit excessive? Probably. I wasn't taking any chances. I wanted this to be as close to perfect as possible. My mind flatlined when a knock sounded at the door, and I rushed over to open it with *probably* enough force to rip a lesser door off its hinges.

Gus was fucking gorgeous in head-to-toe black. He had on a hoodie, familiar faded jeans, and Nike runners. The icing on the cake was a snapback with an embroidered black logo I didn't recognize. I couldn't pull off hats, though I loved it when Gus wore them.

"Hey, doll," I said as I pulled him over the threshold and into a hug. "How was work?"

Gus wrapped me up in his strong arms and kicked the door shut behind him. "Long and boring. But the day is looking better already." He smiled down at me and softly pressed his lips to mine in a kiss. There was no urgency in it, but me being the greedy bastard I was changed that in an instant by grabbing the back of Gus's neck and slipping my tongue past his lips. Gus pulled away first. We were both breathless.

"Jesus, that was one hell of a greeting. Miss me much?"

"More than you know. Look, Gus… I've been thinking —actually I've been racking my fucking brain. Shit, I shouldn't do this out here. Come on." I pulled Gus from the entryway and into my room, rather hastily. I had zero chill and needed to get naked before I lost my nerve. Once in my room, I sat Gus down on the bed and started undressing while he stared at me in bewilderment. "Anyway, I'm ready to… advance our relationship, if ya know what I mean," I said with heated cheeks after I tossed my shirt aside.

Gus's brow creased and his eyes narrowed. "Um, I'm not sure what you're trying to say, Jamie."

"So much for subtlety and my dignity," I groaned. "Sex, Gus. Boning, fucking, getting freaky deaky—whatever. I want to do it with you. Like, right now." I kicked out of my pants and flopped down behind Gus, propping myself up on my elbows. "I'm ready to take that monster cock; fuck me up," I said with a confidence that only slightly wavered.

Gus turned and looked at me like my head had fucking exploded. "Wait, *what*?"

Hmm. Not the reaction I was hoping for. "I'm still scared, don't get me wrong, but I don't want to wait anymore." The deepest fucking sigh I've ever heard left Gus, and I immediately sat up, confused as hell at his reaction. "Do you not wanna have sex with me? Oh God, have I horribly misjudged what's going on here?"

"Calm down, Jamie," Gus said as he grasped my hands and rubbed the undersides of my wrists with his thumbs. "You're not entirely wrong. I do want to have sex with you; I've wanted that since we met. But, Jamie… I'm not a top. I thought I'd made that pretty clear this past month, but maybe I haven't."

"Heh?" I said before I could think not to. I blankly stared at Gus while my mind went back to our previous talks about sex. All those times my dumb ass thought he was joking— the fucking lap dance. "Oh my fucking God. I'm so stupid," I said as I covered my eyes with my palms and fell onto my back.

"Are you disappointed?" Gus asked quietly.

I opened my eyes and shot back up so I could touch Gus and see him better. "Hell-to-the-motherfucking-no. Are you kidding? The only reason I waited this long was because I was deadass scared of how much bottoming for you was going to hurt." Gus huffed out a laugh that sounded more relieved than amused. "You seriously want me to fuck you?"

"Is that so surprising?"

"I guess I'd just assumed that since you're so… 'grr'"—I held up my hands and pointed the tips of my fingers like claws—"and I'm so… not, that you'd want that. I got so stuck on that, and I missed or brushed off all the signs that suggested otherwise. I'm sorry about that," I said sincerely.

Gus shrugged and bit his bottom lip. "It wouldn't be the first time someone assumed that," he replied joylessly.

"Gah, I'm sorry." I leaned my forehead against Gus's shoulder. "I'm an idiot, and I feel shitty about making assumptions, but do know that I still want you. Like, right now."

"Oh, um, today might not be so great."

I whined like a petulant child. "Why not?"

"Well, I just got off work, so I need to have a shower and all that jazz."

"All that jazz? Really?"

Gus sighed. "I need to prep myself, and all my stuff is at home."

"Oooooh," I drew out. "You mean you have to do what I did earlier. That's fine. I can wait."

"I don't have a douche here, Jamie. And I am not using yours," Gus said bluntly.

"I've got two others unopened. Try again."

Gus tapped his fingers against his thigh but maintained eye contact with me. "I feel stupid."

"Why?"

"This isn't sexy. Your first time should be perfect." Ugh. Bless his heart.

"I appreciate your concern, but I know firsthand what goes into getting ready, and I'm still game, doll. If that's all that's holding you back, I'll drag you into that bathroom and get you ready myself." Gus's breath caught, and his eyes went wide. Oh, someone liked it when I got bossy. "Go. You'll find everything you need under the sink. Don't rush." I fisted the front of Gus's sweater and pulled him into a kiss that fanned my desire. When I released him, I lay back down, only so I couldn't reach to grab him again. Gus hummed and stood up, unabashedly raking his eyes over my body while doing so. "Toss me my phone before you go, yeah?"

Gus flicked his gaze toward the nightstand then at me. "Sure. Where is it?" I pointed to the floor, presumably where my pants were, and he got the hint. I connected to the wireless speakers and put on some blackbear as Gus left the room.

Once I heard the bathroom door click, I released a breath I hadn't realized I'd been holding. Holyfuckingshit! It was going to happen; Gus and I were going to have sex finally. And *I* was going to top? Halle-fucking-lujah. I was beyond tickled. It felt like an electric current was running through my body, setting every cell ablaze. All of the uneasiness I'd been experiencing melted away and I felt beyond ready for what was about to happen. I closed my eyes and tried to calm down and be patient, but patience was never my lady. Even so, I got under my duvet, took my trunks off, and lay there pretending to be a version of myself who had some fucking chill.

An indeterminate amount of time passed—it could have been ten seconds or ten hours for all I knew—before I heard Gus clear his throat over the music. I shot up and scrambled for the volume buttons on my phone then took in the feast before me: Gus standing at the foot of the bed with a towel loosely wrapped low around his hips. His chest still had some water droplets glistening on it, and I longed to lap them up. Every inch of him.

"Please just excuse me while I burst into flames."

Gus cocked an eyebrow and smirked. "Is that supposed to be some kind of euphemism for how much gayer you're about to get?"

I barked out a laugh and motioned to Gus with one finger in a "come hither" fashion. "Nah, I'm not worried about that; hit me with that gay shit." Gus knelt on the foot of the bed and crawled up to me. He stopped at my feet and pulled the duvet down until I was fully exposed. I was rock hard, but it was definitely all Gus and not one of my signature anxiety boners.

Instead of advancing, Gus planted a light kiss on the inside of my ankle and continued doing so, all the way up to my knee. He looked up into my eyes and grinned. "What do you want?"

"Shouldn't I be asking you?"

Gus kissed the inside of my other knee then sat up and rubbed my legs from knee to mid-thigh. "Says who? There's no universal sex playbook, *caro*. I just want you to feel good," Gus wrapped a hand around the base of my cock, while he continued massaging my leg with the other. He didn't stroke me, but the pressure from his grip felt damn good.

"I want you on your back," I said with certainty. "Ah, but

I wouldn't object to your magic hands for a bit first." Gus waggled his brows and leaned down, straightening out his legs behind him, then swirled his tongue around my cockhead. My mouth fell slack, and my eyes fluttered at the sudden sensation. The heat of Gus's skillful tongue over my most sensitive skin was altogether too much and simultaneously not enough. He kept up the slow, torturous pace until I was a whimpering wreck before he took pity on me and stretched his lips around my cock.

A slow moan fell from my lips as the heat from Gus's mouth descended upon me, not stopping when my cock hit the back of his throat. I wanted to thrust into that heat more than anything after all that teasing. I couldn't stop myself from flexing my hips up into Gus's mouth, but I needed more.

"Can I fuck your mouth?" I ground out. Gus's reply came as a hum and a squeeze to my hip. My fingers slid through his thick hair until I had a comfortable hold, then I snapped my hips upward, hard and fast. I did it again and again, chasing my own pleasure, and grateful that Gus let me. Tears pooled in Gus's eyes. I tried to stop, but he hummed around me again and gave me a look that told me he was enjoying it just as much as I was.

I threw my head back against the pillow and doubled my efforts. Gus kept his throat relaxed for me and breathed harshly through his nose when he could. My movements lost rhythm as the desperate need to come burned through me. My thrusts became faster and shallower, no longer reaching Gus's throat. Gus hardened his tongue to a point and massaged the underside of my cock on each drive causing my body to shake as I fell apart.

I cried out through clenched teeth and fisted my hands in Gus's hair while I arched my back off the bed. Gus sucked on my tip through my orgasm, not letting a single drop of cum go to waste. He kept up the assault even after I tried to wriggle away from being too sensitive. Gus held my hips still and lavished my spent cock in kisses and licks until I was nearly screaming. He released me with one last swipe around my cockhead and the smuggest grin I've seen on someone other than myself.

"You're all kinds of evil, dude," I whined, out of breath.

"I'm pretty sure you liked it; you've still got a semi."

I held up my head and peered down the length of my body to see that, yeah, I was still half hard. "Traitorous dick is traitorous, and therefore not to be trusted."

"That's a pretty circular explanation, *cretino*," Gus said cheekily.

"You know what? I know what that means, *faccia di culo*."

Gus barked out a laugh and rested his head against my thigh before looking up at me with a smile. "Okay, okay, I'm sorry. You're not a dummy. You didn't tell me you spoke Italian."

"Nah, I don't. I just know the insults. I've had D hurl them all at me on several occasions over the years. But I don't wanna talk about that. I believe I told you I wanted you on your back. Get your ass up here," I said as I patted the bed next to me.

Gus slowly crawled up over me, leaving kisses on my body in his wake. Watching his shoulder blades shift beneath his defined back reminded me of a jungle cat about to pounce. I'd felt like Gus's prey before, but I was gonna change that. I wanted Gus to know that he was *mine* and that I had no qualms in staking my claim. I may have been a little off-balance and reserved in my actions before, but that was about to change. Gus was going to see the confident version of me that I knew so well, and I couldn't wait to please him.

Gus connected his lips to mine in a short kiss before he rolled onto his back next to me. I pinched his nipple then scooted to the edge of the bed, opened the top drawer of the dresser, and fished out two condoms and a small bottle of lube. I kept the big-ass tub under the bathroom sink in favor of refilling smaller pump-action bottles for ease. I tossed the supplies next to Gus then jumped on top of him, knocking the air out of us both.

"Easy there, *coniglietto*."

"That better be something nice," I warned. Gus's reply came in the form of an eyebrow tick. I nodded and made a mental note of how I'd punish Gus accordingly then smoothed my hands over his chest and shoulders, admiring his musculature. He was both firm and soft beneath my hands, a contrast that really seemed to work for me. I leaned down and nipped Gus's bottom lip while I teased his sensitive nipples with my thumbs. A deep moan rumbled in Gus's throat, which was all the encouragement I needed to crank up my seduction game.

I savored Gus's mouth one more time before I inched down his body, tracing a line with my tongue until I reached the towel around his hips. Sinking my teeth into the plush material, I pulled until it came loose, and dropped it aside. Gus was hard and already had some pre-cum glistening at his tip. I hadn't intended to touch his cock yet, but the sight of him leaking was too hot to resist.

With an open grip, I pulled Gus's foreskin back and dragged my tongue flat against his dick from base to tip, making sure to catch the pre-cum. I kissed his glans then pulled back and slid my hands down Gus's thighs. Gus groaned at the loss of contact, but I'd make it up to him.

"Toss me some pillows, doll. I want this ass propped up." Gus obeyed and lifted his hips so I could slide the pillows under him, putting his glorious ass at the perfect height to line up with my cock—and providing my tongue easier access to his hole.

I settled on my front between Gus's knees and pushed them even further apart until he was spread wide before me. His hole puckered as he sucked in a breath and I beamed at the idea that maybe he was just as nervous as I was when he did that for me. I smiled to myself then wrapped my arms under Gus's thighs and gave his hole a tentative sweep with my tongue. It puckered again, and I went in for it. With Gus's balls resting on my nose, I lapped at his hole like a dying man in an oasis, eliciting salacious, low moans from him. Once he was softened up a bit, I slipped my tongue past the tight ring of muscle and probed the sensitive area just beyond it. Gus writhed and got louder than I'd ever heard him, so I pushed deeper.

I'd read up on the prostate—outside of what I knew about it from a medical standpoint—and really wanted to try stimulating it for Gus. I withdrew my tongue and gave his hole a few more passes before I reached for the lube and pumped the bottle twice. I made sure my index finger was sufficiently slicked and rubbed the excess along Gus's perineum and opening.

"You like my tongue, yeah? Let's see if my fingers can do better." Gus growled and smirked while I continued to circle his hole. His smile turned into slack parted lips when I worked the tip of my finger inside him, up to the first joint. There was a lot of resistance—more than I was used to and remembered from the last time I fingered a girl's ass—so I went slow, pushing in until my finger was buried to the knuckle. I nearly blew my load at the thought of how good that pressure would feel around my dick. I gave my balls a firm squeeze to stave off the urge while I slid my finger in and out of Gus's tight heat.

"I've done some research, but you're gonna need to help

me out here and let me know when I find your prostate," I said as I curved my finger upward and felt for that small patch of nerves that would drive Gus crazy, or so I read. I tried different angles and depths until I felt something different. Before I could ask Gus if that was it, he'd clenched down on my finger and gasped.

"Oh, fuck, that's it."

"Nailed it," I said smugly. "Can you take more?" Gus nodded, and I pumped out more lube before slipping a second finger inside him. I alternated between light brushes and firm strokes to his prostate and occasionally spread my fingers to make sure he was getting stretched enough. I didn't have the porn-star dick Gus had, but I still worried about hurting him. Sex wasn't fun if my partner wasn't getting off too, and that was especially true for Gus. I wanted to make him fucking soar. Judging from the pre-cum that oozed from his cock, I was well on my way to achieving my goal.

With more lube, I worked a third finger in. I'd thought Gus was tight before, but he was a vise now. If not for him being boner-inducing levels of vocal, I'd be certain I was hurting him. Wanting to taste him again, I shimmied up between Gus's legs until I was able to claim his mouth. My fingers kept up stroking and stretching while my tongue danced against Gus's in slow, rhythmic movements. Gus threw his head back and cried out when I pressed that little bundle of wonder a bit harder.

"Fuck, you look so gorgeous right now. You ready to take this dick?"

Gus tilted his head forward and dragged his teeth over his delectable bottom lip. "Fuck me, Jamie," he ground out.

It was really happening. Gus and I were about to have sex. Like, *sex* sex. I slowly withdrew my fingers from Gus's heat and noticed my hands were trembling. I clenched my fists for a few seconds, and when I opened them, they were steady. I hadn't gotten pre-sex jitters in nearly a decade. I looked down and saw that I was still hard and raring to go, so that was a blessing.

"Jamie," Gus pleaded, interrupting my thoughts.

"Ah, sorry. I was miles away for a sec. Just a little nervous," I admitted.

"We don't have to do this if you don't want to."

"Nah-uh. I'm good-nervous—excited-nervous," I said as I reached for one of the condoms. I tore it open with my teeth and sheathed up with practiced ease. Unsure of how much more lube to use, I opted for a few more pumps and slicked up my cock then rubbed the excess against Gus. On my knees, I held the base of my cock and pressed the head against Gus's hole. I looked up and my eyes locked with Gus's as just the tip penetrated him. He inhaled sharply then took very deliberate breaths as I pushed harder and sank all the way inside.

I couldn't move right away. Gus was so hot and tight inside; it was like he was massaging my cock, and it felt too fucking good not to relish in it for a hot minute. "Oh, shit. That feels so fucking good. Can I move?" Gus nodded and let his head fall back when I grabbed the backs of his thighs and rolled my hips into him. I kept the pace slow while Gus adjusted to my cock, and even those slow, deep thrusts had me spinning. But the best part was the moans Gus was making. He was so sexy, spread out beneath me, taking my cock with pure lust and enjoyment scrawled across his face.

Once Gus seemed to be able to take me easier, I leaned down over him, buried my hands in his hair, and kissed him as I snapped my hips against his ass. Gus bit my lip and grunted, but didn't tell me to stop, so I did it again and again —faster and harder each time until the sound of our bodies coming together drowned out everything else.

I knew I was being greedy, but I needed it. At that

moment I craved everything he could give me and more. I thrust deep into Gus, wishing I could crawl inside him and take root. Wishing I could always be a vital part of him, something as crucial as his lungs or his heart. He was everything I'd always wanted and everything I didn't know I needed.

"Gus," I panted. I didn't know what I wanted to say, so I just repeated his name until I felt his warm, rough hands on my face. He pulled me into a bruising kiss, and I felt that familiar spark start to burn within, signaling that I was going to come soon. I leaned up, propping myself on one outstretched arm while I took Gus's hard cock in my other hand and jerked him in time with my thrusts.

"Faster, Jamie. I'm close," Gus panted as he pinched his nipple and held my wrist with his other arm.

I dug deep for my self-control and snapped my hips faster, matching the pace with my hand. After a few more seconds of the relentless assault, Gus succumbed to the pleasure and moaned as he shot his load all over his chest and abs. His cock twitched in my hand in time with the pulsations milking my cock. The added sensation was too fucking much. My orgasm hit me like a rogue wave and swept me away. I didn't know if I screamed or if I legit died. I was ephemerally weightless and free.

When I opened my eyes the first thing I saw was Gus's satisfied smile and kind eyes. "You okay in there?"

"Fuck, dude. I don't know where I just went, but it was fucking bliss." Gus laughed, and I sank down on top of him. Well, it was more like a collapse from utter exhaustion, but who was keeping score? I stroked my thumb over Gus's eyebrow scar and smiled back at him. "Can we tape that next time? I need to see you that wrecked every damn day."

"Why tape it when you can have the real thing? If you

rail me like that, I'll let you do it as often as you want," Gus replied with a smile.

I immediately perked up at his praise. "You really liked it? You're not just saying that, are you?"

Gus chuckled to himself and shook his head. "I wouldn't lie to you. When you changed positions on me, you were nailing my prostate. I thought I was going to come hands-free."

"Hands-free, you say. I'll have to try to make that happen next time." I begrudgingly leaned up, slowly pulled out of Gus with a grunt from us both, and tied up the condom. Motherfucker landed right in the trash bin after I tossed it over the side of the bed. *Swish.* I fell back against Gus with a graceless thud, though neither of us seemed to mind. I was playing with his chest hair when something occurred to me. "So, that magic butt-button is really something, huh?"

"What the fuck did you just say?" Gus asked, his voice raising an octave or two.

"The prostate," I clarified.

"Yeah, I know what you meant, but what the hell? Magic butt-button?" His shoulders shook with laughter.

"How else would you describe it? Seems pretty magical to me. Anyway, I want to try that sometime. Maybe you could finger me or something."

"Yeah, I can do that. Just let me know when you want to try it," Gus said as he rubbed my back.

I thought about it for half a second before I said, "How about now?"

"Like, right this second?"

"Fuck yeah. I'm good to go again if you are."

Gus laughed again and kissed my nose. "Give me twenty minutes."

TWELVE

G US AND I ENDED UP fucking twice more before passing out, looking like we'd just played the kinkiest game of Twister ever attempted. I woke up to the sound of my cell ringing. Its location was a fucking mystery to me, but I wouldn't have moved for it even if it was within reach. I was lying practically on top of Gus, drooling all over his chest. Romantic as fuck, right? His heartbeat was strong in my ear, and his skin was hot against mine, creating the coziest of snuggle conditions. Turned out relaxed muscles had just the right squishy-to-firm balance for my head. At least Gus's muscles did. It would have been chick-flick perfect if not for the crusty-ass dried cum *everywhere*—on the sheets, on the blanket, on us—but it wasn't enough to take away from how much I was enjoying being so close to Gus; not even a little. To me, it was perfect, and anyone else's standards could get fucked.

Last night was all kinds of amazing in so many ways that were new to me. At the risk of sounding trite, I felt like things had changed with Gus and me. Yeah, it was sex and sex was great, yet it was more than that. I felt closer to him—

figuratively and literally—and more connected. Jesus, he was still asleep, and I already had those feelings, I could only imagine what it would be like when he was awake.

All the worry and anxiety I carried around about us was gone and in its place was ease and motherfucking serenity. The reality of just how nervous I'd been was revealed after Gus dropped the bottom-bomb on me. I instantly felt better. All of that angst, just because I had my head firmly shoved so far up my own goddamn ass that I couldn't see what Gus had been showing me. I'd gone ahead and took my preconceived opinion and sold it to myself as gospel like others have done to him. Gus seemed to have forgiven me last night, but I was still disappointed in myself. I didn't want to be like everyone else. I wanted to be special to Gus: me and me alone. Was that selfish? Maybe. Did I care? Fuck no.

My phone rang again, that time sounding like it came from under the bed. And under the bed it would stay until I was ready to get up—which wouldn't have been any time soon if I had my way. I shifted my left leg, which was between Gus's, and ended up nudging something soft. Gus grunted, his voice thick with sleep. Oh, balls.

"Sorry, doll. I'm still not used to there being so many balls on the court."

Gus yawned and groaned. "You're not allowed to make sports analogies if you didn't play any sports."

"Track is a sport," I countered.

"There are no balls in track. It's not a sport for the purpose of permitting you to make corny jokes."

I lifted my head up and rested my chin on Gus's chest. "Puh-lease. I always had two balls with me, and let me tell ya, the chafing was awful."

Laughter rumbled through Gus's chest and worked its way through mine. Gus looked at me, wrinkling his nose. "That's gross."

"Yeah, it was. It's part of why I quit. That and, you know, I was lazy."

"I don't buy that you were ever lazy, Jamie. Bored, yes. Lazy? Never," Gus said fondly, making me want to kiss him. So I did, morning breath be damned. I only meant it to be innocent and sweet, but all it really accomplished was making me aware of my morning wood brushing against Gus's leg. A wandering hand traveling down Gus's body confirmed that he was in a similar state. Rock 'n' roll.

I gave his semi-hard cock a firm squeeze and went to work on his neck, alternating between kisses and bites. Gus was super-smokin' hot, and I was a horny bastard, so of course, I wanted to smash again, but the mild throbbing in my ass reminded me that perhaps it would be best to give Gus a break. He'd only fingered me last night—and used one finger because I basically cried like a bitch and wouldn't let him use more—and I was still feeling a bit tingly. It wasn't painful, but the feeling was constant and definitely something I was aware of. I'd fucked Gus three times and assumed he might be a wee bit sore. But making assumptions wasn't always best, so I'd learned.

"How're you feeling this morning?" I asked.

"Sore, but the good kind. It's been a while since I've been fucked and you were pretty damn enthusiastic," Gus said with a grin.

"I'm virile as fuck, what can I say?" I gave Gus a quick peck on the lips then smiled devilishly. "Speaking of, how about we do that thing again where you jerk us both off? My hands aren't as big. It's not as good when I do it."

"You mean frotting?" Gus asked, trying to conceal the laughter in his voice.

"Yeah! That's the one. Sounds gross—kinda reminds me of frogs—but damn, son, it feels pretty great."

Gus snorted a laugh then rolled us over, so I was on my

back. The loss of his heat was a shock I did not welcome. I reached up and wrapped my arms around Gus's neck and hooked my legs over his for more contact. Gus's cock ground against mine, causing us both to hum.

"You really are a clingy spider monkey, *caro*. I can't reach if you won't let go a bit."

I rocked my hips against Gus's and enjoyed the sight of him trying to hang on to his control. "I think we can make it work somehow."

AFTER "MAKING IT WORK" with Gus, he grabbed some damp cloths to clean us up, but really, we needed to shower. We were about to hop in together when my stomach roared outrageously loud. Being the awesome boyfriend he is, Gus told me to go shower while he got a start on breakfast. Wearing just a pair of black briefs, Gus disappeared around the corner as I entered the bathroom.

Taking a long time in the shower was never one of my favorite pastimes, especially not when a scantily clad Gus was cooking—sausages, by the smell of it, which meant he'd be wearing that cute black apron he brought over a few weeks ago. Even more motivated than before, I soaped up, quickly rinsed, and walked out of the bathroom in a towel.

"*Why* are you here?!" I heard Gus ask, sounding surprised and maybe a bit angry.

"Who are you talking to, doll?" I asked as I walked around the corner toward the kitchen. My feet stuck to the floor as if I were glued in place when I looked at the door and saw Gus was talking to Dani.

"*Doll?*" She looked from me to Gus and clenched her fists at her sides. "He's calling you doll? What the fuck is going on here?"

"Um, D?" I eloquently contributed to the conversation.

"How did you find me here? How the hell did you even get in?"

Dani held out her hands and her keys jangled. "I have a key. Now answer me, why are you here, Dino?"

"Dino?" I asked, wrinkling my forehead and looking at Gus. "Who exactly is Dino? What's going on?"

Gus turned off the burners and crossed his arms over his chest defensively. I looked to him for answers, but it was Dani who spoke. "This is my brother, Jamie. Why is he here?" She turned to Gus and crossed her arms, mirroring his stance. "And why the hell aren't you wearing any pants?"

Huh? "Wait, Gus is your brother?" I flicked my eyes over to him, but he wouldn't meet my gaze. His body was rigid, and his jaw clenched tight. He reminded me of how close he was to bolting when I told him about my family's wealth. Not wanting to risk Gus leaving, I closed the distance between us and placed my hand on his lower back.

"*Gus*, huh? Yes, he's my brother, Jamie. Although Gus certainly is a new name for him." Dani uncrossed her arms, pulled out a stool, and sat down. She sighed, seeming to expel the worst of her anger with it. "Dino, you better start talking."

"I didn't know you knew him. It's purely coincidental, Daniella," Gus said solemnly.

I hooked my thumb under the band of Gus's underwear and snapped it, the loud crack getting everyone's attention. "Okay, so you're D's older brother she's been telling me about. Where do you get Gus from Dino?"

Gus uncrossed his arms and tapped his fingers on the island countertop. "My name is Agostino. Dino is a nickname. Gus is a new one," he answered with a shrug.

"Agostino Gallo," I whispered, testing the name on my

tongue. Shit, that sounded sexy as hell. A grin pulled at my lips as my mind took a nosedive into utter perversion.

"No," Dani started, "do not even think about sex right now, Jamie."

"Jesus, is nothing on my mind sacred around you?" I whined.

Dani shrugged. "About as sacred as my best friend not sleeping with my brother."

Gus—Dino? Agostino? No, Gus—winced. I rolled my eyes and huffed. "Oh, come on, D. How the hell was I supposed to know? Gus and Dino sound nothing alike!"

"James. Look at me then look at him."

I stared back and forth between them and felt like an idiot as recognition struck: the freckles, their noses, eye shape, eyebrows, full lips, complexion... goddamnit. I gasped and hammer-fisted my forehead. "OhmyGod, you guys are basically twins. The goddamn freckle pattern is even the same. Okay, so I'm not very astute, but this still isn't my fault."

"No one is at fault," Dani said. "Dino, I'm sorry. I didn't mean to sound so accusatory earlier. This was a big shock, and Jamie"—she cut her eyes at me—"has told me so little about you, so I had no clue."

"He was only respecting my wishes. Don't be angry with him," Gus said, still tapping away. I slid my hand over one of his and squeezed it, reminding him that he wasn't alone. He sighed, and his fingers stilled.

"I'm not angry with either of you—not for being together. God, that sounds weird. I'm mad at Dino for disappearing after moving out, and I'm mad at you for not picking up your goddamn phone."

I tilted my head and furrowed my brow. "My phone? Oh, were you trying to call me?"

Dani hummed and nodded. "I texted you this morning

when you didn't show up at the gym. I finished and still hadn't heard from you. Theo couldn't reach you either, and I got worried. I came over to check on you."

"Oooh," I drew out. "That was you blowing up my phone this morning. My bad. We were… busy."

Dani held up a hand. "Stop there. I can, unfortunately, infer the rest."

"Shit's wild, guys. Also, you"—I poked Gus in the chest —"referred to your sister as a kid, not a twenty-six-year-old woman, dude."

"I called you a kid too, in case you forgot."

"Whatever, doll. Do you want to stay for breakfast, D? I'm sure you already know, but your broski here is basically a chef."

"Oh, I know. He used to work at *Ciao Bella* and taught me a lot of what I know." Dani's small smile lit up her face.

"You bastard, you didn't tell me you worked in a restaurant. No wonder I like your cooking so much, it's all the stuff D's been making for me." I sat down on the stool next to Dani and did a happy seal clap. "This is perfect. Am I allowed to be happy that y'all are related? Because I am. I knew that Gallo snuggles were the best. I fuckin' knew it."

"It's weird, but I'm too hungry to think about it any longer," Gus drawled. "Want some coffee, Daniella?"

"Yes, please," she replied. Gus opened up a drawer and pulled out three K-Cups: two of the Brazilian roast and one hot chocolate, and popped one into the Keurig.

"You guys drink the same coffee," I said aloud, to no one in particular. They both looked at me with a raised eyebrow and the same quizzical expression. "God, I'm the least observant person on the planet," I grumbled.

"Okay," Dani said slowly. "Now that this is all sorted, will you two please go put some damn clothes on? I'm seeing more of both of you than I care to."

Gus crossed his arms self-consciously and practically hid behind the island, while I leaned back on the stool and splayed myself out. "Oh, come on, D, you've seen way more of me than this," I teased. I expected her to roll her eyes at me or scoff, but she surprised me by cutting her eyes at me and subtly shaking her head and mouthing "no." I raised an eyebrow in question, thoroughly confused by her reaction.

"What are you talking about?" Gus asked me, his voice sharp.

Oh, right. Gus was a protective big brother. "Um, nothing. I'm going to go get dressed." I slid off the stool and sprinted for my bedroom as Gus called after me.

"Have you been sending my sister those Snaps? Jamie!"

"I'mma flex my fifth amendment right and not answer that for my own well-being," I called out before slamming my bedroom door and leaning my back against it. I heard Gus and Dani rapid-fire arguing back and forth in a mix of English and Italian that I had no hope of following. I slipped into some lounge pants, retrieved my phone from under the bed, and texted my brother to let him know he could meet Gus today, and that I had a surprise for him. Might as well get all that shit out of the way in one go. Gus might want to kill me, but what was life without a little risk?

GUS STOOD NEXT TO me while I knocked on Theo's door. I held his hand for reassurance and to keep his fingers still. It was kinda cute that he was so nervous to meet my brother, but it also broke my heart a little bit. I told Gus I thought they'd get along since they're so similar, though he was worried regardless. We didn't get super into it on the way over, but I had a feeling it was due to all the shit he told me about his past. Theo wouldn't judge him for any of that, but I understood why Gus was antsy.

Theo opened the door, and I greeted him with a big smile and a drawn-out "surprise." His smile fell when he looked from me to Gus, at the same time Gus painfully squeezed my hand. "Ow, are you trying to break my fingers, dude? I have delicate hands." Gus released my hand without taking his eyes off Theo.

"Agostino," Theo gasped with what sounded like a hint of fear.

"*You*," Gus ground out, his voice thick with anger. He took a step toward Theo, but I inserted myself between them and stopped his advance with my hands on his chest.

"Hold up. Why do you guys know each other? And why did this just go from zero to one hundred in, like, two seconds?"

"Jay, this is Dani's brother," Theo said from behind me.

I looked behind me and saw that he was tense from head to toe, ready for a fight. "Um, yeah, so?" Then it hit me. Again, I wasn't fucking astute. "Oh, shit, Dani. I take it you two have met." I turned back to Gus and slid one hand around the back of his neck, teasing the short hair at his nape. "And you must know that things ended kinda ugly between them and are clearly not happy about it. Okay, I'm up to speed. Righteo. This is what's going to happen: you two are going to find some chill, and we're all going to sit down like civil adults and not make things difficult. Is anyone remotely unclear on that?" I looked back at Theo, and he shook his head, taking a few steps back. I returned my attention to Gus, and he still looked at my brother with flared nostrils and murderous intent in his eyes, but he said he understood.

This man was going to be the beautiful-death of me.

I heard the shower running and made a wild fucking guess that Masa was in there while Gus and I sat on the couch. Theo pulled over a chair from the bar and sat on the other side of the living room table, giving Gus a wide berth. I couldn't say I blamed him; Gus was still shooting silent daggers, and probably only being so quiet not to upset me.

"All right, one of you guys needs to start talking and get your shit out so we can all be civil. My boyfriend and my brother aren't going to be aggro toward each other. I don't need that kind of drama in my life. Who wants to go first?"

Theo cleared his throat and apologized for hurting Dani the way he did. He explained to Gus that he should never have dated her, since, you know, he liked dudes, and that he was in a bad place when they were together. To his credit, Theo was being a lot more forthcoming than he would have been in the past, and I appreciated him legitimately trying to patch things up with Gus.

"I know my personal problems don't excuse my behavior, but I've tried to make it up to Dani and be a good friend to her. I hope you and I can achieve the same."

Gus rubbed his eyes with the palms of his hands and sighed. "Last time I talked to you I told you I'd kill you if I ever saw you again. Obviously, I won't do that. For Jamie's sake, I'll try not to be an asshole," Gus grumbled.

Theo nodded as the bathroom door opened and a still dripping, towel-clad Masa walked out of the room in a burst of steam and sexiness. My jaw might have actually hit the floor before I could think to stop it. Gus growled next to me, breaking me out of my creeper trance, and I smiled innocently at him.

"Jamie," Theo warned.

Ah, shit. So much for me keeping my mini-crush on Masa a secret. "Yes, brother dearest?"

Masa coming back down the hall—thankfully fully

clothed—saved me. "What's going on out here? Oh my God, this must be Jamie's Gus," he said excitedly, making his way around the table to extend a hand in greeting. "I'm Masamune, but everyone calls me Masa."

Gus stood and shook Masa's hand, not seeming to harbor any ill-will toward him as a result of my not so subtle ogling. "Jamie's Gus," Gus replied with an amused lilt. It was silly, but hearing him say that, even jokingly, made me buzzy and happy. I bit my lip to hide my smile, but Theo was watching me, and no doubt saw my reaction. He flicked his gaze over to Masa and Gus then back to me and bowed his head with a smirk. I guess he liked what he heard as well.

"So, what did I miss?" Masa asked the room at large.

I clapped my hands once then snapped my fingers, and pointed friendly finger-guns at Masa. "About that. Grab a seat. I'll fill you in. You'll probably think it's a riot."

APRIL

I GAVE GUS A BREAK before unleashing my friends on him a couple of weeks later in what turned out to be a spectacularly wonderful brouhaha. We started out with drinks at my place to get Gus acclimated to their vibe in a controlled setting and then rolled through a few bars and ended up at a club. Roz spent most of the night climbing Gus on the dance floor, but he took it like a champ. In fact, if I hadn't had him moaning my name beneath me hours before, I'd have thought they were gonna split and go make some babies in the back.

Watching them move together in the throng of sweaty bodies, pounding music, and alternating colored strobe lights was entrancing. It got even better when Roz tagged me in and left Gus and me on the floor. I'd danced with guys before, but it was different with Gus—everything with him was different. The music hit hard and fast, though we moved to our own rhythm, moving together in a sensuous grind that sent my pulse pounding. Gus's arms were wrapped tight and low around my waist, pulling our bodies close. With one arm wrapped around Gus's neck and the other holding his hip, I was able to pull him down and kiss him as often as I wanted. I was indeed a greedy bastard, so I tasted him more often than not, just because I could. I'd have devoured him right there in the crowd if not for closing time and reality setting back in. Then I remembered that it was a Saturday night and the reality of that was Gus and me going back to his place and finishing in bed what we'd started on the dance floor.

Those first couple weeks of April were fuckin' wild. With nothing to do, I spent a lot of my free time bugging Dani down at the restaurant and waiting for Gus to get off work. His days were long, and he was always tired when he got in, but he always had time and energy for me. I tried my best to give him whatever he needed from me, whether it was my awful attempt at making him dinner, massaging his tired muscles, fucking his brains out, or just being a snuggle-bug.

I tried cooking pan-fried steak and roasted potato wedges for dinner, which means I burned two steaks and almost set some potato wedges on fire. I disposed of the evidence and cracked open that big-ass window by the bed to get rid of the smell before Gus got home. By the time he showed up, I had a large pepperoni and sausage pizza waiting on the counter, and was sitting on the bed in my underwear, wearing one of Gus's hats, and playing *GTA: V*. Gus glanced over at the counter then walked over and stood next to the bed, looking down at me.

"Nice to see you had a rough day," he said, his tone dripping with dry sarcasm.

"Bruh, you have no idea! I've been stuck on the same delivery mission for hours, and it drove me so fucking batshit that I snapped and just ended up running and cutting people down with a katana. But look at how much money I picked up! Baaaaallin'." A smile pulled at Gus's lips, and he ran a hand through his hair, messing it up in the cutest way. "Get naked and hop in with the pizza," I said, schooching over on the bed.

"Soon. I need a shower first."

"Come on, you know I like it when you're all dirty."

Gus shook his head, but his smile remained. "I'm not touching that one right now. I won't be long." With that, he disappeared around the corner, and I went back to wreaking mayhem on Los Santos while I played through all the ways I'd like to wreak mayhem on Gus after dins.

I heard the bathroom door open but didn't take my eyes off the game. Gus's heavy footfall stopped in the hall that separated the bathroom and closet from the main space. I peeked over and was bombarded by the sight of head-to-toe dampened skin. The water must have been hot because there was a red tinge to his chest and shoulders. His towel was nowhere in sight, lucky for me.

"You are delightfully nude right now." And he was. He so fucking was.

"I have enough laundry to do—thought I'd take a page out of your book," he said with a grin before heading over to the kitchen area. He came back with the pizza box, a handful of napkins and four cans of beer then sat down on the bed next to me.

I immediately turned the game off, leaned over, and gave him a slow kiss. "I'm sorry it's pizza again. I tried to make something new, and it didn't end well for me or the poor steak." I held up my index finger and sulked. "I burnt my finger on a hot pan."

Gus took my hand in both of his and brought my finger to his mouth. He ran it along his soft lips then gently sucked on it while giving me his best "fuck me" eyes. After one last swipe of his tongue, he pulled off of my finger and rubbed my wrist with his thumbs. "Is that better?"

"Is what better?" I asked in a daze. Gus chuckled and opened up the pizza box, taking out a slice and handing it to me before taking one for himself. "You're too good for me, dude," I said sincerely.

"What are you talking about?"

"You spoil me more than Dani and Theo do, and that's saying a lot."

Gus grunted, but there wasn't any joy in it. "How can you spoil someone when you have nothing to offer them in the first place?"

"Okay, my turn to ask, what are you talking about? You offer me plenty." Gus grunted again and took a bite of pizza. I knew him enough to know when he was brushing me off, and I wasn't gonna take it. No one liked talking about hard shit, but too fucking bad. "I don't know where your esteem issues stem from, Gus. You make me feel like I'm something worth treasuring. You make me feel wanted, secure, and free, but you don't try to suffocate me or police what I do. You pick me up when I'm down—figuratively and literally, which I love by the way—and you've been so patient and under-standing with me." I nudged Gus's thigh with my knee and flashed him a sympathetic half smile. "I know you've had some shitty luck with bi guys in the past, and I'm really happy you gave me a shot anyway. Dating you has made me a better person, which if you think about it is truly impres-sive, because I was already perfect before," I teased.

"Gee, how did you get so humble?" Gus deadpanned.

"I'm perfect, remember? And don't try to change the subject. You're important to me. Tell me why you think you don't have anything to offer me."

"Anyone can give you those things, Jamie. It's the things I can't give you, things that you deserve, that remind me of what a loser I am. I can't offer you any kind of stability or financial security. I can't provide for you like a man should— not how I am now. You deserve to have so much more than I'll probably ever be able to give you," Gus said, his voice dropping almost to a whisper at the end.

"Wasn't it you who told me that there wasn't a universal playbook for how shit should go? You were talking about sex, but it applies to this too. Everything you told me you can't give me? That's all stuff I don't need from you. I've casually dated people who could easily provide those things, and it didn't ever work out. I've never had an emotional connection with someone before now, and that's worth more to me than anything money or status can get me. That shit is all superficial, trust me, I know. If you're kicking yourself over what you think I need, please stop. I'm already getting everything I need and more from you. I wanna be that for you too. I want you to be able to lean on me and rely on me and stuff. And talk. You have to talk to me. I can infer that you're not happy with your job, but you never want to talk about it."

"What's there to say? I took the job that paid the most out of all the menial ones I could find. It's not something I'm particularly proud of and not something I like reminding you of. Sometimes I feel like I'm in a pit that I can't escape from, and I don't want to drag you down there with me."

I thought about what Gus said and, in a way, understood. He was lost. It wasn't quite the same, but I felt lost too when I was faced with having to pursue a career I had no interest in being part of. I had my brother to show me that I could do anything I wanted, but whom did Gus have? He'd been keeping his family at a distance, but I was sitting right there in front of him. I could help him if he'd let me.

"Let's switch gears. If you could do anything in the world, what would you do?" I asked.

Gus snorted and rolled his eyes. "I honestly don't know. When I was a kid I wanted to be a pianist, then I wanted to have my own restaurant. I don't know anymore. Those things aren't plausible, so I haven't thought much about them."

"Why did you quit at *Ciao Bella* if you like cooking so much?"

"You're really not going to let me off easy, huh?"

"I told you I was persistent as fuck when I found you again. I wasn't saying it to be cute."

"You were cute though," Gus said with a reverent grin.

My cheeks prickled with heat at the compliment and how much Gus seemed to mean it. I wanted to jump him and kiss him until we were both kiss-drunk, but I had to stay focused for a bit longer. "Thank you. But I'm not going to get distracted that easily."

"I left the restaurant because it wasn't something I worked for. Going to work for my father every day made me feel like a charity case. I'd failed on my own in every city I'd moved to in one way or another. Coming home to lick my wounds and get a pity job didn't exactly make me feel like…"

"Like a man?" I guessed.

"Yeah. I wanted to make my own way, even if it meant doing things I didn't want to do. I don't have much, but I can say that everything I have is mine. I've worked for it and earned it."

Yet he still wasn't proud of himself, nor was he happy—things I'd work on in time, but he'd had enough for one night. I picked up the pizza I didn't even realize I'd set down and took a massive bite. "You work too hard, doll. You need a break."

"I can't afford a break, Jamie. Not right now."

I pondered that for half a second before the lightning struck. "Remember when I said my mom invited me over for dinner and I told her about you?" Gus nodded, and he took another bite of his slice. "My parents are leaving for a trip next week, and Mom asked me to keep an eye on the house. Usually, that means popping in occasionally to make sure nothing is on fire or that we haven't been robbed, but I was thinking of staying over at the house this time." Gus nodded and popped the last bite of crust in his mouth. "I was hoping you might stay over with me for the week. It's not Necker Island, but there's a hot tub and a piano you could play for me. Pleeeeease." I leaned against Gus's arm and batted my eyes up at him. It was a childish tactic, but that shit worked on everyone—except Dani.

Gus sighed, but the happiness in his eyes revealed his true feelings. "Okay. I'll come."

I sat up straight and reached a triumphant fist in the air and shouted, "Yaaaas!"

Gus shook his head again and got another slice from the box in front of us. "I just got played, didn't I?"

"Oh, totally, but you're not backing out. I won't allow it. I promise we'll have fun," I said with the utmost confidence.

"I trust you."

Gus's trust—something I'd been trying to earn and deserve. I hoped he truly meant that and wasn't just saying it casually. Gus's trust was important to me, and that wasn't something I was going to take lightly.

THIRTEEN

"Y OU GREW UP IN LINCOLN Park? In a mansion, no less." Gus asked as our car parked in front of my family home.

"Yeppers. You excited to see my bedroom?"

"Behave," Gus warned quietly. Our driver made eye contact with me in the rearview mirror and smirked.

"If you're trying to be discreet for Miranda's sake, it's too late. I fear she's already been privy to me trying to climb in your lap and panting in your ear." Gus flushed, grabbed our bags, and exited the car so fast you'd have thought it was on fire. "He's a little shy sometimes," I said as I pulled a Benji out of my wallet and passed it to Miranda. "You were stellar today, love. Drive safe." She thanked me for the tip, and I scooted out of the back seat to join Gus. "Thanks for grabbing my bag. She was a nice girl, wouldn't you agree?"

"I could strangle you right now."

I placed my index finger to my lips and hummed in contemplation while I started walking toward the house. I heard Gus's steps behind me then spun back toward him and said, "You know, I don't think I'd mind trying that. I've always been curious about erotic asphyxiation but didn't trust anyone enough to try it. And you know, I didn't really want to do it alone and end up as an unfortunate statistic. The last thing anyone in my life needs is to find my body with my dick out. No, thanks. But," I started slowly, "if you were interested, I would be too." I took Gus's hands in mine and kissed his fingertips. "No pressure, of course. If that's not your thing, it's all good. I frankly don't know if it's even my thing."

Gus licked his lips and pulled me into a hug. His familiar scent and warmth made me purr. It wasn't cold outside anymore, but the spring weather had nothing on how hot Gus was. "If you want to experiment with breath play, we can. We'll need to discuss it a bit more, and I'm not going to do that in the driveway." I laughed, and with that, we went inside.

It had been a while since I brought someone new home —years, in fact. I'd forgotten the effect the place had on people. Gus dropped our bags on the freshly polished white marble floor and gaped at the super high ceilings, and the especially bougie black and gold railed spiral staircase that went up three floors. Mom liked Victorian-style furniture, so that's what filled the house, with the exception of the overly classically masculine woody rooms Dad frequently used.

"Holy shit," Gus whispered.

"Can I interest you in another tour?"

"Do I get to keep my clothes on this time?"

"Do you want to?" I countered with a quirked brow.

"Perhaps until I'm sure there's no one else here. This place is massive, Jamie," Gus said, taking in the foyer again.

A small laugh rolled through me as Gus's eyes darted around us. Was he looking at the crown molding? Maybe the usually fresh, but now likely three-day-old flower arrangements adorning inlets in the walls? Or perhaps any of the other overly decadent features that made this room look like it was from a magazine spread instead of somewhere people actually lived. Whatever it was, it wasn't me, and I wanted to remedy that.

"I can assure you that we're alone here. I had groceries delivered yesterday, and there's going to be a cleaner coming twice during the day while you're at work. So, if you want to be butt-ass naked, go for it. Although, I would recommend staying at the rear of the house after dark, so you don't give everyone on the street a free show."

Gus's Adam's apple bobbed as he swallowed, but he otherwise didn't move before he picked up our bags again. "I'm good for now. Where are we sleeping?"

"Wherever you want. We don't have to stay in my room. There are six bedrooms, and I'm okay with using any of 'em, aside from the master. Theo's old room might be kinda weird too. It's basically a tribute to his high school achievements. Oh." I paused as something occurred to me. "You can have your own room if you want space. Of course, I hope you'll sleep with me, but yeah, you don't have to."

"We can take your room. Then you can show me the rest of the house before I start on dinner."

I let my glee show unrestrained and launched myself at Gus. He dropped our bags and managed to catch me as I wrapped my arms and legs around him. "Damn spider monkey," he murmured as he held one hand under my ass and the other on my back while he took a couple steps back to regain his balance.

"You didn't have to catch me," I said playfully.

Gus didn't smile back and looked at me as earnestly as he ever had. "I'll always catch you, Jamie."

I felt his heart beating through his chest, steady and sure. The conviction of his words stirred up my feels and left me with no other recourse than to kiss him. I leaned down and pressed my lips to his, hoping for… fuck, I wasn't hoping for anything. I just wanted to share the moment with Gus. His taste was on my tongue, his scent overwhelmed me, his heart pounded against my chest, and he was all I could see. I stroked my thumb across the freckles on his cheekbones then kissed the small scar there.

"Kiss me all you want, I'm not going to carry you up those stairs."

"There's an elevator; you don't have to. And thanks, I will kiss you all I want," I said before claiming Gus's mouth again. He indulged me until I started to get hard. My crotch was pressed tight against his abs, so I couldn't really hide it.

"Okay, time to get down. Show me around, and then we'll relax and have some fun after dinner."

I held on tighter. "Are you sure you don't want to carry me?"

"I'd carry you through fire, but I'm not carrying you up those fuckin' stairs."

"All right," I huffed. "'Twas worth a try."

After dropping our bags off in my room, I showed Gus around the spare bedrooms on the upper and middle levels, skipping over the master and Theo's room. I never realized how many useless rooms there were until I found myself having to explain them to Gus. I mean, eleven bathrooms? Sure, we didn't look at all of them, but it just seemed so… excessive. It wasn't something I gave much thought to before going room by room with Gus and imagining how it must all look through his eyes. Even so, I couldn't do a thing to change my upbringing, and I wasn't going to feel guilty about it. I understood Gus enough to know that he wasn't that brand of petty and wouldn't think any different of me after seeing all this—not negatively, anyway. I'd worry about that later. My main priority was making sure Gus relaxed as best he could.

We skipped over the piano room on the second level. I wanted to save that for last and surprise Gus. I wasn't at all smooth about redirecting his attention away from the stained French doors, but I managed. All was forgotten once I showed him the kitchen and liquor room. Mom hated it when I called it the liquor room, but it had a bar, tons of alcohol, and all the mahogany known to man, so what else would I call it? It was connected to a room with a pool table that I—you guessed it—called the game room. The table was more there for show since it was handcrafted and pretty fancy, though that didn't stop Theo and me from using it when we were home alone.

It was about four when I finished showing Gus around. We ended up back in the kitchen while he dug through the groceries to see what we were going to have for dinner. When Gus asked me if I wanted to help him make Margherita pizza, I planted my feet firmly on the floor to keep from flinging myself off the bar stool and at him once again, and simply nodded enthusiastically.

I was put on tomato cutting duty while Gus started on the dough. Whatever he was doing looked a trillion times more fun, and I found myself creeping over to his section of the white marble counter. My wanting to help turned into Gus showing me how to knead and toss dough, which turned into me throwing it too high and having it land in the flour, thus making a huge mess. Whoops. Then I dropped it on the floor and gave up, fully expecting Gus to scold me. He never did, though. He laughed at me, cleaned up my mess the best he could, then showed me how to do it again with fresh dough.

Dinner was delicious. It was the same recipe used at *Ciao*

Bella, so it was familiar to me. God, I couldn't believe I was dense enough not to notice Gus and Dani. Perhaps if I'd asked for his last name, we could have avoided that surprise. But then maybe we wouldn't be where we were, so I was kinda glad that my stupid brain didn't think to ask, you know, basic questions that any normal person would ask.

After we tidied up the kitchen, we took a shower in the bathroom off of my room. I really wanted to make it quick and get Gus in the piano room, but once he was all naked and wet and soapy, I said "fuck it" and opted for indulgence. As if I could've kept my hands to myself in a situation like that.

I got out of the shower first so Gus could finish washing up, which was code for getting that ass squeaky clean for me. We both knew what he meant, but he got embarrassed when I broached the subject without tact. My sweet, shy Gus. Also, go Gus for making the decision that we were going to fuck later. He really was more than I deserved.

Drying off was a half-assed effort at best, but it was paramount that I got ready before Gus came out. I slipped on some comfy pants and slipped a condom and some individual lube packets in my pocket. I found those bad boys on Amazon a few weeks ago and knew there would come a day. I straightened up and gave myself an evil chuckle in the mirror. It was a little chilly, so I raided Gus's bag for one of his comfy hoodies and zipped it halfway up. The one I chose still smelled like him, which made it the best one.

Gus came out of the bathroom about ten minutes later, naked and mostly dried off. I sat on the edge of my bed and had to look away; otherwise, my plans would be foiled, and we'd just end up screwing in here for the rest of the night. Not that there was anything wrong with that, but I had something else in mind.

"I appreciate you giving me some privacy, but you really

don't have to look away," Gus said. "In fact, I came out here naked because I figured you'd just try to steal my towel anyway."

"A towel is a cruel device to cover your body in, Gus." I turned my head toward him, and thank fuck, he was wearing pants. "I will always try to free you from your cottonous bonds."

"Cottonous bonds, huh?"

I got up and pulled Gus into my arms. "Mhm. They're a serious thing. Come with me. I want to show you something."

Around the corner from the French doors to the piano room, I stopped our advance and asked Gus to close his eyes.

"Should I be worried?"

"Absolutely not," I replied. "It's a pleasant surprise."

Gus closed his eyes and held his hands out, palms up. "I trust you."

There was that word again. I took Gus's hands in mine and slowly led him over to the doors. I asked him to wait while I opened the doors and turned the lights on, then guided him over to the piano bench. The marble floor was cold on my bare feet, perfectly contrasted with how hot my hands holding Gus's were. I contemplated having Gus take a seat, but I figure he might want to look at the piano first.

"Okay, you can open your eyes now," I said after releasing Gus's hands.

Gus opened his eyes, squinting from the light at first, then wide. The faintest of smiles tugged at the corner of his mouth, but he mostly looked awestruck. "Oh my God. You didn't mention that you had a fucking Steinway."

I shrugged one shoulder. "I said there was a piano."

"Yeah, not the same thing." Gus reached out but pulled

his hand back before making contact with the instrument. "Can I touch it?"

"Of course. I hope you'll play it too," I said encouragingly. Gus ran his fingers along the keys, light enough not to produce a sound. Seeing how carefully he handled the piano reminded me of how he treated me, like both were precious things. It made me feel like a million bucks—Gus always did. I watched as he circled the piano, ghosting his fingertips over the surface. "You know, I did say you can touch it."

"I don't want to leave smudges. This thing is pristine."

"Nah, don't worry about that. There's a dude who comes and takes care of it. I'll make sure he drops by before we leave to shine it up or do whatever it is one does to a fancy piano. Please, sit," I said, gesturing to the bench. Gus did so, and I sat down next to him. It was a tight fit, but we made it work. I squeezed his thigh and leaned my head against his shoulder. His skin always seemed to be hot to the touch in the best way. Gus was like a sexy heating pad or something. Well, that probably wasn't the best way to describe him, but I did really like heating pads, so it wasn't the worst either.

"Do you know how to play?" Gus asked me.

"Nah-uh. I had lessons, but my instructor said I was 'insufferably hopeless.' It wasn't my fault that I got bored quickly, but whatever. Theo picked it up like the good, diligent son he was. He used to play for Mom."

"My ma liked to listen to me play too. She'd stay for my lessons when she could and always be smiling," Gus said with a smile that I now recognized as the one Mrs. G wore when she gushed over Dani.

"Yeah, I think I know the one. I've seen it a bunch when D and I would talk about how well school was going."

"You've met my mom?" Gus asked, turning his head toward me.

"Gus, I've met your whole family. I'm D's best friend; I've

been over for dinner countless times and sometimes just hang out, or study at the restaurant. It's only by chance that we haven't met before."

"Well, I haven't been around much in the last few years. Wait, if you've been to my parents' house, you should have seen my pictures."

I thought about it, and yeah, I had seen pictures of Dani and her brother hung on the walls. "Dude, you guys were kids in those photos. And sorry, but I was focused on how cute D was with those straight-cut bangs and those adorable buck teeth," I said teasingly.

Gus snorted a laugh and nodded. "Yeah, she was always pretty cute. Tell me something. Have you and her ever…"

"Fucked?"

"I was going to say dated, but sure," Gus asked, with a hint of tightness in his voice. The poor guy was worried that I'd screwed his little sister, not that I could blame him.

"We went on one date that ended in disaster. And that was only because I'd begged and begged and she got tired of it. We talked and laughed and had a great time, and I kissed her at the end of the night." Gus wrinkled his nose, making his freckles look like they were dancing. "Don't worry—it didn't do anything for either of us. She laughed at me, and I told her it kinda felt like what I'd imagine kissing my sister to be like. After that we were pretty inseparable—in a super affectionate yet wholly platonic way. The kiss didn't have tongue, if that helps." I bit my lip and smiled, hoping I was cute enough for him not to be angry. He sighed, but it was the good kind that meant I was in the clear. "Aww, yeah, I'm not in trouble."

"You talk too much sometimes," Gus said flatly.

"Shut me up then. Play something," I replied, nodding my head toward the keys. "And don't even try to tell me you can't. If you won't, that's okay, but don't say you can't."

Gus grumbled under his breath. "You can't let me stand behind my bullshit just once, huh?"

"Nope. Not today, doll."

"Okay. I'm just letting you know upfront that it's been years since I've played, and it's going to suck," Gus said nervously.

"Relax. You could play me 'Twinkle, Twinkle Little Star' with one finger and I'd be impressed." Gus turned to me with a raised eyebrow. "It was what my instructor was trying to teach me before all hope was lost. I couldn't even manage that." I rolled my eyes at the memory.

"Wow. Okay. I do feel better now. I can do a bit better than nursery rhymes, but there will probably be mistakes." I smiled and squeezed Gus's thigh again encouragingly.

He took a few deep breaths to steady his trembling hands then the first few notes reached my ear.

"Hey, I know this one!" I exclaimed excitedly, forgetting that Gus might need concentration and not me yelling in his ear.

Luckily, he grinned at me and said, "I'd sure hope so. It's 'Ode to Joy.' Well, a very simplified version of it."

I watched Gus's skilled fingers move over the keys in utter adoration. He made me wish I knew how to play so I could play for him. That line of thought hardly surprised me anymore. I found myself wanting to do everything for Gus as of late. It just kinda happened, which was wild. I couldn't say with any certainty when I started caring so deeply for Gus, but that didn't matter. It was the way I felt, sitting there on the bench with him, and that was what mattered.

The song ended, and Gus released a deep breath as if he'd been holding it the entire time. I clapped for him and showered him with praise that made his ears burn red. He played another song that was familiar to me and that sounded a bit more complex. When I realized what it was I blurted out

"Black Swan!" and Gus laughed and corrected me. Appaaaaarently it was from Swan Lake. Minor technicality. Gus made a few mistakes during that one and the song that followed, but he never stopped or lost tempo. He cursed under his breath the first couple times, but I was right there with a reassuring hand on his thigh.

After the last note of the third song, Gus dropped his hands in his lap and smiled at me. "Thank you for this."

With my hand still on his thigh, I leaned over and dropped a soft kiss on his inviting lips. Gus kissed me back and slid his hand around the back of my neck, keeping me close to him. I sometimes wondered if he wanted me as much as I wanted him, but then he'd do things like catch me or just pull me closer, and I knew the feeling was mutual. We weren't always the best with words, but the feelings were definitely there—scary, exciting feelings that made me wonder what more we could have. What would a future with Gus look like? If it was half as good as kissing him on a piano bench or snuggling and watching Netflix, sign me the fuck up.

Gus brushed his thumb against my earlobe, sending tiny currents of pleasure through my body, and inevitably making me start to get hard. I'd planned on getting freaky-deaky with Gus tonight, hence the condom and lube in my pocket, but I hadn't narrowed down where. Until I opened my eyes and saw that wonderfully huge piano sitting right there, holla.

I let Gus lead the kiss and moved my hand up his leg, giving his balls a light squeeze. He moaned into my mouth then pulled back. "My playing make you hot?" He was totally teasing me, but yeah, it had. I kissed him again and let my hand slipping under his waistband answer for me. I gave his soft cock several squeezes and tugs until it began to harden in my hand. I slipped the tip of my thumb under Gus's foreskin and circled his highly sensitive tip, making him shudder and moan. The sound was worth savoring, but I was too fired up to take things slow.

Once Gus was fully erect in my hand, I withdrew my thumb and stroked him with a firm grasp from root to tip, easily sliding his foreskin over his cockhead and back down. I gave my wrist a small twist at the top of each stroke, just how I learned Gus liked and was rewarded with his pre-cum and satisfied sighs. His breaths were coming out a bit too ragged for us having only just begun, so I thought it best to give him some warning.

"Don't you dare come yet, not until I'm balls deep in that sweet ass," I rasped in his ear.

Gus stilled my hand with both of his and swallowed hard. "I can't hold off if you keep going."

I narrowed my eyes, both tickled and aroused at Gus's admission. "Stand up and take those pants off then."

"Right here?" Gus asked, surprise clear in his tone.

"Not quite," I said and nodded my head to the left, toward the piano. "Up there."

Gus looked at the piano and back at me with wide eyes. "No."

"Um, yes," I replied as my other hand found and tweaked his nipple, causing him to flinch.

"No, Jamie."

I sighed and withdrew both of my hands, letting them drop in my lap. "Why not?"

"We can't do that."

"I assure you, we can."

Gus rubbed a hand through his hair and squeezed the back of his neck. "That's a one-hundred-thousand-dollar piano, Jamie. We cannot fuck on top of it."

"Hmm. For clarity's sake, lemme double check something here. Are you saying no to me or are you saying no to here?" I motioned around us, toward the piano in particular.

"Definitely not you."

"Oh, good. We can't have my self-esteem taking that kind of hit," I said half-jokingly yet completely relieved.

Gus tugged on my sweater and brought our foreheads together before kissing me. "You're not the problem, *caro*."

"You told me you trusted me when I asked you to follow me in here blindly. Do you still trust me?" Gus nodded, and I bit back a grin. "Then trust when I say that I'm going to fuck you up there or right here against the keys. Choose wisely." I stood up and leaned against the edge of the piano, Gus's eyes tracking my every movement. I dragged the zipper of the hoodie down, ever so slowly, and heard Gus groan once it fell open. I was free-balling, so my VPL game was strong as fuck with how rock hard I was. I imagine I looked like quite the snack.

Gus eyed me appreciatively but made no efforts to move. I wasn't in a particularly patient mood, so I circled around behind him and ran my hands over his chest, paying close attention to his nipples. I leaned down and whispered in his ear while I worked my hand back down his pants. "Come on, Agostino. Stand up," I ordered. Gus whimpered and rose to his feet, and I spun around to stand in front of him, only letting go of his dick to reverse my hold. I stroked him with one hand and shoved two of my fingers in his mouth, which he sucked on with the same effort he used on my cock.

Once my fingers were sufficiently wet, I withdrew them and guided them down the back of Gus's pants, into the cleft of his ass. I rubbed my middle finger over and around his hole then pushed the tip of my index finger inside. I waited for the resistance to ease up then slid my finger inside as far as I could, while still jerking Gus off. I rubbed his prostate a few times, just to drive him crazy, and then backed off so he wouldn't come. He whimpered in my ear again, so I nailed his prostate again, with a bit more pressure. His cock twitched in my hand that time, which I always found so damn sexy.

"You're going to do as I say, understand?" I ground out. Gus nodded, but that wasn't good enough. I squeezed him hard, drawing out a gasp. "Tell me you understand."

"I understand."

"Good," I said as I pulled both hands out of Gus's pants and eyed the open piano lid behind me. "Close the lid," I instructed. I picked up the bench and carried it to the side of the piano where Gus was following my order. I'd have done it myself and got him to get the heavy-ass bench if I knew how to close the lid. Oh well, what mattered was that this was actually gonna happen.

And obedient Gus was just as perfect as bossy Gus. Fuck me.

Gus turned to me once the lid was closed then stepped one foot up on the bench when a brilliant idea came to me. "Hold up, doll," I said, reaching for Gus's arm with a sly smile. "Me first." Gus stepped aside and placed a hand on my lower back as I climbed up. I assessed the limited space to be found atop the piano and opted to lie lengthwise with my head up by the keys. I shimmied out of my pants but kept them next to me. Gus pushed his pants over his ass and let them pool around his ankles before he climbed up to join me. I'm pretty sure he was tall enough just to scoot up, but I appreciated him not making me feel inferior. He was considerate and shit.

I propped myself up on one elbow to get a good look at Gus kneeling and leaned back on his haunches with his cock lying heavy against his thigh. His erection had flagged a bit—likely due to nerves—but I'd be sure to remedy that in good time.

"Come over here," I said as I lay flat on my back. I patted

my hips twice and couldn't stop the smile twisting my lips. "I want you to ride me."

Gus didn't hesitate. A couple seconds later, he swung a leg over me and lowered himself down in my lap. My cock rubbed against his ass, and I had the overwhelming urge to fuck him raw. I made a mental note to bring it up any time but right then and jerked Gus back to full hardness.

He leaned forward then back up against my cock, again and again, making my eyes roll back. I'd have shot all over his ass if not for his helping hand in the shower earlier, but I was still way too close for not having yet been inside him. I grabbed my pants and dumped the condom and lube packets out next to us. Gus looked surprised for a second, which made me wonder if he thought I wanted to take him without a condom. Of course I did, but I'd never do it without talking to him about it first.

Gus got back in the zone and smirked when he flipped over the cutest little lube packets. "Did you plan this?"

"Not exactly this. I knew I was going to fuck you some-where... interesting tonight." Gus ripped open the condom, reached behind him, and rolled it down my cock like a motherfucking boss. "Done this before?"

The smug bastard shrugged and cocked his eyebrows at me. "Maybe once or twice, but never quite like this." He leaned down and kissed me, brushing my hair out of my face.

"Slide up a little and let me stretch you a bit. I need to get in there before I embarrass myself."

"I'll be fine. I just want to feel you," Gus said before tearing open two packets of lube. He used one to slick himself and the other to lube up my cock. After turning back to me, he held my cock at the base and slowly guided himself down on my length. He went achingly slow, so I felt every involuntary spasm of his inner sphincter milking my cock.

"Fucking hell," I ground out. Gus moaned low in his throat once he'd taken all of me and dragged his teeth over his bottom lip. "I want you to fuck yourself on my cock. I want you to shoot all over me."

Gus took my words to heart and rocked his hips from side to side, then in circles, while he adjusted to the intrusion. I always spent a good deal of time making sure sex would be as painless for him as possible, so I was worried about him feeling discomfort. But he was in total control, and I trusted that he'd stop or slow down if it wasn't good for him.

When Gus's breathing evened out, he began to rock up off his haunches then back down, feeling like he was driving me deeper each time. The angle must have worked for him because he was moaning and leaking pre-cum on my stomach. I couldn't resist and swiped my thumb over his tip to collect it then brought it to my mouth for a taste.

"You taste so good," I said as I traced my bottom lip with my thumb and squeezed Gus's thigh with my other hand. He smiled down at me through heavy-lidded eyes and came down harder with each pass. I had to use every bit of my strength to hold off on coming until Gus found his release. It was the hardest thing, but I knew it would be worth it in the end.

"Jamie," Gus said through ragged breaths. He flattened his hands against my chest and ran one down the expanse of skin while he found purchase with the other and fucked harder and faster. He panted my name again, with more urgency, and I blew without warning, closing my eyes and straining as my orgasm ripped through me. I cried out when Gus dug his blunt nails into my chest and pulsed around my cock. I opened my eyes in time to catch him still riding the high of his release, looking like an actual god, and coating my chest with his spunk.

"Fuck, dude. That's a lot of baby-batter," I said as I tried to catch my breath.

Gus groaned. "Please don't ever say those words again."

"No promises. But seriously, you drenched me. I think another shower is in order then maybe some snuggles?"

"We can do that. I just need a minute to breathe," Gus said.

I remained silent for about five seconds before the need to speak ate a hole through the seal on my lips. "You ride dick like a fucking champ. Please feel free to do it again any time."

"Thanks. Now stop talking."

"Aaaaand the gold medal goes to… Gus Gallo, who scored a perfect ten out of ten from the only judge who matters."

"I'm going to smother you if you don't stop talking."

I tried. I really fucking tried, but I couldn't do it. Just as I opened my mouth to say something dumb, Gus's lips were there to silence me; that was a silence I would take any time.

We ended up snuggling outside on a couch on the back balcony, surrounded by trees in our own private slice of paradise. Gus had the brilliant idea to bring a blanket out with us, so it was super cozy.

"It's gorgeous out here. This whole place is amazing," Gus said, pulling me closer.

"Yeah, this huge-ass balcony is definitely one of the best perks. The pool down there is also really nice in the summer."

Gus hummed and rubbed my arm. "We'll have to try it anyway before we leave. Jamie," he started, "can I ask you something?"

"Of course. You can ask me anything."

"You told me your family was 'kind of loaded.' This

doesn't really look like kind of."

"Okay, so maybe I downplayed it a little. Talking about it is weird for me. I'm never really sure what to say. To be blunt, there are at least eight figures in my parents' personal account at any given time, not counting savings or investments. I have a very generous mid-eight figure trust that I haven't touched yet that's just sitting at the bank, garnering interest." I might as well lay it all out there.

Gus was quiet for a while, continuing to rub my arm. The silence killed me, but he deserved time to figure out what he wanted to ask me. "Which bank is it? That your family owns."

"Rey Financial."

"Makes sense. That's the bank Pop switched to a few years ago."

"I made sure the banking fees for the fam and business were waived, and that any lending is done at or below prime. Well, I don't really have any pull with the company, but Theo took care of it as a favor to me," I explained.

"Jamie Rey, huh? Nice to finally meet you. I'm Agostino Vitale Gallo."

"Fuuuuuck, that's sexy. Nice to meet you too. I'd like to spend the rest of our time here thoroughly getting acquainted with you. Inside and out," I said very seriously.

"Inside and out, you say."

"Yes. Especially inside."

Gus snickered and kissed my forehead. "I'm certain I can fit you in tomorrow morning around, oh, say, ten?"

"Wunderbar. Get lots of sleep tonight because I'm gonna acquaint the fuck out of you tomorrow."

"I don't think that's quite right," Gus said. I couldn't see his face, though I could tell he was smiling.

"Shh. Shush your pretty mouth. I'm almost a doctor; trust me."

"Yes, *caro*."

The rest of the week went by in a blur. A ridiculously fun, sexy blur. Gus and I had sex in nearly every room in the house, played pool, watched plenty of bad TV, made good use of the hot tub, and even attempted to swim in the pool out back. It was way too fucking cold, but chillin' out there in the evenings with hot chocolate was the best.

On the last night, Gus and I were watching some episodes of *Friends* on Netflix, just relaxing. Gus was lying on his stomach with one arm and one leg hanging over the edge of the couch, and I was lying on top of him. I'd discovered how comfy he was as a full human cushion on day two of our stay and had taken advantage of it every day after Gus assured me it wasn't painful or uncomfortable for him. I even lay on his back while he did push-ups one day—now *that* was hot.

I'd almost fallen asleep when Gus laughed at something from the show, the robust vibration from it, echoing through my chest. I drew little hearts on his shoulder with my fingertips then scoffed at myself.

"What is it?" Gus asked.

"Nothing, doll," I said, having no intention admitting to what I was just doing. "I had a lot of fun this week. I'm glad you decided to stay with me."

"Thank you for convincing me. This week with you has been amazing, even if you did coax me into defiling a Steinway. I'm going to go to hell for that, you know."

"Shh. I won't let the devil take you. You're mine and mine alone, and I'll take on anyone who thinks otherwise," I said through a yawn.

Gus chuckled, the sound lulling me further into sleep. "My hero."

"You're damn right I am."

FOURTEEN

G OING BACK TO REALITY after that perfect week with Gus was way harder than I thought it would be. When Gus went to work while we were at the house, I spent my days reading, watching movies, and browsing social media, and I didn't have a single complaint. Now that I was back in my own place, I felt like pulling my hair out. I was so fucking bored. I'd cut back on smoking after Gus told me he was subjected to random drug tests at his job. He never asked me to stop or begrudged me smoking, but it felt like the right thing to do.

I was seriously bored and needed to mix things up. I still had some shatter left, which would be perfect. Dabbing alone was fine, but I fancied some company, so I sent out a message in the group text to see who was free and up for a sesh. Dani didn't smoke, and she was working anyway, Roz had an engagement party to go to, Pat went with her, but my man Scotty came through in the clutch.

An hour and a half later, I heard a knock at my door and was greeted by Scotty, holding bags of what I hoped were tasty snacks. We greeted each other and fist-bumped as he walked inside and made himself at home in my kitchen. He emptied the two bags, pulling out three bags of tortilla chips, salsa, queso, and a container of sour cream.

"Bruh, nachos? You know me so well."

"You're hosting, man. It's the least I could do," Scotty replied.

We caught up on some of the new girls he'd been after, and how much harder it was to pull when he wasn't at the hospital. "Chicks really dig the lab coat" was what he'd said to me, and it was a goddamn fact. I'd have been lying if I said I hadn't taken advantage of that fact on occasion in the past. I'd have to bust out the coat for Gus and see if it worked on him too.

"Dude, stop thinking about your guy," Scotty said through that perma-grin of his.

"Jesus, are you D now? How did you know?"

"You're standing there with this look on your face that's a weird mix of dopey and pervy. It was pretty fuckin' obvious." He grabbed half of the snacks then headed for the couch.

I snagged the rest and followed. "All right, ya got me. I'm sorry, I can't help it!"

Scotty unzipped his green sweater and shucked it off, revealing a white V-neck over fitted knee-length jean shorts. I could never pull off denim shorts, but Scotty was cute as fuck in anything he wore. I hadn't bothered to get dressed. I slipped into a pair of boxers and one of Gus's hoodies. I was a little bit exposed, though it wasn't anything Scotty hadn't seen before on several occasions—including via Snapchat just that morning.

He sat down on the couch and shook his head at me as I flopped down next to him. "You don't have to be sorry. I'm glad you're so happy. I didn't think you had it in you."

"Being happy or being with a guy?"

"Neither, *oyinbo*. Commitment. You never let anyone tie you down, and as soon as they tried, that was the end of it. But you're so happy right now, and we've all been trying to figure out what's different this time around."

He was right, and it was something that hadn't occurred to me. Why were things different with Gus? It wasn't because he was a guy. That would have lost its allure if that was all it was. So, why Gus? I picked at the sleeve of Gus's sweater and chewed on my bottom lip, trying to think of something profound to say. "You know, things with Gus are just easy. I think I don't have a problem committing to him. It doesn't feel like work. I want to do it. He's supportive of me, though he doesn't tie me down whatsoever. I still feel like me, but now I have him as well, and it's pretty fucking rad."

"Deep shit, bro. You already have a few dabs without me?" Scotty teased.

I scoffed and rolled my eyes, but couldn't help smiling anyway. "Whatever."

"I'm just playin'. Everything you just said was perfect. Have you told him how you feel?"

I stretched out and rested my head on Scotty's leg and looked up at him. "He knows how I feel about him."

"Still. You should tell him. It's nice to hear, even if you already know," Scotty said knowingly.

"Goddamn. When did you get so smart with relationships?"

"I have four sisters, dude. You pick shit up through osmosis."

We were deep in NBA playoff season so I reached for the remote on the table and turned on some sports highlights without even asking, knowing Scotty would be interested. I'd brought two glass rigs out and cleaned them for something to do while I waited for him to arrive. I laid out the six remaining strains I had leftover, as well as some San Pellegrino. As much as we both enjoyed indulging in adult beverages, shatter was best enjoyed without the influence of alcohol, at least for us.

"Yeah. I guess so." I sat up and cracked my neck from side to side. "Bust open them chips, let's get this shit going. If your sober advice is this fire, I can't wait to hear your stoner wisdom."

"Oh, you're in for some wild shit. I'll probably have you wanting to marry the guy by the time I leave."

We both laughed at that, but if I was being honest with myself, it truly didn't sound so terrible to me. That said, there was no need to rush or get ahead of myself, so I set up a rig, lit the torch, and inhaled to clear my mind.

GUS WAS COMING over that evening, which was a Tuesday or Wednesday or some shit. I really didn't know. I was a mess all day and remembering what day it was didn't register as important. After Scotty went home the night before, I felt even more restless. I went to the gym in the morning with Dani for our class and tried to work out all of my extra energy, but it wasn't enough to tire me out. The only thing that really drained me anymore were the body weight exercises Masa and I did, and he was in Japan with my brother on their sweet-ass Valentine's trip. I tried doing the workout on my own, but I needed to be pushed, and Masa had this particular brand of inspiring that was firm and got my ass moving. Dani didn't care for the routine Masa and I did. She preferred cardio machines, which was where I found her when I rejoined her. I snagged the treadmill beside her, starting out with a brisk walk.

"What's wrong?"

"What makes you think something's wrong?" I wasn't

sure why I was deflecting. That's not who we were. "Fuck. I don't know."

"Is there something wrong with you and Dino?"

"Not even a little bit. I feel antsy, and I can't relax. I don't know why. Everything was great while we were at Mom and Dad's then I got all weird when we got back. It's only been a couple days, but they've been brutal, D. I had a great sesh with Scotty yesterday, then as soon as he left, the feeling came back."

"Do you miss him?"

"Of course I do, but it's only been a couple of days, so that can't be it. Anyway, I'm seeing him tonight, so I guess I'll see how I feel then," I said as I worked up to a run that matched Dani's.

"You should talk to him tonight. Tell him how you're feeling and don't hold shit in. You'll feel better after."

I whipped my head over toward her and stared in disbelief. "Have you been talking to Scotty? He basically said the same thing."

"He's not just a pretty face—do not tell him I said that. His head is big enough already," Dani grumbled. "Try to be as direct as possible when you talk to him. He's a stubborn goat, and you get distracted too easily. Keep it concise, and you'll be fine."

"Thanks for the advice, D. I'll try it—anything to get back to fucking normal."

"Any time, *fratellino*. I was really surprised initially, but I love you and Dino, and I want you guys to be happy. If that means together, then I don't have an issue with it." With that, we finished our run in silence while I tried to figure out what the fuck I was going to say to Gus.

THE MOMENT I SAW GUS, I lost my nerve to talk about anything. I pulled him into a kiss, purring at the smell of him. He'd gone home and taken a shower and smelled like my birthday and Christmas combined—the best if that wasn't clear.

Gus grabbed my ass and picked me up, which was all I needed to know that we were gonna be having a late dinner in favor of some fuckin'. In the past, I'd have said that I loved food more, but Gus easily came before it. I'd fast for a week if I got to see him every day. Fuck, I'd do it for twenty-four uninterrupted hours. I'd take the twelve or so I had and put them to good use.

After I blew Gus's mind with my ever-improving oral skills, he wanted to ride me again. I'd normally be all for that, but I was craving control after feeling so very out of it lately. I pushed him onto his back, using more of my strength than I usually did with him. He totally noticed and growled in response, which always sent a jolt straight to my cock. I pushed his legs wide and sank in as deep as I could. Gus inhaled sharply, but I knew that sound enough to know it was a good one. I slowly rocked my hips into him after a few moments of just feeling his body around me.

I set a good rhythm and targeted Gus's sweet spot, just how he liked it, but I couldn't lose myself in the experience like I usually did. When I looked into Gus's eyes there was so much I wanted to say, so many emotions roiling inside me, screaming to get out. It was worse than how I'd been feeling without Gus around. I felt sick to my stomach in a moment when I shouldn't have been thinking about anything other than the gorgeous guy in bed with me. The guy who made me happier than anyone ever has.

Gus squeezed my back and cried out for me to go faster, to fuck him like I wanted to. I tried to shake off my thoughts and give him what he wanted, but they still swirled around in my head. My body knew Gus's enough to act on sex muscle memory—if that was even a thing—and gave him exactly what he'd asked for, making him come hard.

Even distracted, I couldn't ignore Gus's body trembling, and how he felt, hot and tight around my cock. With a strangled cry, I blew, filling the condom between us. Leaning down, I dragged my lips across Gus's jaw, enjoying the prickle from his beard before I kissed him slow and sweet. When I pulled back and looked into his eyes, the noise in my head quieted, and I *knew* what the problem was and how I could fix it. I stilled my hips and maintained eye contact with Gus while the weight of what I needed to say began to dissipate. I knew, I fucking knew what this was, and I wasn't scared or confused anymore. I opened my mouth to say the words, but the sound came out muffled with Gus's hand covering my mouth.

"Don't you dare tell me you love me," he said—because all the fucking Gallos were mind-readers. I squirmed, but Gus wouldn't move his hand from my mouth, so I did the only other thing I could; I bit that motherfucker, and I bit him hard. He cried out and pulled his hand back to shake it out.

"What the hell, Gus?! I was trying to tell you—"

"I *know* what you were going to say, and I'm not going to hear it while we're fucking." He was still breathing hard from having just come.

"I love you, Gus," I blurted out. Gus groaned and whacked me on the side of the head, once again reaffirming that he shared blood with Dani. "Ow! What the hell?"

Gus pushed a hand against my chest. "You're still balls deep in my ass, you idiot."

"Ugh, I'm sorry." I carefully pulled out, tossed the condom onto the floor, and propped myself up on outstretched arms over Gus so I could see him clearly. "I'm not kidding. I do love you, Agostino Gallo."

"Jamie…"

"You don't have to love me right now, but trust me when I say that you will."

"You're a cocky sonofabitch," Gus said dryly.

"Damn straight I am. Ah, hell, phrasing."

"You can't call yourself out for phrasing."

"I can. I did. Fight me."

"This isn't a joke, Jamie." Gus turned away from me and clenched his jaw. His brow was furrowed, and he actually looked angry.

"What's the big deal? Why are you mad?" I asked genuinely.

"You don't take anything seriously."

"That's not true."

"It is, Jamie. You walk around like everything is one big fucking joke and I can't—I won't—allow myself to trust that." Gus pushed my arm aside and slid out from underneath me. He sat up and wiped the cum off his chest and stomach with his T-shirt, never once looking up at me.

I rolled over and sat up next to Gus, our elbows just barely touching. I wanted to climb into his lap in case he tried to bolt, but I didn't think that would stop him right then. A cheap trick would never be enough to make him stay if he really wanted to leave, so I sat quietly next to him and listened to his breathing, which was soon joined by the light tapping of his fingers against his leg.

"I'm the second son in my family, Gus. My brother was the one burdened with responsibility and, frankly, expectations. My brother did everything our dad asked of him and in doing so, took the pressure off me entirely. He worked hard to keep Dad happy, so I could be carefree and unburdened. I'm sure you can relate to that with what you've done for Dani.

"Theo spent a lot of his youth being miserable and feeling trapped, partially so I wouldn't have to. So, yes, Gus, I like feeling carefree. I enjoy not having to restrain myself. And as annoying as I might sometimes be, my no-filter-having ass brings a smile to my brother's face like nothing else." I chanced a glance over at Gus and was relieved to see he was looking back, listening to me speak sincerely. "There have been a handful of instances in my life where I couldn't be shielded, and as terrible as they were, feeling them made me cherish what Theo sacrificed to give me all the more. Look, Gus, I don't know how to convince you that I'm sincere. This is just who I am. If you can't trust that, then the problem here isn't on my end."

"It's not that simple, Jamie," Gus said somberly.

"But it is for me. My brother taught me to be fearless. Perhaps a bit too much, but that's not the point here. This is pretty black and white for me. I like you, Gus. A lot. Hell, I was trying to tell you that I love you! It's not because you're the first guy I've messed around with and it's not because you're smoking hot—but believe me, you are toooootally hot enough to scorch the earth. I like *you*. And when there's something I like, I go after it until it's mine. That's what I want you to be, Gus. Mine. And I wanna be yours."

Gus's jaw ticked, and I thought he might say something, but he bowed his head and rolled his shoulders. I had to do more. "We can take it slower if that's what you need. I'll do anything I can to show you how serious I am." Gus looked pained. Like the more I spoke, the more it hurt him. Hurting him was the last thing I wanted to do, but this wasn't a talk we could shelve for later now that we'd started. "Last week you told me twice that you trusted me. Was that bullshit?"

Gus shook his head. "No. I wasn't lying to you."

"Then why can't you trust me now?"

"It's not you I can't trust, Jamie. It's myself. I believe you when you say you love me and that you're willing to take things slow. The problem is me. I fell for you weeks ago. I can't trust myself to go slow with you," Gus said.

"Weeks ago," I echoed. "What's wrong with that?"

"I believe you when you say you love me right now. But I need to be able to rely on myself to not get too attached when things…" Gus trailed off and looked away, but I already knew what he was going to say.

"You mean when I come to my senses and break your heart, like your douchebag exes." Gus didn't respond, though his silence said enough. I crawled in front of Gus and sat back on my haunches. "Look at me, Gus. I'm not confused or in any way ashamed or embarrassed to be with you. I know you've had some shitty luck with relationships, but it's not fair to lump me in with your exes. You're assuming I'm going to change my mind and hurt you, just because I'm bi. That's fucked up, doll. You're doing the same thing to me that I did to you; making wrong assumptions and acting based on those wrong assumptions. It felt shitty when I did it, and it feels even worse having you do it to me." Gus's eyes widened, and he grabbed my hand, rubbing the underside of my wrist like he has so many times. "What I'm feeling, Gus, I-I… I mean this more than I could ever fucking say. Will you give me the chance to show you? Please." Fuck it. I crawled into Gus's lap, crossing my ankles behind his back. I would repeat myself until he fucking heard me loud and clear. I held his face in my hands and forced him to look at me, looking past the war raging in his eyes and point blank asked, "Do you love me?" I want to say I sounded confident and in control, but my voice came out as not much more than a shaky whisper.

"Yes." His big, warm hands enveloped my wrists, stroking lightly at the sensitive undersides.

"Tell me. Say it for me."

"I love you, Jamie. I really do."

A rush of air left me, but I swallowed back my happiness and steadied myself for the hard question I had to ask. "And why isn't that enough? Tell me the truth, Gus. I know you enough to know when you're making excuses because you don't want to confront something. This is your chance to tackle that shit head-on and be honest with me. Why isn't our love enough?"

Gus tried to look away, but I held him in place. His grip on my wrists stayed slack, never once trying to subdue me when he so easily could have. "I'm scared, Jamie. *You* scare me," he said, as his eyes welled with unshed tears. "Things have been too easy with you, and I'm waiting for it all to come crashing down on me like it always does."

"Just because it's easy for me doesn't mean I'm not sincere. I'll fiercely fight for you until you no longer want me to, and then I probably still will because I'm fucking persistent. You're holding yourself back from me, and it's making you hurt unnecessarily. I get why you've been living that way, I do. You don't have to now. Let me have all of you, and I promise I'll take care of you however you need me to. It goes both ways, Gus. I need you to take care of me too. You've been doing it so well already. I don't know what I'd do if you left. And I really don't want to find out. I know I have some growing up to do, but please, please…" I leaned my forehead against his and kissed him. I froze when Gus's hands let go of my wrists, though was flooded with an instant wave of relief when his arms circled around my waist and pulled me tight against him.

"I'm sorry. I'm so sorry, Jamie. I almost let my cowardice ruin this, and I'm sorry. I'm not as strong as you think I am."

I ran my fingers through Gus's hair and shrugged. "I never asked you to be perfect. Just be mine. That's all I want, doll."

"Okay." Gus nodded then kissed me. I felt his warm tears against my cheek and kissed him until they stopped falling. "What do we do now?"

I shrugged again and smiled, finally feeling the heaviness of the situation lift. "Whatever we want. There's no playbook, remember? We'll do whatever feels right for us. Everyone else can go get fucked," I said with certainty. "Does that work for you?"

"Yeah." Gus gently brushed the hair at my temple behind my ear and grimaced. "I'm sorry I hit you. I promise I won't ever do something like that again."

"Hit me?" I asked. "Oh. No, no, you don't have to be sorry about that. That wasn't, like, a real hit. There was no malice there. Besides, D hits me harder," I added in hopes of lightening the mood.

Gus's eyes narrowed, and I thought I heard a rumble in his throat. "Daniella hits you?"

"Well, she does when I deserve it. She legit punched me in the jaw when I told her I was bi. Like, in public and everything. But it's all good."

"It's not okay. I'll be having words with Daniella next time I see her." Gus kissed my jaw all over then the side of my head.

"I always liked the way you treated me. It's like I'm something precious or delicate. But, like, not in a condescending, patronizing kind of way. I feel safe and cared for if that makes any sense."

"You *are* something precious." Gus sighed and leaned back against the headboard. "Look, if we're really doing this, I'd like you to meet my family. I keep too many secrets from them."

"I already know your family, Gus."

"I mean as my boyfriend."

"Oh, duh. When do you want to tell them? Oh my God, Mrs. G is gonna flip! She adores me," I said, my voice climbing higher with excitement.

Gus laughed for the first time in forever, and I just had to kiss him again. "We can go to Sunday dinner and tell them then. I'll make sure Daniella and her boyfriend come as well."

"Ouu, Indy might hate me less if he knows I'm with you."

"You mean Andrew?" Gus asked.

"Yeah. I prefer to all him Indy. Kinda like with Scotty."

"Indy I get. Indiana Jones, right? But what about Scotty?"

"His name is Adeoye." Gus cocked an eyebrow at me and eyed me skeptically. "Yeah, I know, Scotty isn't close to that. He did his undergrad in engineering, and I was really drunk when I met him and kept butchering his name like some uncultured swine, so I just started calling him Scotty because of Montgomery Scott, chief of engineering on *Star Trek*."

"Are you serious?" I gave a single nod, and Gus shook his head. "He lets you get away with that?"

"Well, it's been a couple of years, so there's no going back now. Besides, he calls me *oyinbo*, which basically means 'white boy,' so I think we're even." Gus found that fucking hilarious, and I didn't mind him laughing at me. We ended up staying in bed, cuddling and talking about nothing in particular until my stomach rudely reminded us that it was well past feeding time.

Gus made us dinner then we went back to bed and made out like a pair of high-schoolers until I was too tired to keep my head up. Gus pulled me into his arms and held me all night until he woke up for work. I saw him off with a quick kiss at the door followed by an "I love you," which I didn't think could ever get old. Especially not the feeling of hearing him say it back.

"WAIT, SHOULD WE KNOCK?" I asked as Gus reached for the doorknob to his parents' house.

"Of course not. They're expecting me," Gus said, opening the door and ushering me inside. We'd decided not to tell them I was coming and explain everything in person. Well, that was how Gus wanted it, and I was okay with that. He was super nervous and jittery on the way over, similar to how he was before he met Theo. I understood why he felt the way he did, but I didn't think he had any reason to worry. His family was some of the kindest people I'd ever met, and they already loved me like a son because of my relationship with Dani.

Gus even dressed up, which was adorable. He came out of the bedroom wearing a dress shirt and tie, which I promptly took off of him. I picked out one of his sexy fitted long-sleeved shirts and had him wear that. The last thing he needed was to feel uncomfortable because of his clothes, so I made that decision for him all executively and shit. I opted for a flannel over a white tee and jeans stylishly ripped at the knees. It just felt like a plaid kind of day.

I waited for Gus to lead us through the house so he could have control over how this went. The Gallos had a really cute place. It was an older bungalow on the south side on a block with a dozen others that looked exactly like it. The inside was what made it special. Pictures of the family, both in the US and back in Italy, adorned walls and shelves. There were a ton of them, though it was super tasteful and really homey. A large area rug covered most of the hardwood floor in the living room, as well as one in the dining room. The house wasn't overly large or flashy, but it was organized, felt lived in, and was cozy. I could already hear Mrs. G, her sister, Rosa, and Dani talking animatedly in the kitchen, which typically meant Mr. G, Rosa's husband, Luciano, and Andrew were in the living room or dining room. We'd just walked past the living room, and they clearly weren't there, which left the dining room.

Gus entered the kitchen first, and the talking was replaced with excited gasps from Rosa and Mrs. G. "*Ehi, Mamma*!" Gus said, so fucking cheerfully that it made my mouth fall open. Guess he wasn't nervous anymore.

"*Mio patatino*," Mrs. G replied, just as enthusiastically. Gus scooped her up in a hug and kissed her on each cheek before setting her back down. They showered each other in a mix of English and Italian greetings, and it was so fucking sweet. Gus momentarily turned his attention away from his mom to say hello to Rosa and Dani, then returned to showering Mrs. G in affection. I saw a new side of Gus, and goddamn, it made me love him more. Love. It was still wild to say that, but in the best possible way. I hadn't told anyone yet, telling Gus's parents first seemed best. Theo and Masa got back from their trip a few hours ago, so I figured I'd give them the day to get settled back in before I go over and force them to drink with me.

"Jamie, dear, Daniella didn't say you were coming today." Mrs. G patted Gus's chest then came over, hugged me, and kissed my cheek.

"Yeah, it's a bit of a surprise, actually. I hope that's okay."

"Nonsense, dear. You're always welcome. Oh"—a smile lit up her face, and she turned to Gus then back to me—"have you met Agostino?"

I opened my mouth then closed it and looked to Gus for help, not wanting to say the wrong thing. Rosa smiled at me, and D wore my second-hand embarrassment on her face. "Um, I, uh—"

"Mamma, I have something to tell you," Gus said, saving me from further verbal diarrhea. "Where's Pa, he should hear this too."

Mrs. G breezed by Gus and opened the oven, releasing a smell so good it made my mouth water. I was terrible at identifying spices, but I definitely smelled cheese, and that meant dinner was going to be phenomenal. "You boys go sit down. We can talk in a little bit, *patatino*."

Gus nodded and waited for me before leaving the kitchen. Once we were halfway down the hall, I whispered, "What does that pati thing mean?"

"*Patatino*? Um, the literal translation would be 'little potato.'" I snorted a laugh before I could stop it, spurring Gus to growl in my ear behind me. It sent shivers down my spine in a way that was not at all appropriate for being in my boyfriend's parents' house. "It's a term of endearment, *caro*." There was an edge to Gus's voice, which did absolutely nothing but push my buttons more.

"You know, it would be best if you just didn't talk to me right now. I'm two gusts of wind away from tenting these jeans, and I really don't want Mrs. G to see that."

"Jesus, Jamie."

"I'm sorry! It's not my fault you're so fucking hot. And growling in my ear really isn't helping," I whisper-shouted.

Gus grabbed my hip, stopping me, just before the entryway to the dining room. He tightened his hand around my throat, just tight enough to really get my attention. He pressed his lips against my ear and whispered, "Be good. I'll show you something new tonight if you can be good for the next couple hours." I nodded my head like an obedient dog and was rewarded with a kiss to my temple. "Go on. Let's get this over with," Gus said after taking a deep breath.

I rounded the corner and was met with wide smiles and greetings from Mr. G and Luciano. Andrew smiled and nodded, his eyes going wide for just a second when Gus came in behind me. Clearly, Dani had told him about us, or he had super accurate and speedy deduction skills. I went with the former.

I said hello to everyone and shook Mr. G's hand like I always did, then took a seat, saving the spot next to him for Gus. Luciano began explaining something to me, though my attention was on Gus, and how stiff he was as he embraced his father at the head of the table. Mr. G said something to Gus, but I missed it when Dani came in with another place setting.

"Today, huh?" Dani asked me quietly as she quickly set up the area in front of me.

"Yeah. It was Gus's idea."

"I'm going to have to get used to that name."

I shook my head and noticed Andrew watching us out of the corner of his eye. "He likes it when you call him Dino." Dani finished her task and rubbed my shoulder. I leaned up and kissed her cheek then stealthily checked on Andrew after Dani left the room. He gave me his version of a glare, which was really a look of mild irritation. I smirked at him because it was too easy to get him going. Yes, he would like me better if I wasn't a dick, but he was just too fun to not fuck with.

The sound of a chair scraping the floor got my attention, and I turned toward Gus to see he was holding his chair out and looking at me with a knowing—and disapproving—eye. Busted. I turned away from him bowing my head, remembering I'd agreed to be good not even five minutes before.

"Who is scratching up my floors?" Mrs. G demanded as she entered the room, holding a tray of hot entrees. Dani followed her in with some salads, as well as Rosa with an armload of red and white wine. "Agostino, you were raised better than that."

"I'm sorry, Mamma," he replied as he sat down next to me. Dani took a seat between her father and Andrew, and Rosa sat next to Andrew, across from Luciano. Mrs. G came over, hugged Gus, and kissed the top of his head before taking her place opposite Mr. G at the other end of the table. Everyone at the table bowed their heads, and Mr. G said a prayer. I wasn't remotely religious, but the Gallos were Catholic, and I respected that when I was in their home.

Mr. G finished the prayer, which mentioned how happy he was to have Gus home, and he even mentioned me—and winked at me when he did, because he knew I'd be peeking during grace. Whoops. Everyone picked up their forks and shit and started talking, but Gus cleared his throat and got everyone's attention before the food was touched.

"I have something I'd like to tell everyone," he said, projecting his deep voice in a way that would have made my knees buckle had I been standing. Dani grabbed Andrew's hand on the table and smiled at her brother while everyone else looked on expectantly. "I found someone. He, ah, makes me happier than I can remember ever being and he makes me laugh. And for whatever reason, he loves me. It's still new, but I wanted you all to know."

Mrs. G gasped and unleashed a flurry of Italian I had no hope of following. The rest of the table, excluding Andrew, laughed and Gus smiled. "*Sì, Mamma. Sono innamorato,*" Gus replied.

"Where is he?" Mrs. G asked, pure elation in her voice and conveyed in the smile on her face.

Gus turned to me, smiled, and took my hand on top of the table. "Right here." Gus lifted our joined hands, kissed the back of mine, and smiled.

"*Oddio!* James?" Mrs. G asked in shock.

"James? Oh, yes. I guess that is probably his full name. Yes, it's Jamie." A silence descended on the table, and I wanted to say something to break it, but I kept my mouth shut, tightening my grip on Gus's hand. He looked between his parents, fingers twitching, but unable to tap. "Say something."

Mrs. G got up and came over. Instead of going to her son, she pulled me up and into a hug, topped off with three kisses to each cheek, followed by one to my forehead. "You're an angel. Thank you for making Agostino happy." She gave me one more kiss, smoothed my hair, then went back to her seat, talking rapid-fire with Rosa. I turned to sit back down but stopped when I noticed Mr. G behind me. I stepped around to stand in front of him, not sure what to expect. He was a serious-looking man, but I'd only ever seen him be kind.

"You're in love with my son?" he asked me evenly.

I nodded and licked my lips. "I am."

He stepped closer and wrapped his arms around me, in that all-encompassing way Gus hugged. It took me a second to recover from my shock and return the gesture. My scale for being shocked was re-evaluated after Mr. G kissed each of my cheeks and followed it up with, "*Benvenuto nella nostra famiglia.*" I knew that one; welcome to the family.

"Th-thank you, sir."

He released me and chuckled. "Don't go getting all formal on us now. We love you as you are, Jamie."

"Fuck me, thank God," I said, feeling insta-relief. Everyone laughed, including Gus, although he may have cringed a bit as well. Once we were seated, everyone else gave their congratulations, and I felt so at home and happy. Gus had a beautiful family, and I was stoked that they still liked me after the news.

"Eat! We have more to celebrate now," Mrs. G

announced proudly. Gus smiled at me and offered me the
garbanzo salad first. As if I didn't love him enough already.

GUS and I were grilled after dinner. I remembered what it
was like for Dani when she first brought Andrew home, so I
prepared for it by drinking all of the wine within reach. At
one point, Gus had snatched my glass from me, but Luciano
had my back and gave me his. Muhahaha. I learned a lot
about him during the questioning, though. The motherfucker's birthday was at the end of the month, and he didn't think
that was important to tell me. Dani spilled the beans, and for
that, I would be forever grateful.

It was dusk when we left, and a little chilly, but the air
felt great. I wanted to walk for a bit, so we didn't call a car
and headed toward the train station. The sounds of the city
served as an ambient hum, making the perfect backdrop to
Gus's deep voice.

"Are you okay, Jamie?"

"What do you mean?"

"My family can be a lot," Gus started, "and not everyone
wants that. My mom and Rosa have already started planning
our wedding, I'm sure."

"If you're asking if I still wanna be with you, the answer
is yes. I've probably been over a hundred times, and Mr. G
has never hugged me, let alone kissed me. That's, like, a big
deal. I'm basically your betrothed now," I gasped.

Gus chuckled and held my hand in his, our fingers twin-
ing. "You ready for that responsibility? It's all harmless talk
about cake and color schemes until she tells you she wants
grandbabies."

"Oh, heeeeeeell naw. Fuck, you don't want kids do you?
Because—"

A hard shoulder check made me stagger and bump into Gus. I whipped around to see the guy who did it walking away, but nah, fuck him. "Excuse you," I called out.

Gus pulled on my arm, but my focus was on the asshole that turned around. "Leave it alone, Jamie." Maybe I would have if I was sober. I'd been bumped enough on the street before, but this time really pissed me off.

I was fully prepared to lay into the guy when I noticed the oomph in his step, the twitch of his hand, the sweat on his brow, and his dilated pupils once he was in my face. Dude was lit as fuck—and jonesin' for another hit if the fresh scratches on his arm were any indication. Gus must have seen it too because he took a step back and brought me with him.

"What're you sayin'?" the man asked, scratching at his already sore arm.

"Nothing, dude. My bad," I said holding my hands up. He eyed my watch—the one Theo got me—and I could have kicked myself for drawing attention to it.

"You guys have any money? I need to catch the train."

Except you're heading in the wrong direction, was what I wanted to say, but didn't. Gus beat me to the punch before I could think of something appropriate. "Sorry, man. No change on us." Gus tugged on my wrist and nodded his head for me to keep walking. Our tweaked-out friend had other ideas.

He pulled a knife out—oh, great, a fucking switchblade —and pointed it at me. "I'll take his watch."

"No fucking way," I blurted out. The man narrowed his eyes and stepped closer, still aiming the knife at me. Gus tried to placate him, but it was like he didn't even hear him. The man stared me down with sole focus and a face twisted with anger and desperation.

I saw it coming when he pulled the knife back and plunged it forward aiming for my neck. I saw it coming head-on, but my feet wouldn't move. My hand went cold, then I was pushed to the side, out of reach from the knife. I stumbled then looked up to see Gus holding his bicep and blood on the sidewalk.

I shouted Gus's name, taking a step toward him. "Stay back," he hissed, freezing my feet in place once more. I watched in horror as the man took swipes through the air at Gus, thankfully not connecting.

More blood colored the sidewalk—too much. I pulled my phone out of my pocket with the intention of calling the police and an ambulance to see to Gus when the guy charged in my direction. Gus stepped between us and grabbed the guy once he'd slammed into him. He twisted the attacker's arm until I heard something—likely his shoulder—pop. The guy screamed and staggered back, holding the shoulder. His arm was dangling limp, and the knife was nowhere in sight. He eyed Gus one more time, then cursed and took off running.

"Oh my God, Gus, are you okay? Your arm is bleeding." I walked over to Gus and reached him as he turned around— with the knife sticking out of the right upper quadrant of his abdomen. His fingers were clutched around it, and he was breathing heavily. "No, no, no, don't touch that," I said, carefully prying his fingers off the handle. I dialed nine-one-one, never taking my other hand off Gus's chest.

"It hurts," he choked out.

"I know, baby, but please, don't touch it." A calm voice came through my phone's speaker, and I relayed the situation and our location to the dispatcher then hung up. I needed to assess Gus's injuries and stop whatever bleeding I could as quickly as possible. His parents' house was too far back for him to walk, so I led him to the grass and helped him sit down, wincing when he did.

My hand on his arm came away dripping blood,

reminding me of how much I saw on the sidewalk. "Listen to me. I need to look at your arm and stomach. Try to be still." I tore the shirt open from the hole where the knife entered and felt my stomach flip. The wound was gushing blood, meaning that knife was fucking sharp and had cut clean through the brachial artery.

"Are you all right, Jamie?" Gus asked.

"I'm fine, doll. Don't worry about me." I wanted to curse and scream at the top of my lungs, but I needed to stop that bleeding more than anything. The abdominal wound had likely hit his liver, which was bad, but the blood rushing out of Gus's arm was much worse. I ripped off my flannel and pressed it firmly against Gus's arm, merely slowing down the bleeding. EMS should have arrived in a couple minutes since we weren't too far from St. Bernard Hospital.

My full-blown panic nearly set in when Gus started to lose consciousness. He was losing too much fucking blood. I really wanted to freak out, but I knew what to do, and I needed to be calm and collected to fucking do it. I begged him to try and stay awake and promised him he'd be okay; I always kept my fucking promises.

FIFTEEN

THE LAST NINE HOURS were hell. Gus didn't regain consciousness in the ambulance and was rushed in for surgery to repair his severed brachial artery. The stab to his abdomen did, in fact, nick his liver, resulting in a Grade Two laceration. After a round of blood work, X-rays, and a CT scan, it was determined that the bleeding had stopped and surgery on the liver wasn't necessary. It would heal on its own; it would just hurt like a bitch for about six weeks. The exterior wound was stitched up, not quite to my standards, though it shouldn't leave a bad scar. I was just relieved to know that he was going to be okay.

I stroked my fingers over the back of Gus's hand, careful not to bump the IV sites, and rested my head on his hip. I was starved for any type of contact, just the physical reassurance that he was still with me—that he was safe.

A nurse told me he woke up earlier when they were setting up the IV blood transfusion, but I was out in the hall calling Theo. I called Gus's parents and Dani as soon as Gus was admitted for surgery, and they came over immediately. I hadn't even thought to wash his blood off my hands. Mrs. G hugged me as soon as she saw me, and I lost it. I cried in her arms and told her again and again that I was sorry. It didn't seem like enough, but she held me and comforted me while I ruined her shirt with my bloody hands and my messy face. She patted my hair out of my face and sent me with Dani to get cleaned up and checked out by a nurse.

They left after getting word that surgery went well. Dani had made a compelling argument that Gus wouldn't want to be fussed over and have the family miss work. I promised them I would stay with him and call them as soon as he woke up, which I hoped would be soon. I wanted nothing more than to talk to him and just hear his voice.

"You're mumbling," a familiar voice rasped, snapping me from my reverie.

"Gus," I said, sitting up taking in his open eyes. "Fuck, you're okay." I bowed my head and felt tears sting my eyes again.

"I'm okay. Are you all right?" Damn him for being concerned about me, even after he was fucking stabbed twice.

"I wasn't harmed, doll. You made sure of that."

Gus tried sitting up, wincing at the pain in his core, then abandoned the idea and fell back. "I was so scared he would come back for you. I tried to stay awake, but I felt so tired."

I ran my fingers through Gus's hair and rubbed his forehead with my thumb, keeping my other hand on his. "You dummy, you could have died last night. Why would you do something so stupid?" The tears burned down my cheeks, leaving a cool trail in their wake. I wiped at them with a clean sleeve from the shirt Dani brought over for me after seeing what a mess I was.

"I had to keep you safe. I'd die before I let anyone hurt you, Jamie," Gus said, squeezing my fingers.

"Thank you. You're still a crazy idiot, but you saved me."

"From what the nurses told me earlier, you saved me too. They said my husband pinched off my artery and gave me a tourniquet on the sidewalk," Gus said with a smile, placing emphasis on the h-word.

"Yeah, about that... I kinda lied and said we were married so they'd let me ride in the ambulance and come in the room. Your mom and dad backed me up on that." I wiped my eyes again and laughed weakly.

"Thank you. I heard you, you know. Your promise."

I shook my head and cried more because that's who I was apparently. "I only say shit like that when I'm confident and in control. I was the complete opposite last night. I don't know if I said that for you or to make myself feel better about having no control."

"You did your best, and I'm right here. It's okay, Jamie." Gus cupped my cheek, and I leaned into his warm touch, thankful to feel him again. "I wish I could hold you right now."

"You're too banged up for that. Your mom would kill me if I aggravated your injuries. Shit, I need to call your parents —I promised I would when you woke up."

Gus raised an eyebrow in surprise. "You mean they came and actually left?"

"Yeah, once we got word that you were all good and rest-ing, D convinced them that you wouldn't want everyone fawning over you while you slept."

Gus snorted a laugh, followed by another wince. "She knows me too well."

"You and me both," I replied. "Do you need anything? I can call a nurse if you're in pain or hungry." Gus shook his head weakly and groaned. I looked around and spotted the bottled water I bought earlier and never drank. I twisted the lid off and scooted up closer to the head of the bed. "Drink some of this. You need to keep your fluids up, and it'll feel better on your throat."

"Yes, Doctor," Gus said with a smirk.

"Nah-uh, you're not allowed to call me that. I can't be getting a Pavlovian boner every time someone calls me doctor after you've gone and perved the shit out of it. Nope. Not happening."

Gus's smile grew wider, and he licked his lips. I tried and failed not to be turned on. "That's really too bad. I was hoping you'd fuck me while wearing a lab coat and stethoscope."

"What the fuck kind of doctor-kink porn have you been watching?"

"I can demonstrate for you when I get out of here."

"You're not going to be doing anything like that when you're released. You were stabbed in the liver, dude. You're not going to be doing much of anything."

Gus furrowed his brows and his smile faded. "I need to call my boss." He tried to sit up again, and I pushed him back down.

"Stop moving. Your liver didn't need to be stitched, but you need to be still and let it close. I already called your boss and explained what happened." Gus didn't try to get up again, though his worry was still evident on his face. "This is actually something I wanted to discuss with you when you got released, but maybe we should talk about it now."

"Talk about what?"

I seriously did not want to have that conversation at the hospital, but oh well. "You're going to be in here for at least a week, and when you get released you won't be able to do anything strenuous for at least a couple months. Going back to your job right now isn't really an option."

"I have to. I need to pay my rent and whatever this bill is going to cost. Shit… I can't stay here for a week, Jamie."

"Easy, calm down. Don't worry about the hospital bill." Gus eyed me suspiciously, which would have been adorable under different circumstances. "Theo is paying for your treatment." Gus sucked in a breath, but I continued before he could protest. "Don't even try to refuse it. I was going to pay for it myself, but Theo insisted. It's his way of thanking you for protecting me. He said paying for your treatment was the least he could do. Say thank you and move on, Gus. I'm not going to fight with you about it," I said firmly.

He sighed and nodded, which was a serious win. "Thank you."

I grinned at my victory and leaned down and gave Gus a chaste kiss on the lips. "Good. I'll pass on your thanks to Theo and let him know that you for sure won't be murdering him now." Gus huffed and mumbled under his breath, so I kissed him again. I hoped it would make what came next a bit easier. "With respect to your job—"

"No," Gus interjected. "I need to work to survive. I'm not moving back home."

"Are you happy? With your job, are you happy?" I asked evenly. I already knew the answer because Gus had told me he wasn't happy or fulfilled at work. He did it merely to get by. Perhaps not wanting to repeat that, he tensed and looked away from my eyes. "Because if you are, that's more than enough for me, dude. But I don't think you are. You have it in that thick fucking skull of yours that in order to be successful you have to be a doctor or lawyer or some shit—"

"*You're* a doctor."

"Not the point, Gus. I don't care what you want to do, whether it's working at the restaurant, doing what you're doing now—whatever. I just want you to be happy. That's all that matters to me, doll. I'm not going to push you to do something you're not into. That's not what I'm about. Though, I do want to help you find something you love if you haven't already. Whether that help is moral support, networking, just being there for you to lean on, or fucking your brains out, I'm in. Whatever you need, I'm in." I bowed my head and looked at our joined hands before turning back to Gus. "So let me ask you again: are you happy?"

"No," Gus ground out.

"Quit. Call tomorrow and quit. Let me help you, Gus. You support me in so many ways, let me do the same for you, just for a little while, doll."

"Support me… what, you're going to pay my rent? My bills? No." Gus broke eye contact with me again, looking in the complete opposite direction. "I can't do that, Jamie," he said in a low voice.

"I'm trying to ask you to move in with me, here. It's not a grand romantic gesture, and I'm sorry about that, but I mean it. I love you, Gus. Please let me help you. And if it helps, it's also for my own selfish reasons. I want you close to me."

"Jamie…"

"Let me frame it this way. If it had been me who was injured, would you want to help me any way you could?" I asked, already knowing the answer.

Gus turned back to me with wide eyes. "Of course I would."

"Then why does it have to be different for me? I want to take care of you the same way you do for me. If you move in, that'll become super easy. It would make me the happiest guy if I could wake up next to you every morning," I said before kissing Gus again, this time with more heat. And maybe some tongue. Okay, a lot of tongue.

"Are you sure you're a doctor and not a lawyer? You're too good at swaying me," Gus said quietly.

"You know, I thought about going to law school, but I —" I cut myself off when the implication of Gus's words revealed itself to me. "Oh my God, is that a yes? You'll move in?" Gus tipped his chin down and smiled at me before I launched myself at him, assaulting him with an overabundance of kisses and Eskimo kisses. I pulled back and sat my ass back down in the chair, grinning like a fool and savoring the taste of Gus lingering on my lips.

"You're so fucking cute when you smile like that."

"Pfft, I'm fucking cute all the damn time."

Gus chuckled and stroked his thumb over my cheek. "You're right, *caro*. My mistake."

I shifted my attention over to Gus's right arm, where he was bandaged. "You should be pleased to know that none of your sexy tattoos were marred. Well, the initial stabbing didn't touch them. The additional slicing and dicing for surgery did kinda mess up some of the flowers under the skull. Wolfie is okay."

"Slicing and dicing, huh? Is that the official medical terminology?"

"Absolutely. Super official. Seriously though, I should call your parents. They're probably freaking out."

"Can I be selfish and have you alone for ten more minutes?" Gus asked.

"Fuck yeah, you can."

Gus brushed my hair back, and I leaned into his touch once more. "I love you, Jamie."

"I love you too, Gus."

MAY

GUS'S HOSPITAL stay lasted for eight long-ass-motherfuck-ing-days. During that time, Theo, Masa, and I moved Gus's stuff into my loft, which basically meant I supervised while they moved stuff and argued. It was great. Gus and I also gave our statements to the police and were told we'd be informed of any developments in the case. Yeah, good luck finding one junky in a city this big.

In preparation for Gus coming home, I cleaned everything and stocked up the fridge with food I could manage to cook, and snacks he liked. I got some grass too, in case Gus wanted some. He'd kept his word and called his boss to say he wouldn't be returning, and I was so proud of him. He didn't like relying on anyone, but I wasn't just anyone, and I was tickled to know he was willing to trust me like he said he would.

We took an Uber from the hospital to my—our—place. Gus wanted a shower immediately, which was understandable. We had to keep him from overextending, which meant I got to help. I offered to give Gus a sexy sponge bath, but he declined and opted for a shower. I was a little salty about not getting to administer the sponge bath, though I forgot about that once Gus was naked and wet in front of me. I soaped him up from head to toe, even the parts that made his ears burn red with embarrassment. Especially those parts, since that was essentially what I was needed for, so he wouldn't be stretching. Despite me being a trained medical professional, Gus was super shy when I came at him with a soapy washcloth. I promptly informed him that if I wanted to lick his hairy crack, I had no problem washing it either. *I* thought it was pretty funny—Gus did not.

We got in bed after the shower and carefully snuggled for a few hours before I got up and made us some dins. Gus's birthday was two days ago, but he didn't want to celebrate in the hospital. Dani and I baked him a chocolate cake, which means Dani baked it, and I did the taste test. I also put the raspberries on top of it—in the shape of a heart, no less.

After we ate, I cleared the dishes away and loaded up a

tray with the cake and nonalcoholic sparkling wine. You know, alcohol and liver lacerations weren't really a great mix. I opened the cupboard and took out the cute little bouquet of flowers that looked like the ones from Gus's tattoo and put them in a washed-out Patrón bottle with water in it. I stashed them there earlier when I found out Gus was being released. It wasn't anything big, just six little flowers, but it was cute, and I hoped he'd like it. I loaded everything on the tray and got halfway to the bedroom with it when I remembered the actual gift. I carefully returned to the island and retrieved an envelope from a drawer. Inside was a cheesy card that put into eloquent words how much I loved Gus, and courtside NBA playoff tickets for next week. We just… weren't going to mention how much those cost. Ever.

Gus was looking at his phone when I came in, tray in hand. He locked the phone and set it on the nightstand, twisting in a way that agitated his wound. "Shit," he hissed under his breath, readjusting to a comfortable position. "What's all that?"

"All this," I said as I carefully sat down next to him while balancing the tray, "is your belated birthday surprise."

"What, you mean you singing for me while I was bedridden wasn't enough?" Gus teased.

"You know what, I'm great at a lot of things, but skating and singing aren't among them. I am, however, a master cake decorator. Check these raspberries."

Gus tilted his head and eyed the cake then flicked his eyes up at me. "Did Daniella bake this?"

"Um, no, clearly I did. D might have helped. Just a little bit. She said it was your favorite."

"She was right. I taught her this recipe when she was seven. She asked me what my favorite cake was so she could make it for me. But she didn't know how to bake a cake, so I spent the afternoon showing her until one turned out perfect," Gus said fondly.

"Y'all are just the cutest. I get why you said you had a kid sister now. She's still that sweet little girl to you." A half smile pulled at Gus's lips, and he nodded. "You're a good big bro. How you talk about D reminds me a lot of my brother. I sincerely think you guys would be great friends once the, um, awkwardness is gone."

"I'll try. Now, what's all this here? Did you get me flowers?"

"Fuck yes, I did. I wasn't sure what to get, and I totally felt like I dropped the ball by not bringing flowers to the hospital. These aren't very big or flashy, but they reminded me of your tattoo. You know, therefore, they reminded me of you."

"They're beautiful, thank you." Gus gently brushed his fingers along the petals of one of the white flowers.

"Here," I said, indicating to the two glasses full of golden, bubbly liquid, "we have virgin sparkling wine—which is all you're getting until your liver is fully healed. And here"—I picked up the envelope and handed it to Gus—"is my gift to you. And don't bother saying I didn't have to get you anything. I know that, doll. I wanted to get you something."

Gus took the envelope from me, deliberately caressing my fingers as he did. "Thank you. If this is a bunch of sex IOUs, I'm going to be very happy," he teased.

"Fuck me sideways, that's a great idea. I'mma remember that."

Gus laughed and ripped open the sealed paper, pulling out the card. The tickets were inside yet another envelope that was open at the top. He read the card with a smile then laughed at my handwritten note at the bottom, scrawled in my best doctor-writing. He leaned over, despite the pain, and kissed me after reading the card.

"What do we have in here," he said, tipping the envelope so the tickets slid out into his hand. He gasped, he fucking gasped, just like how he did when I first slid into him when we had sex. Gus's gaze met mine with a look of sheer surprise. "You didn't… Tell me you didn't."

"I sure did."

"How did you know I liked basketball?" Gus's voice was pitched a bit higher due to his shock.

"*NBA 2K18.* It was sitting out the first time I went over to your place. I conferred with Scotty to see which game would be best to pick. I don't know your team, so I went with his judgment based on what he said would be a good match-up."

"I really wish I could move right now."

"Why?"

"You deserve a blowjob," Gus said, deadass serious.

"As if I don't always deserve one."

"Thank you, Jamie. You're going to find out in a week how much I love basketball." Jesus, he was beaming—so adorable.

"Me or basketball?" I asked. Gus stroked his chin and hummed, so I flicked his earlobe. "You're deliberating too long!"

"I'm just messing with you. Come over here," Gus said, patting his lap. I set the glasses on the nightstand and pushed the tray to the side then carefully flung a leg over Gus's and lowered myself onto his lap, draping my arms around his neck. He snaked one hand under the waistband of my lounge pants, just resting it on my ass, and stroked my neck and jaw with the other. "It's always going to be you, Jamie. I'd never watch another second of basketball if it meant I could spend it with you instead."

"Damn, that's a good answer." I leaned forward and pressed my lips to Gus's in a slow-and-sweet-turned-sensuous kiss. Gus wasn't supposed to do anything strenuous or that got him out of breath just yet. So, sex was definitely off the table, but maybe those rules could be bent. Just a little bit.

The days leading up to the game were beautifully uneventful. Gus and I lazed around and enjoyed each other's company way more than I thought possible. He forced me to go out without him, and even though I whined like a petulant child, he was right. I kept up on my gym commitments and went out one night with my friends. They came over once as well to check on Gus, which I thought was hella sweet.

Theo and Masa came by as well, and Theo expressed such sincere gratitude toward Gus for what he did for me. It totes made Gus borderline uncomfortable, though I thought it was a good step for them. Gus also gave an awkward thanks to Theo for covering his medical fees and started going on about how he'd pay him back one day, which signaled my time to interject. Gus had a lot of pride, and I understood why he wouldn't want to feel like he was indebted to Theo, but he needed to learn how to accept help. And not hate my big brother. Baby steps.

The game was a motherfucking riot. Basketball in real life was way more entertaining than on TV. Like, I was screaming, almost as loud as Gus was. He overdid it and made his stitches sore, but he refused to have any chill and toughed it out like a trooper. I sat on his right side to protect his arm and torso from getting accidentally bumped, which meant I didn't get to sit next to the super-hot-as-fuck blonde model on Gus's left. He didn't even bat an eye at her, but he sure did enjoy laughing at my anguish.

We went for a slow walk after the game and enjoyed the warmer spring air. We stopped for ice cream and tacos and made out in the back of the car the whole ride home. After taking a mutually enjoyable shower, Gus and I crawled into bed, ending up with me resting on the left side of his chest. I usually slept on the right side, but the left was pretty dang comfy too.

GRADUATION DAY WAS UPON US—WHICH also fell on Mother's Day—way to steal my thunder, Mom. In addition to wearing a dumb hat, getting my papers, and officially becoming Dr. James Rey, it was the day I'd decided my parents should meet Gus. The entire Gallo clan was in attendance, and it just seemed like the perfect time. Dad would never make a scene in public, so it was guaranteed to go over relatively smoothly.

During the pomp and circumstance portion of the day, Gus sat with his family and Theo and Masa sat next to Dad. Mom's wheelchair was next to Dad's chair in the aisle of the auditorium. She held a massive bouquet from Theo and me, and cried when I walked across the stage. I waved to her then found Gus next to his mom and blew him a kiss. 'Twas a good time.

After everyone was called and speeches were given, I was free to celebrate offstage with my crew before we split up and returned to our families. Scotty, with all his bravado, cried like a baby when he hugged me. Pat tried to school his emotions, but he wasn't entirely successful in keeping a smile off his face. Roz went with natural-looking makeup that would make her parents happy and she'd done Dani's before the ceremony. They were both goy-geous.

Theo convinced me to get a haircut a few days ago "so I wouldn't look like a shaggy mop." His words. With Gus's approval, I went with a much shorter style than I'd had in years: short, but not shaved, on the sides and back, and wavy and flowy up top. It was similar to Theo's haircut, just a bit longer and wilder. And cuter, if I was being honest. Gus really seemed to enjoy it too, if the hickies under my collar were any indication.

Dani and I broke off from our friends and strolled over to our waiting families to receive our congratulations. I went over to Mom first and leaned down for a hug, but I'd definitely be circling back to give Mr. and Mrs. G hugs and those cheeky kisses.

"Congratulations, honey. You looked so handsome up there," she said, starting to cry again.

"Don't cry, Mom." I leaned into her ear and whispered, "Gus is here, and I'd like you to meet him." Her breathing hitched and she jerked her head back in surprise. Surprise shifted into a smile and a nod followed by a glance over at Dad, who was standing a couple feet away with his eyes glued to his work phone. I shook my head and shrugged to show I gave zero fucks. "Too fucking bad. I don't care what he thinks anymore. I'll bring Gus over in a bit."

"I can't wait," Mom said, still smiling. "Go pose with your brother; I want to take some pictures." I kissed Mom's hand like the queen she was, and strode over to Theo and Masa, hugging each of them. We all posed for way too many pictures, which only turned into more damn pictures when Dani came over.

The rest of the Gallo clan, including Gus, followed shortly after, presenting the perfect opportunity for some very important introductions. I said my hellos to Mr. and Mrs. G and hugged Gus when I finally reached him, even going in for a kiss. He flinched for a second before he returned the affection, but I wouldn't blame him for being taken aback. We broke apart, and I held his hand, leading him back over to my mom.

"Mom, this is my boyfriend, Gus. Gus, this is Mom."

"Agostino Gallo. It's a pleasure to meet you, Mrs. Rey," Gus said, maintaining eye contact with Mom while formally shaking her hand.

"Oh, please call me Suzy. My son is terrible with introductions, so you'll have to forgive him for the shoddy introduction." Gus laughed

"Jamie didn't tell you about my chair, did he?" Mom asked.

Gus looked at me then back at Mom and shook his head. "No. I'm sorry if my gaze was wandering."

"You're fine, dear. Jamie is a sweet boy, but he can be rather clueless sometimes. He tends not to disclose the chair when he talks about me."

"Why would I?" I asked.

"It's sweet, but shocking people isn't nice, honey."

I shrugged. I didn't deliberately avoid telling people about Mom's accident, it just never seemed like a relevant thing to focus on. Though, I did see her point. She was pretty accepting of the chair now, but it was tough when I was younger. Mom wasn't herself for years. Things really turned around last year when she and Theo repaired their relationship. I guess I was still a bit overprotective of her— something for my otherwise perfect self to work on.

"It's all right. Jamie has a big heart, I know he means well." Gus shot me a wink and turned back to Mom, a flash of pain flitting across his face at twisting suddenly.

"Are you okay, Gus? Jamie called me last night and told me about what happened to you."

"I'm fine. It doesn't hurt much anymore," Gus replied.

Mom took Gus's hand in hers and thanked him with fresh tears in her eyes. He leaned down and hugged her, which I knew had to hurt, though he didn't let it show. Gus whispered something to Mom that made her smile, but I didn't catch what it was.

"Who is this?" Dad asked from next to me, startling the shit outta me.

Gus stood up straight, and Mom tensed. I wasn't nervous. "This is Gus Gallo, Dani's older brother, and my boyfriend." Dad's eyes widened for half a second before his cool, hard expression returned. "Before you even think about saying anything rude, don't. I'm not looking for your approval in any capacity, just simply letting you know what's up and who's important in my life. I also want to make it very clear that any disrespect toward him, Masa, Theo, or me will not be tolerated. I should never have sat back and let you treat Theo so terribly. I'm sincerely sorry about that," I said as I looked over to my brother for a moment and gave him a half smile. "If you're good with all that, I'd love for you to properly meet Gus, and Masa as well."

The tick in Dad's jaw was the only outward sign that he was mega pissed. Let him be. "How dare y—"

"Jim," Mom interrupted in a sterner tone than she'd ever used on me growing up. "We'll discuss it later."

I sidestepped over to Theo and whispered, "Since when does Mom talk back to Dad like that?"

"You see her more than me, how should I know," he replied, just as surprised as me.

My parents exchanged a few more whispered words, resulting in Dad excusing himself to ready the car. She wheeled over to the rest of us and merely said, "Your father and I are going to have a long chat tonight. This has gone on long enough. Gus, dear, I hope you'll be joining us at the house for the party? I'd have sent you a formal invite when I mailed them to the rest of your family had I known you were Daniella's brother."

"I wouldn't miss it, Mrs. Rey. Ah, Suzy," Gus added quickly.

I nudged Gus's left arm with my elbow and waggled my

brows at him. "Come on, doll. Don't be nervous. She already likes you." I turned to my right at Theo and Masa and asked, "You guys are coming too right? I'll bail on my own damn party if you say no."

Masa bit back a grin while Theo turned to Mom wordlessly. "Don't worry about your father. It's time to come home," she said in that comforting way only a mother can.

Theo exchanged a wordless glance with Masa then made me super happy by saying they would come. I clapped my hands together, snapped up some finger-guns at no one in particular and said, "Rock 'n' roll. Let's go get fucked up in the backyard."

I changed from my T-shirt and gown into a cream-colored all-over floral print Gucci suit with purple, rose, and orange flowers. Was it a bold choice? Yes. Did I look insanely fuckable? Fuck yas. I went with a plain white dress shirt with two buttons undone under it to keep the focus on the gorgeous print. No belt, no socks, and tan and white wingtips. Theo helped pick out the shoes, and I had to admit, they were pretty dope. Satisfied with my outfit, I ran my hand through my hair to fluff it up, and headed down to the party.

On my way down, my attention caught on the cracked door to the piano room, and I just knew I'd find Gus in there. I pushed the door open farther and peeked in, pleased to see Gus standing by the piano, his fingers caressing the keys. He was hella handsome in cream slacks and a crisp white dress shirt with the sleeves rolled to his elbows. I walked in and closed the door behind me, the click alerting him of someone else's presence.

His head shot up quickly, though he relaxed and smiled when he saw me. I made my way over to him, where he pulled me into a hug and melted against me. Something so simple filled me with an array of complex feelings, which, like Gus, never ceased to amaze me. I was indescribably happy, but it was more than that—more than anything I'd experienced before. I knew now that those complex feelings had a name: love. Motherfucking love. I had to laugh to myself.

"What's funny?" Gus asked as he pulled back and stroked his thumb over my bottom lip.

"Nothing, doll. I was just thinking."

"Don't hurt yourself," Gus teased. I feigned offense, but even that was hard with Gus smiling at me so fondly. "I'm proud of you, Jamie. And you look sexy as hell in that suit, but I really don't want that to take away from what I just said."

"Don't worry; you made the compliment even better. Wait till you see how cute my ass is in these pants." I pecked Gus on the lips quickly then turned around and shimmied my ass against his crotch. A loud crack echoed through the room, followed by a sting I'd felt once before. The suddenness of it all made me jump, but I wouldn't have minded another. "If you want to spank me like you mean it, I'll gladly lie over your knee," I said, looking back at Gus. I bit my bottom lip and waggled my brows at him for added flair.

"Whatever you want," Gus replied, wrapping his arms around my waist from behind and kissing my neck.

"What about you? What do *you* want?"

"You."

"Let's go downstairs and have a good time, and when we get home, you can have as much of me as you want."

"You mean…"

"Mhm." I spun around in Gus's arms. "I'm clearing you for bursts of light to moderate activity."

Gus snorted a laugh. "You're clearing me for sex?"

"Isn't that what I just said? Rough, hard-core fucking is still off the table, though. Sorry."

"How will I ever manage?" Gus deadpanned.

"With me, silly. Always with me." I leaned up and pressed my lips to Gus's, intending on going in for a short kiss, yet unable to pull away from him. But fuck it. That was okay. The rest of the world could wait a little bit longer.

EPILOGUE

AUGUST

"I'M GONNA BLOW IF you keep doing that."

Gus pulled off of my cock with a loud, wet pop that almost made me lose it, and narrowed his eyes at me. His lips were wet and plump from being wrapped around my painfully hard dick, and his eyes were glassed over with unshed tears. A string of spit connected his bottom lip to my tip before it fell away when he ran his tongue over it. Gus gave my balls a firm squeeze then massaged them in his palm, just how I liked. He looked utterly debauched, and I wanted to commit that image to memory for future solo endeavors—not that there were many anymore.

I wondered how he might look with my cum all over his face before he took me back into the perfect wet heat of his mouth and my thoughts fizzled. He took me down fast and hard, bringing me to the edge in mere seconds. I grabbed the back of Gus's hair and wrenched his mouth off my cock, just in time to unload all over his face. While panting desperately, I wiped up a stream of cum from Gus's cheek with my thumb and ghosted it over his lips. Without me needing to ask, he sucked on it with the same effort he would my cock, which always got me going.

I leaned down and replaced my thumb with my tongue, kissing Gus as hungrily as I could muster in my post-orgasm haze. I could faintly taste myself on his tongue, which only made me want to kiss him more. Not wanting to be wasteful, I licked Gus's cheek and almost fell backward when he crashed his lips against mine, seeking out the cum I'd just licked off his face.

"Holy fuck-nuggets, that was great. Woo!" I looked around my old room and grabbed a discarded towel, wiping Gus's face clean as best I could with a dry towel. Getting cum out of facial hair properly required water, but I tried. "Sorry if I pulled too hard."

"It was good. You know I like it when you get rough."

"Yeah, shoulda let me smash. I could've licked the cum out of your ass. I know how much you get off on me doing that." After a relatively short chat and a trip to my doctor, we stopped using condoms last month and, fuck, what a difference.

"No. I told you, we're not having sex here when your parents are home." Gus wiped his fingers on the towel then discarded it in the corner, and pulled out his phone. "Your father already hates me enough as is. He caught me looking all disheveled after we, uh, played pool, and I was so embarrassed. He was just standing there in the doorway with a glass of scotch, told me my behavior was unbecoming and left. I don't need to give him any more ammo."

"So now I'm getting cock-blocked by Dad? I can't believe this shit. He's such a twat-waffle sometimes." Dad was way better than he was before, but it was all obviously superficial. He was still a dick to Theo at work and was even more dismissive of me, but whatever. Instead of being outwardly disrespectful and hateful, he resorted to excusing himself to go work in his office when things got too fucking gay for him. It was a big step for him, and Mom was diligent about continuing to work on him. At least we were able to do family shit at the house again. We got together for dinner every two weeks since my graduation, and it was typically a really nice time. Mom loved being around "all of her lovely sons"—as well as Dani, Andrew, and Scotty on occasion. It was also the weekend of my birthday, so we were having a barbecue.

"I know you're frustrated, and you have every reason to be, but I can't really take you seriously when you talk like that. On that note, your brother and Masa are here."

I snatched my phone from my pants on the floor and wrinkled my nose when there were no notifications. "Why the hell did they text you and not me? Are you and Theo secret best friends now?" Gus barked out a dry laugh. Nope, still working on that. I gasped and held my hand against my chest. "You're not trying to steal Masa away from me, are you? I won't let you have him."

Gus sighed and pecked my lips quickly. "Stop talking, *caro*. Daniella texted me because you're awful at replying. They arrived just after she did."

"Oh my God. That was one goddamn time that I didn't reply to her!"

"You can go argue with her about it. I need to go wash my face," Gus said before he got up and strode into the bathroom, not bothering to close the door.

I got up with the intention of putting my pants back on, but my brain was not yet communicating effectively with my legs, so I flopped down on my old bed. I was fucking tired. Not just from coming, but from my residency. It was extremely fulfilling, but sixty to ninety-hour fluctuating work weeks sucked ass—and not the good kind. I wasn't seeing Gus as much anymore, which was hard for me after spending so much time with him while he was healing. The upside to being at the hospital was that I was constantly on the go or too tired to mope about missing him, so I was able to do my job and not be distracted.

Gus healed up nicely and started going back to the gym last month, which has made him happier and hornier at home. The police never contacted us with any leads in the case—surpriiiiiise. That free time did not go to waste, though. Gus figured out that he wanted to go to culinary school, but he wasn't super confident about how he'd look on paper. I encouraged him to apply, and, of his own merit, he was starting at Washburne Culinary & Hospitality Institute in September for a two-year program. He applied for financial aid and was stressed about the waiting, which resulted in our first real fight when I told him I'd pay for it. We got tired of going in circles and being mad, so we dropped it for the time being, but it was a conversation we'd be returning to.

After Gus was medically cleared, he went back to work at *Ciao Bella*. He overcame feeling like it was a handout from his dad, seeing it instead as career experience—which made him enjoy it more. Dani said he and Mr. G weren't fighting anymore—unless it was over what specials to run or what ingredients to order. With the money we were both earning, we made enough to live comfortably—excluding the payments on the loft—and not have to spend my parents' money. Gus taught me where to cut back, though sometimes I slipped up and splurged beyond what my paycheck could cover. But I was trying for him. I respected that he didn't want to live off my parents' money. That said, I'd definitely be happy once I was making more than forty-four grand a year so I could spoil him like I wanted to. One day.

"You're still up here?" Gus asked. "And you're still naked. Okay."

I lifted my head and grinned at him. "My legs weren't

cooperating. Come 'ere for a sec." Gus came over, and I pulled him down and snuggled in against his back, getting a good whiff of that yummy Gus smell from his nape. It was even better since he smelled like sex too. I got a little too relaxed and squeezed out a fart. Luckily, it was silent, so I was sure I'd get away with it—for all of three fucking seconds.

"Oh, fuck me dead, that's awful," I said, perhaps sounding a little too pleased with myself.

"What are you talk—Jesus Christ, Jamie." Gus jumped up and took several steps away while I lay on the bed, basking in the foulness I'd created. "Did something die in your ass?"

"Oh, it's not that bad." But it actually kind of was.

"It *is* that bad. I think I'm going to throw up." Gus made a show of opening a window and fanning the air in front of him. "Are you okay?"

"Actually, I do think I need to take a shit now," I managed to say while laughing at Gus's reaction.

"I'll be downstairs. Don't even think about coming down until whatever is going on is out of your system." Gus headed for the door and had his hand on the knob, ready to turn, when I called out for him to wait. He froze in place then turned toward me.

I got up and walked over to him, stopping just before we were touching. "Do you still love me?"

Gus's features relaxed in an instant, his whole demeanor shifting. "Of course I do." He wrapped his arms around my waist, and pulled me against him. "I love you too much, even if your ass is rotten."

"Good. Because I think it's from that new fried chicken I picked up last night, and sorry-not-sorry, there's still more of it at home." An evil smile spread across my face, while one of disgusted horror twisted Gus's features. I leaned up and kissed him before saying, "I love you, doll." I headed for the bathroom with a spring in my step as laughter rolled through me.

"I'm throwing that shit away as soon as we get home," Gus called out in a raised voice that carried no malice.

I spun around and pointed at him from the bathroom doorway and shouted, "You'll do no such thing. I bought that with my own money."

"*Che cazzo*, I'll make you new food!"

I closed the door and continued to argue anyway, our voices getting louder and louder until we were downright yelling. Fighting about stupid things was another new thing for me, and I'd be lying if I said I didn't like fighting with Gus sometimes. Of course, I'd throw away that chicken. It probably gave me food poisoning, but getting Gus riled up sometimes was way too fun. He'd always catch on after a bit, and then we'd have some straight-fire make-up sex. I was looking forward to that later.

ALSO BY SERENE FRANKLIN

ACKNOWLEDGMENTS

I'd like to give special thanks to a few people in particular. First, Cass and Jenny for alpha reading again.

To Jason for awesome date advice, and for always indulging me.

To Steven for even more Chicago help—as well as other fine details.

To Caitlyn and your inspiring, beautiful marriage.

To Stefan for being a really cool dude.

ABOUT THE AUTHOR

Serene Franklin lives in Halifax (Nova Scotia, not California), but has fallen in love with Chicago through research and writing. She has a political science degree, and--more importantly--two adorable and mildly irritating dogs: Tai the Goldendoodle and Fynnian the Irish Wolfhound.

When not writing, she enjoys reading, cooking spicy food, thrashing to music, losing at crib, and watching movies. Serene is a proud otaku and collector of anime figures in addition to novels and yaoi manga.

Serene currently writes contemporary MM romance, but has plans to branch out into other subgenres.

Email: sfwrites801@gmail.com

 twitter.com/serenitydarko

 instagram.com/serenity_darko

 bookbub.com/profile/serene-franklin

CPSIA information can be obtained
at www.ICGtesting.com
Printed in the USA
LVHW101524260722
724458LV00016B/113

9 781999 472733